WEB OF TRUTH

A DREAM WEAVERS & TRUTH SEEKERS NOVEL

CECILIA DOMINIC

ABOUT WEB OF TRUTH

The final bounty was supposed to be the easiest. So why is she the one being hunted?

Morgan le Fay, once the most promising priestess on Avalon, lost her powers due to her unwitting role in the fall of Camelot. She's survived by becoming a bounty hunter for Faerie Queen Tatiana. After she completes her tenth, and final job, she will be free to live her own life and regain her powers.

The problem – the situation isn't as simple as it seems. Her final target, the fledgling vampire Philippe, turns out to have ties to her family, and her handler isn't telling her everything.

The answers Morgan seeks lie with her aunt Margaret the Truth Seeker, who has her own history with Philippe and her own regrets around her part in Morgan's fall and Philippe's situation. Nightmare creatures, faerie plots, and murder follow the two women as they navigate their own past hurts and attempt to unravel the truth. Will they be able keep their friends safe and find forgiveness in time to figure out what the faerie queen wants with Philippe? And will Morgan deal with her old wounds and risk her powers – and her heart - to secure her future?

COPYRIGHT

Web of Truth

Copyright © 2018 by Cecilia Dominic

ISBN: 978-1-945074-43-1

All rights reserved.

Edited by Holly Atkinson
Line edited by Angel Durham

Cover art by Best Page Forward

ACKNOWLEDGMENTS

Thank you once again to Officer Josh Speed for your invaluable help on clarifying some procedural stuff. I hope you continue to enjoy "magic Decatur," as you described the setting of these books.

Thank you as well to my critique group for your feedback on the earlier parts of this book and especially to Kimberly and Denise for the beta reads of the final draft.

I am, as always, eternally grateful to my family for their support, especially my husband Jason and my parents, who are always there with encouragement. I'd also like to thank my sister Elle for being my first and biggest fan.

Finally, thank you to my readers! Y'all keep me going when I'm feeling down or discouraged, and I really couldn't do this without you.

1

One more week.

Morgan crossed October 31 off her calendar. Sure, it was only noon, but the revelry in her normally quiet—if there was such a thing—neighborhood just outside New Orleans said people were already partying like it was nighttime, so she may as well count it. She hoped she wouldn't have to hose too much vomit off the sidewalk in front of her magic store the next morning. But it was Halloween, one of her busiest days, so she didn't dare close.

She'd need a source of income once she retired from being the Fae queen's bounty hunter in, oh, a week. While calendars might have changed and shifted in the ten centuries since she'd made her agreement, she always remembered the date—a week after Samhain. She hadn't bargained with the devil, although the Fae queen was close enough, and her messenger handsome as sin.

Just one more week, and she'd be free. Ten jobs or ten centuries, whichever came first. Then she'd have her powers and her retirement, and she could finally live life without always looking over her shoulder.

The bell over the door tinkled, and a dark-haired young man walked in. Morgan's heart joined her stomach in a free fall of despair, and she barely kept herself from letting out a disappointed moan. Of course she wouldn't get off that easily.

Ten centuries or ten jobs? Ten jobs it is.

She leaned her elbows on the glass case that displayed the objects that were either nicer or small enough for easy shoplifting—typically crystals, fossils, and wands. Their magic auras wafted up to her through the glass, steadying her.

"Decided to skip the drama today, Elric?" As much as she hated what his appearance meant, she fought a sly smile. Fine, she liked the adventure, both of the chase and of him in bed, and it had been a long time. "Since when do you come in the door like a normal person?"

He grinned, his teeth perfectly straight, and the thoughts of what he could do with his lips made her cross her legs where she stood. He always dressed congruent to the century he appeared in. Today he wore skinny tan corduroy pants, pointed-toe boots, and a dark green cashmere sweater under a brown faux leather jacket. Although he appeared neat, he'd allowed his hair to grow long enough to cover the pointed tips of his ears, which made it shaggy and gave him a bohemian— or rebellious—air.

She liked, and she licked her lips at the thought of getting him out of the outfit and raking her fingers through his hair.

His intense expression—was he as hungry for her as she was for him?—gave his words a delicious double *entendre*. "I have a job for you."

"From you or the queen?" There was always the possibility he'd missed her, after all. Maybe he wasn't here for official business. Maybe they could finally be—

"From the queen." He nodded, but his gaze flicked up and to the left before he returned it to her, his smile more dazzling. Yep, he was walking sex, and her mind clouded with both memories and hopes for what would happen when she got those pants off him—

She waved away the glamour. The power to see through Fae spells had come back after job number six, much to Elric's irritation and her relief. But she'd always been able to sense when he was lying. "And this will help me fulfill my deal with her."

"This will count toward your ten."

"*As* my tenth." She stood so she could look him in the eye. She'd made it through nine jobs so far by ensuring there was no Fae trickery.

"As your tenth," he agreed through clenched teeth. He didn't look nearly as pretty now that she'd irritated him. She almost sighed as the ache between her legs eased. Good.

"And after this, my obligation will be finished, and I'll get the rest of my powers back," she pressed.

He gave her a curt nod.

"No, say it." She leaned forward and pressed her palms to the counter, heedless of the hand-prints she'd have to clean. Otherwise she'd grab his shirt and shake him. "I need your word that this is it, Elric."

He sighed, and she almost applauded the drama of it. "Fine. When you deliver this bounty to the queen, you will fulfill your obligation to Queen Tatiana, and you will get your powers back."

"Once I deliver it. Say it again."

"Yes, once *you* deliver the bounty to her," he repeated. He rolled his eyes. "Do we have to go through this every time?"

"Yes." She rubbed her hands together, already pondering what she would need to do with the store while she chased down whoever or whatever had caught Tatiana's interest this time. Sometimes there were insults to avenge. Sometimes it was simply a matter of the queen seeing in someone a pretty, shiny thing she wanted. Even after all these years, Morgan couldn't understand the queen's whims or how she could treat living, thinking beings as objects. Morgan made it a point of pride that she hadn't let her almost-immortality make her unsympathetic to those whose lives were but a blink. Well, assuming they didn't get in her way.

"Who are we after this time?" She looked at him through her lashes. "And when do we leave? I want to get this over with as soon as possible, although I need a day to get things settled here." She waved her hand. "One does not simply abandon one's magic shop on Samhain."

But her mind already sorted through details. She could call Lacey, her assistant and a talented magic-wielder who had figured out Morgan was more than she let on. Killing people had gotten too messy in the twentieth century—damn forensics —so she'd decided to make the girl an ally rather than elimi- nate her as a threat. Lacey would be happy to help and to watch things while she was away.

"Understood, although I don't see why you bother. Silly mortals, thinking that trinkets can make them into powerful magic-makers." After the seventeenth century, they both instinctively avoided the word *witch*, although it had lost some of its negative connotations since. Elric walked around. "What kind of wards do you have on this place? You've gotten better at them."

Heat came to Morgan's cheeks and frustration to her chest that she still preened under his praise. Was that why he'd used the door rather than just appearing as he usually liked to do? Discreetly, of course. He wouldn't just appear in the middle of a store or someplace else where humans would see him. Nor would he typically pick up objects and put them down without even looking at them.

Or was he complimenting her? Elric's restlessness said he wanted to be away quickly. And he'd apparently done some Earth-crossing before arriving rather than using the connec- tions between the Faerie realm and human ones to expedite his trip. The sense of something being off, like milk just on the cusp of souring, made her hesitate. If there was a loophole that would allow her to not take the job and wait out her time, she aimed to find it.

"And who are we after?" she asked his back as he stood and studied the bookshelves to the right of the door.

"Some vampire." His shoulders lifted and dropped with what she assumed was another sigh. "The queen wants a new pet."

Morgan pulled the glass cleaner and a roll of paper towels from the shelves under the register to rid herself of the hand-prints on the formerly clean case. "What the heck does she want with a vampire? She doesn't typically bother with the nightmare creatures."

"Indeed." He bent to examine a book more closely.

"Let me know if you have any questions," she said automati-cally. Her mind worked as she cleaned the top of the case. Then the front, since no matter how much she tried, she couldn't keep fingerprints from gathering on it. She'd put away the glass cleaner and found the duster for the shelves inside when a weight on her shoulder brought her back to the present.

"It's fine," Elric said. The impatience and irritation had gone from his tone, and now he looked at her tenderly.

She put away the duster and clenched and unclenched her fists to distract herself from the gritty feeling on her fingers. "Where are we going, anyway?"

He put his arms around her, and she stiffened before she snuggled into his chest. She remembered their mutually agreed-upon rules. Anything more than an ongoing fling was impossible, but she'd take what she could get. Even his smell contradicted itself—the odor of plants in a rainstorm over sun-warmed rock.

"There's an island in the Caribbean owned by a man you may have heard of—Merlin. The vampire is being held there."

"Merlin?" Morgan pulled back and looked up to study Elric's face. "We're going up against the Truth Seekers?"

Elric traced a finger over her cheek. "Not necessarily. This vampire poses some sort of threat to them. That's why the queen wants him."

Morgan shivered, both from the journey of Elric's hand, which traced down her cheek and along the line of her jaw, and the thought of what she'd be getting into. No one wanted to be in the middle of the ages-old conflict between the Truth Seekers—the self-styled supernatural law enforcement agency that more than a few paranormal creatures considered to be a band of well-organized vigilantes—and the Fae. She should've known her final job wouldn't be that easy.

"GOOD, NOW MAKE THE CLOUD BIGGER."

Audrey frowned as she focused on the cloud that hung above them in an impossibly bright blue sky. The grass she laid on tickled the backs of her arms and legs, and she had to keep from being distracted by the waving leaves on the nearby trees. Her spirit guide, a small silver dragon, made for a comforting weight on her belly. Maggie, who lay next to her, had explained that this part of the Collective Unconscious, or C.U., remained in a state of eternal summer, hence the green. But it was also a good place to practice a variation of what Audrey had done as a child, only this time she made the shapes in the clouds. Or tried to.

The vaguely cat-shaped white and gray puffball above them suddenly expanded, then dissipated. Audrey sighed, and the dragon squeaked in protest.

"I'm not very good at this." She turned her head to Maggie.

Maggie smiled and patted Audrey on the hand. "You're doing fine. You can't be good at everything on your first try."

"But this isn't my first try." Audrey turned her face back to the sky. "We've been at this for a week, and I can barely manipulate the clouds. How am I supposed to be of any use?"

"A week is nothing. It took much longer for some of us to master even the most basic magic on Avalon." Maggie snorted. "At least if you make something blow up here, it won't hurt anything."

"True." Audrey turned back to her. "Tell me about Avalon."

Maggie shook her head, but behind her, an island shaped cloud appeared. It looked like a semicircle with rectangular things sticking up at the top—standing stones? "It's gone into the mists, although there is a reflection here."

Wispy gray clouds covered the island-shaped one, and it all blew away.

"Do you ever try to go to the reflection, to see what happened to the people there?"

"No." Her tone had gone flat, and Audrey drew back, stung.

"I'm sorry," Maggie said as she patted Audrey's hand again but didn't look at her. "I made one of my biggest mistakes there, and it changed the course of history."

"I'm sorry for asking. By the way, nice cloud work."

"What?" Maggie looked to where Audrey indicated. "I wasn't doing it." She sat, and Audrey did as well. "What did you see?"

"An island with standing stones on the top, and then gray clouds covered it and took it away."

Maggie grinned. "Avalon didn't have standing stones. That must have been your version of it."

"Oh!" Audrey clapped. "But I wasn't trying."

"That means you've been trying too hard." Maggie stood. "And you need a break." She helped Audrey to her feet, and the dragon made lazy circles around them.

Audrey sighed. She'd never get used to this topsy-turvy world, which Maggie had told her was like a dimension. No one had figured out why only humans could reach it in their sleep. Or why they could stash their collective cultural memories here in the forms of gods, goddesses, and other mythological beings. Or why dream weavers like Audrey could—supposedly—manipulate the C.U. and therefore influence the waking world. Audrey wondered if she'd meet Thor someday, but she wouldn't rush it. She hadn't felt quite right since her encounter with Zeus, but she couldn't describe how, except that she often had the sense of someone peering over her shoulder and waiting. For what, she didn't know.

She followed Maggie to the edge of the woods, where the reflection of the sky filmed the surface of a small pool of water about three feet in diameter. The sky darkened, and Audrey looked up to see that dark gray clouds had rolled in. A cold breeze teased the hair at the back of her neck, and she remembered she wasn't the only one engaged in supernatural pursuit. Or, in Damien and Charlie's case, pursuit of something supernatural and nasty.

"Time to check in on the boys?" Audrey asked. Maggie would never admit it, but they were both nervous about the guys hunting a rogue were-bat that day.

"Yep." Maggie pulled her hair back and secured it with an elastic band. "I wish I knew how the nightmare creatures keep getting through like they are. The barriers between the C.U. and the waking world should be mostly healed by now."

Audrey had pictured the barriers as stone walls, but in reality—or what passed for it—they were more like sheets of elastic that could heal like skin. Or that's what she imagined now that Maggie had explained their nature. "Is there another way?"

Maggie shook her head. "Not unless a neighboring realm is letting them through, but the rulers like the nightmares as much as we do, which is to say, not at all."

"Oh." She had to prove she wasn't a total failure. "Can I try to summon the vision?"

Maggie smirked. "Feeling confident after your accidental cloud-work?"

"Yes. Plus it's easier for me to do this because I truly want to see Damien."

"Go ahead then." Maggie stepped back.

Audrey took a deep breath, even though she didn't need to breathe here, and looked at the pool, allowing her eyes to blur their focus. "Show me Damien," she whispered, the desire to see him and make sure he was safe thick in her chest. The surface of the pool shimmered although no breeze stirred the leaves of the plants around its edge, and it cleared to show late fall woods, the trees almost bare. She could make out a couple of dark-clad figures crawling along, but a gray film covered the scene.

"I think I have a bad connection." She huffed. "Is nothing going to work right for me today?"

"There's no such thing here." Maggie stood beside Audrey and looked at the vision. "That's a cloud of obfuscation. Something doesn't want us to see them."

Panic crawled up Audrey's throat. "They're in danger?"

Maggie squeezed her hand one more time and disappeared, leaving Audrey to worry.

2
____

Charlie crawled through the autumn-cool mulch and tried not to think about what that wet spot that soaked the edge of his sleeve could be. The acrid odor that broke through the woodsy smell of forest floor enlightened him anyway—cat piss. While he'd been told about a feral cat colony, he'd yet to see any, likely because they'd scattered when their new neighbor had moved in. No kitty wanted to become the blue plate special. That there was still cat pee to find meant the bat hadn't been there that long, which was a good thing. Less chance of someone seeing the supernatural creature, which would look like a Halloween decoration that had been left out too long come to life.

Finally his destination, an old chimney, came into sight. As he'd been told in his orders, the stones had fallen out at human eye level. Hence why he and Damien had to slink along the ground in case their quarry woke early and watched from inside. The problem with the bat being holed up in the chimney was the danger of a stray shot ricocheting around and injuring one of them, so they would have to wait until evening when it woke and emerged. Plus, even though he knew it was much more dangerous to hunt were-bats when they were awake, Charlie couldn't bring himself to shoot a sleeping creature.

A tug on his pants leg made him turn, and Damien gestured toward a large wild azalea bush to their right under a majestic magnolia tree. The shrub's blooms had long fallen off, but its leaves made for good cover. Charlie nodded. He wanted to get a look around the structure, but it was almost dusk. He would have preferred for them to have done recon during full daylight, but he'd only gotten the orders that afternoon after someone had reported something strange in the woods near the new PATH trail. Now the sky darkened under heavy clouds, the heaviness of twilight near. They crawled behind the bush and sat with their backs against a tree. Charlie stretched out his legs and grimaced at their complaint.

"You're getting old." Damien mouthed the words rather than saying them aloud.

"We're the same age," Charlie grumbled, but also silently.

Damien wrinkled his nose. "What is that on your sleeve? You smell like burning rubber and hot metal had a love child."

"You didn't crawl through it?"

Damien shook his head with a grin.

Charlie frowned. Yes, the odor in the air resembled that of the liquid that had found his sleeve, but it was too heavy to be just that. He and Damien looked up simultaneously. The werebat snoozed in the lattice of the branches about fifty feet above, its B-movie monster face peaceful. Charlie's orders had been for the right creature, wrong location.

Damien stiffened beside him. A snicker made Charlie look to his left, where a child-like creature about two feet tall stood. It wore what looked like blue and green garden gnome clothing stood and held a slingshot and stone in its hands. Its eyes the lurid color of a Sprite bottle sparkled with amusement.

Charlie kept his own jaw from dropping. A faerie? What

was it doing here, in the middle of the city? How had it gotten past the ring of sun-baked metal and concrete-encased girders that formed I-285, Atlanta's perimeter? He'd been told of pockets of the forest creatures in the deep woods of the North Georgia Mountains, but one shouldn't be here.

The child-like creature armed its slingshot and aimed it at the were-bat. Torn between needing to stop the faerie from waking the were-bat and not wanting to move so suddenly as to wake it himself, Charlie could only watch as the stone arced over his head and hit the tree trunk with a thwack.

The were-bat plummeted toward them, its wings spread as much as possible within the confines of the branches and mouth open to reveal its yellowed, shark-sharp teeth. Charlie and Damien scrambled out of the way just in time. They each took a shot, but missed, further angering the creature. Charlie cursed. They needed to draw it out into the open.

Charlie and Damien darted in different directions. That was the plan—if they didn't get a clear shot when it first charged, split up, and whoever wasn't followed would then circle back and kill the bat before it killed his partner. The acrid breath on the back of his neck and the gusts of fetid air from the beating leathery wings told Charlie he'd been the unlucky one in that lottery. He dodged around trees, trying to make it get itself tangled in branches so Damien could get a clear shot.

A bullet whizzed by his head, but it came from the wrong direction. He dropped and rolled to his left just before the were-bat dove for him and missed. Charlie landed with a splash in a stream. Two shots happened so close together they sounded like one with an echo, and the creature fell with a thud to the ground, bursting into flame. Charlie resisted the temptation to bury his nose in the stream to escape from the stench of the combusting corpse. Instead, he rolled to his hands and knees and peered over the embankment. Damien stood back, his arms crossed, but his facial expression didn't give much away beyond mild anger.

The figure that stood on the other side of the body blended in with the colors of the forest in its skin-tight clothing, a knit cap on its head. Charlie groaned when he saw the pale oval of her face with eyes hidden behind purple glasses.

Maggie.

She must have heard him because she turned in his direction. "Charlie! There you are. Did you decide to go for a swim?" Her teasing didn't help his mood.

He staggered to his feet and mentally checked himself for injuries. Just bruises and scratches and the discomfort of wet britches, as his mother would have said.

"Ha ha ha." He didn't know whether the pressure that reached from his chest to his throat meant anger or happiness at her appearance. Nothing was ever clear with her. She'd essentially rejected his offer of a romantic liaison due to the curse that had dogged her for several hundred years. Typically he'd been able to move on from rejection, but not this one. For the first time in years, he hadn't been on a date in several weeks. None of the women on the internet compared to Maggie's ethereal beauty, not even with their professionally done photos and clever camera angles. Or maybe he'd just gotten cynical.

"Would you like to explain why you almost shot me?" he asked, his voice gruffer than he intended. "I felt that bullet go by."

"I had to get you to duck," she explained, her hands palm up. "It was gaining on you, although you're an impressive runner." She looked at his red mud-caked black jeans. "I didn't realize you'd go into the stream—sorry."

"I had it," Damien said.

"You didn't have a clear shot," she told him. A brown tabby

cat emerged from behind one of the trees, and Maggie bent over and held a hand out. "Here, kitty."

"Careful, the ones around here are feral," Charlie warned her. "They're not going to be all nice kitty, soft kitty for you." Then he noticed the creature had very bright green eyes. Maggie straightened, her eyes narrowed.

"That's no cat." Her expression mirrored the same confusion he'd felt earlier. "But one of *them* shouldn't be here."

Damien, apparently having caught on that their supernatural adventures were not over yet, said, "Shouldn't we go?"

The creature shimmered and grew, expanding into a brown and black tiger-like creature. Its growl resonated deep within Charlie's gut.

Oh. Crap.

Maggie grabbed his hand, and he had the familiar sensation of something clicking into place, the sensation he'd hoped would disappear after she'd told him she couldn't be with him. The forest faded around them, and he found himself standing in the middle of Maggie's living room. Part of his brain observed that she'd redecorated, going from white couches and blue carpet to blue and green furniture on tan carpet. It looked homier than previously.

The other part noticed that while she held both his and Damien's hands, she released Damien's first.

❧

Two days after Elric found her at her shop, Morgan stood at the edge of the surf and let the waves wash over her toes. The sun set over the ocean and painted it and the clouds above in mirroring shades of pink, orange, red, and finally purple. She smiled when the sky turned gray. Tomorrow she would be a free woman, no longer having to wait and wonder.

She closed her eyes and reached out to the surf, allowing

the energy of the dusk to wash over her. Then her eyelids snapped up when someone grabbed her right hand and planted a cold kiss on it. A man stood in the surf in front of her, his feet hidden by mounds of sand, his golden hair catching whatever light remained. Lapping waves darkened his uniform dress pants beyond their usual black, and the red stripes on his sleeves told Morgan he served the faerie queen directly. Electric dismay tingled through her—this could only mean trouble.

"Greetings, le Fay," he said and bowed, but he didn't release her fingertips.

Morgan snatched her hand away and crossed her arms. "What do you want?"

He smiled, and she had to tell her mind to still so her internal speculation wouldn't drown out his words.

"I come to you with your final mission. But it seems we have a problem."

She swallowed against the pressure at the back of her throat. The ceviche and margaritas that she and Elric had shared for dinner threatened to make a reappearance. "What's the problem, Captain?"

"It seems that you have accepted the mission without knowing all the information." He gloated as only a Fae who'd just caught a human in a verbal trap could.

"Tell me." She could only squeeze out short sentences around the spreading panic in her chest.

"Well, I was to offer you a choice." He held out his right hand, palm-up. "You could complete this final task, and the reward would be the rest of your power plus enough riches to keep you comfortable for the rest of your immortal life. Or..." He matched the gesture of his right hand with his left. "You could retire with what you have and receive your powers at the end of the time. Queen Tatiana is fair—she acknowledges your deal was ten jobs or ten centuries, and this last one came close to the end and will be more difficult than the others. You'll be attempting to steal something from Merlin, after all."

Morgan's stomach sank into the soft sand beneath her feet. She could have refused the job and gotten her powers back anyway? No, it couldn't have been that easy, and she held back her scoff at him calling the queen fair. She also heard what he hadn't said. "And if I fail?"

He shrugged. "You walk away with what you have, and the queen keeps the rest of your powers."

Well, at least there was that.

But he continued, "Or she may take what you've regained to this point. You did have a deal, after all."

Now anger flashed through her, and steam wreathed her ankles. Damn, he'd know she was losing control—she only heated when she couldn't help herself since she hadn't yet fully regained her power over fire. "That's not fair. I've done nine jobs for her. I should be paid for those."

He shrugged and started to bow. She knew he was about to disappear.

"Wait, can I step back from this job and walk away?"

He straightened. "You've already accepted it. You and Elric spoke the words of binding."

"But he didn't tell me everything!" A familiar stinging feeling sank from her heart to her stomach—betrayal. She'd been a fool to ignore her instincts and trust him when he'd given her the assignment, even after he'd given her nine centuries' worth of reasons why she could. But how had Elric come to her without the queen's knowledge?

The soldier bowed again, and as he faded, his words hung in the air between them. "Take it up with the queen, then. I've done my duty."

Morgan put a hand to her throat to stop her heart's panicked beating and took gulps of the sea air. Then coughed. The breeze held a hint of sulfur, and she turned when something other than the waves moved in her peripheral vision. A gnarled creature covered in wet seaweed emerged from the waves, its eyes a glowing red. It inclined its head when it saw her, and Morgan stepped back. The nightmare creatures had always treated her with respect, which she had alternately appreciated and found curious. But what was one doing here? It crawled back into the waves and was gone.

She clenched her fists and turned back to the surf. She knew one thing—she'd never trust anyone again, and Elric would be the first to be turned into a crisp once she finished this damn job and regained her full abilities.

3

———

Maggie released the breath she'd been holding as the woods faded around them, and they transferred to her apartment. She'd rarely stayed anywhere as long as she had in this place, and it had come to feel like a sanctuary.

"What are we doing here?" Charlie's clothes had dried during the shift, but his mood had not improved, and he took his hand back. "And what was that in the forest? Was that a faerie? And why was it trying to kill us?"

Maggie heard his last question even though he didn't ask it —*and what the hell were you doing there?*

She removed her knit cap and shook out her long red hair. "To answer your questions in order, you're here because it was the place that I felt was safest for now, yes that was a faerie, and I suspect it was trying to mess with us. They're mischievous like that."

She looked at him with her full gaze behind her glasses. "And I came because I knew you were in trouble."

Damien put a hand on Charlie's arm and said, "Thanks. What matters is that the were-bat is taken care of."

Charlie nodded once. Curtly.

"Please," Maggie said and gestured to the couches, "make yourselves comfortable." She escaped into the kitchen and grabbed three bottles of water from the fridge. The awkwardness of her and Charlie's last conversation stood like a presence between them. She took a couple of deep breaths to steady herself and watched the two of them from behind the counter.

Damien removed his hand from Charlie's forearm but didn't move otherwise. Charlie took a step and then looked down at his own attire.

Maggie shook her head—she'd forgotten they'd been crawling through the woods. Any motion made dirt and leaves flake off their clothing, and the mud on their boots had stained her carpet. She returned to the living room, handed them the bottles of water, and waved her hand. The visible dirt disappeared, but she couldn't do anything about the grit beneath their clothes and in between their toes. At least not without getting too personal.

"Sorry, now you can sit. Thanks for being considerate of my stuff."

They both sat, and she noticed that Damien avoided the couch that had replaced the one where his girlfriend Audrey had been sleeping when her spirit had gotten trapped in the C.U. Charlie perched there. She hesitated—would he be more or less annoyed if she sat with him? Or with Damien? She elected to stand.

Charlie stuck to business, his tone devoid of any of the tenderness she recalled. "Did the faerie come through from the C.U.? Is that how it was able to get into the heart of the city?"

"I don't know." Maggie fidgeted with the cap of her water bottle. "I'm not sure what's going on. I haven't gotten my next assignment yet, and my bosses are being strangely quiet." She glanced at Charlie, and he flinched and looked away.

Did he hate her so much he couldn't stand for her to look at him? She took a swallow of water to ease the tightness in her throat.

"You still haven't explained why you appeared in the forest," he said.

She hadn't thought this one through. Only dream weavers and Truth Seekers were allowed the knowledge that they could spy on people from the waking world. "I just had the feeling that something was up." She bit her lip. "Sorry, that was a lie. I can't tell you now why I was there, but I'm glad I was."

Charlie glanced at Damien, who just drank his water and watched the exchange, the wrinkles at the corners of his gray eyes giving away his amusement. Normally he would have jumped in by this point to defend Charlie's ability and aim—both of which were damn good, from what Maggie had seen. She smiled. Being with Audrey had settled Damien. He'd gone from being a talented officer skittish about the supernatural to a talented were-bat hunter with a healthy respect for other-worldly danger.

"We had it under control." Charlie gestured toward Damien. "I trust *him* to have my back."

Ouch. Maggie shifted her weight. Did she feel she needed to make up for having left him to the mercy of the magically drugged champagne at Lyle Ames's party? It had all worked out, but she'd allowed him to be in a vulnerable position.

She needed to talk to Merlin to see what was up. Did the nightmare creatures'—and there had been more than one—appearances mean she'd be sticking around for a while? Her intuition said yes, but not with any detail or clarity.

"I need to check into some things before we talk about this situation further," she said. "C'mon, I'll take you to your car."

Charlie sighed, and she stopped herself from echoing with her own dismay. *Looks like we'll probably be working together again. Hopefully we can keep it professional.*

Morgan stared into the surf, trying to convince herself that what she had seen was real. Oh, she had no trouble believing Elric had betrayed her—it always happened eventually, a hard lesson she'd learned as a child—and she would figure out what to do with that information once she could think around the heartache. Even though she'd lived more than a millennium, she still berated herself for being a foolish girl.

But what had the sea creature been doing there? Morgan had felt the walls of the Collective Unconscious weaken, as had most non-mortals, she guessed, but the cracks should be fixed by now. The sea monster had smelled enough of sulfur to tell her it had been freshly released.

Something more was going on. And her eyes stung from not blinking so she wouldn't miss the creature if it made a brief reappearance. Like the ocean, her life had tides and currents that ran deeper than surface appearances. And it seemed Elric's motivations ran deeper than she had suspected.

Yes, she'd been a foolish, foolish girl.

"Penny for your thoughts?" Elric asked when he approached but she didn't acknowledge him. He'd been hinting all day that once they made their arrangements, they could satisfy their mutual lust—again—but she was no longer interested. Fine, let him guess.

"I just saw a lagoon monster. I think that's the correct term." She turned away from the sea, finally blinking moisture into her stinging eyes. "It appeared from the waves, saluted me, and disappeared again. One of those shouldn't have gotten through. The cracks aren't that big anymore."

Elric shrugged. "There are always anomalies. I've heard some points still had more difficulties than others. The Truth Seekers are on it." He gave her a fake grin and a double thumbs-up, and a giggle escaped around her hurt. He had the same like for Merlin's organization that she did, but then she sobered. They were going up against Merlin's defenses on the island where the vampire was being held. And now she didn't know if she could trust Elric to have her back.

"Did you get the boat?" she asked.

"Yes, it wasn't too hard. At least once I glamored him."

Morgan shivered. She hated to watch the Fae operate their magic on mortals. She had often wondered if mental clouding and manipulation were among the powers she hadn't regained yet, but she didn't think she would use them if she had them. She preferred to convince people in a way that allowed them a chance to refuse. Of course, there could be consequences for refusal, but there were consequences for everything in life.

"We can go when you're ready." Elric tried to put an arm around her, but she shrugged him off. "What?"

The question of why he hadn't told her she had a choice in taking that last job tottered at the end of her tongue, but she held it in. She didn't need to let him know she knew about his deception, at least not until she figured out what he was up to.

"Nothing." She smiled even though it hurt her face. "Where's the boat?"

"At the marina." He arched an eyebrow but didn't ask anything else.

"And I can count on you, right?" She put a hand on his arm. "You wouldn't keep anything from me about this job, would you? I'm nervous taking on Merlin's magic, even if he isn't there."

His gaze briefly flicked left like it had in her store before he answered. "You've totally got this. I—the queen is counting on you."

She nodded, directing her attention ahead as they walked, her mind working in double time to their hurried steps. She would have to be extra careful. And not hand the target over to him. She wondered if she could get away from him somehow once she picked up the vamp. A nightmare creature. There had to be a connection.

"Any idea as to the island's defenses?" She felt safe asking that question, at least. The beach was strangely deserted, likely due to the lagoon creature. Humans might not always be the smartest, but they often surprised her with their survival instincts.

"Some security spells, but from what I could gather from the intel, not a whole lot. It seems that Merlin was trying to keep the vamp from getting to people, not the other way around."

"So it's a particularly dangerous one. Young and hungry?"

Elric nodded, his lips set in a grim line. "So I understand. Turned in January."

"January? What does Tatiana want with a fledgling?" The question burst out of her before she could catch it.

"That's *Queen* Tatiana, and I don't know, only that she wants him." His gaze flicked away so quickly she almost didn't see it.

His confusion sounded almost genuine, but she'd caught the lie. He knew exactly what the queen wanted the vamp for, and he was planning to double-cross Morgan for...what? She balled the fist on the far side of her body from him. She had the sense that if she could step back and look at the whole picture, she'd figure it out, but she didn't have the proper perspective. Thus she'd have to grab the quarry and see what it—he—knew. Then maybe she'd discover what was up.

They reached the marina, and Elric led her to a bay boat. A bearded man sat under the canopy at the controls. He wore a captain's hat, which looked comical with his other attire—a blue and white tropical shirt open to show his gray-haired tan chest and cargo pants.

"So you're after some late-night fishing?" he asked. The only clue that Elric had messed with his perceptions was that his eye contact seemed off. Too long when he spoke, too short when she answered.

"Yes, we're after a big one tonight."

"Then hop aboard, and we'll get you going." He tipped his hat. "You can call me Captain Bob. Welcome aboard the Bullfinch."

Morgan smiled at the old-fashioned gesture and accepted his invitation. Elric followed her. They sat in twin bucket seats in the small area behind the cockpit, and Morgan tolerated Elric putting his arm around her. She didn't mind the anchor to this reality as the captain maneuvered the boat out of the marina and to the open sea. She'd hated crossing water since that last fateful trip from Avalon, when she had been forced to leave without her son. She'd lost her powers, and she couldn't part the mists herself, so a "friend" had taken her. A friend who'd betrayed her.

Why did she have to repeat the same lesson? Each time it grew more painful.

"So what are you going to do with your retirement?" Elric asked. The wind whipped around them, and the engine was behind them, so Captain Bob couldn't hear them.

She almost laughed in his face, his question ridiculous now that he'd set her up to fail, but she had to stay calm and collected. "I don't know." At least that was an honest answer. "I don't remember what life was like before."

Not that she wanted to recall, anyway. Dread that had nothing to do with Elric's Fey games or the nightmare creature situation curled in her chest. She'd lived with the purpose of getting her powers back for centuries. But what would she do once she had them and therefore didn't have anything to strive for? Would she go back to having to make up things to keep herself busy, like the silly Knights of the Round Table had? Maybe she could find the Holy Grail. She'd gotten an archeology degree at one point.

"Really? There's nothing you've been just dying to do?"

Was he being cruel, or just curious? She shrugged. "Modern life is pretty darn comfortable, in case you haven't noticed."

"So you'll be going back to your little store? Is there a man waiting in the wings? Or woman?"

Morgan shook her head. "Neither, at least not this time."

He attempted to engage her in further conversation, but she put her earbuds in and put on music that would get her pumped up—Heart's "Barracuda". She ducked when he swatted at something.

"What was that?"

"Don't know. But I took care of it."

He put his arm around her. Morgan figured she could at least use his shoulder if nothing else and forced her muscles to relax to conserve her strength. She didn't recall anything until he nudged her and said, "There's the island. We're here."

4

———

Maggie dropped Charlie and Damien off where they'd parked their cars and returned to her apartment. She locked the door, closed all the blinds, and whispered incantations at each one to reinforce her privacy. No telling what could be watching, especially with it being after dusk. She hoped she didn't catch Merlin at dinner —he hated to be interrupted when he was eating. He'd been a foodie before the term existed.

She took a deep breath and headed to her spare bedroom. Ghosts of memories flitted around her, warning her to avoid the space and the recollections of one of her major mistakes. She stopped at the threshold and shook her head, not wanting to look inside. There had been so many mistakes already in her past. Why had she allowed herself to be caught unprepared again?

Only one person besides Audrey had stayed in her spare bedroom, a young man named Philippe who had developed feelings for her. She'd done her best to push him away. And had failed. And he had been doomed—in his case, turned into a vampire. Merlin had "taken him to a place where he couldn't hurt anyone," whatever that meant. But had he been hurt? Was he okay?

She'd put on her big immortal pants and ask Merlin when she talked to him. In a minute.

She took a deep breath and opened her eyes. The room looked the same as it always had—cream-colored carpet, dark blue bedspread, light wooden nightstands with plain brass lamps atop them. Cozy but neutral, designed to be comfortable for the Truth Seeker's very occasional guest. She walked in, prepared for something to pounce on her from the recesses in her brain, but only the tightness of regret washed through her.

Yes, she would insist Merlin tell her where Philippe was.

One unusual feature was the locked door of the walk-in closet. Maggie unlocked it and stepped inside.

White candles on the small altar along the smaller wall to her left flared to life when she breathed a short spell. They illuminated but didn't reflect in the oval obsidian mirror between them. Maggie made sure her altar accoutrements were arranged on the black satin cloth. She had the expected small dagger and bowl but had added other meaningful objects. A spiral snail shell from the bank of the lake that surrounded the island of Avalon and various rocks and shells from other places she'd visited and lived helped to both ground her and allow her to draw strength from her long history. She gripped the rough sides of the mirror and murmured the words that would put her in touch with Merlin.

A blurred ghostly image, the reflection of her own face, appeared in the mirror, and she waited for it to morph and change into that of the most ordinary-looking of men, Merlin the Magician, Counselor of Kings and Director of the Truth Seekers.

Maggie counted her breaths, and on breath five, she said the calling spell again. Nothing, and her shoulders grew sore from the awkward arm position. Finally when her fingers tingled in anticipation of numbness, she dropped her hands and shook them out. The mirror's surface returned to eerie blankness.

"That's odd," she said aloud, her words loud in the small space. Merlin always answered a mirror summons unless he was indisposed. And even if so, he would always call back. She waited for the tingle at the base of her skull that would tell her he tried to reach her, but there wasn't anything for ten, twenty minutes. She crossed her arms and leaned against the wall, looking at the mirror like a fool, for another ten to make it half an hour of waiting for a call-back.

Nothing, not even the wisp of a magical signal, came to her. For the first time in over a millennium, she wondered if Merlin had succumbed to some sort of illness or vulnerability. He was the most powerful of them all, except for maybe Morgan le Fay —wherever she was, if she'd regained her powers—but he could still be killed if not careful.

"Time for the emergency protocol." Saying it aloud made it more official. She braced her hands on the side of the stone and said in her most authoritative voice, "Mirror, mirror on the wall, who's the most powerful of them all?"

She couldn't help but roll her eyes. At least Merlin only made them stroke his ego in an emergency.

Her ghostly reflection came into view again, and this time it did morph, but not into Merlin. It showed the image of some sort of fishing boat racing across a moonlit ocean. Maggie found she could pan, zoom, and move around the boat to see who was in it. A guy in cargo pants, a tropical shirt, and captain's hat drove, and behind him sat two people who looked familiar.

Then memory snapped into place. The one on the left, a beautiful twenty-something-looking girl with long dark hair and blue eyes, had barely aged since the last time Maggie had seen her. At that time, she'd looked a teenager. That a thousand years looked like ten on her was a testament to her inherent magic and faerie heritage—Morgan le Fay. And the young man beside her looked about the same age, but his appearance was twice as deceptive. That was Elric, cousin and favorite of Queen Tatiana.

Where were they going? Maggie's vision seemed tied to the boat, and she couldn't move more than ten feet from it in any direction. When she zoomed back to the couple, Elric seemed to look straight at her and waved his hand. An electric shock jolted her hands off the mirror, which cracked in the middle. Maggie dove to the floor and covered her head as its magic dissipated in a burst of thick black smoke that coated the walls above knee-height. Maggie crawled from the closet, her back, arms, and legs coated with the stuff. She lay on the carpet, panting.

"This isn't good." Voicing the feeling didn't help her feel better. What was Morgan up to now? And worse—since the mirror had shown her to Maggie—how was Maggie going to become involved?

Worst of all—where was Merlin?

Audrey looked up from the stove when someone turned the key in the lock to her front door. She made sure the pasta water wouldn't boil over and walked from her small kitchen into the living room. Damien, freshly showered and in street clothes, smiled at her, but the tension around his eyes told her he'd had a rough day.

They both had.

Relief washed over Audrey, and she blinked so she wouldn't cry with the release of the tension and anxiety that had tied her heart to her gut all day since she'd found out Damien and Charlie were hunting the were-bat. And had ratcheted up to almost unbearable tension after Maggie had told her about the obfuscation spell. She ran to him and threw her arms around him.

"Hey, hey, it's all right." He rubbed her back. He hadn't told her what he'd been doing—Charlie's assignments were top secret until they were over, but when he'd told her he'd be out of touch from late afternoon to shift change, she'd guessed. And then Maggie had confirmed her suspicion and given her the details.

"Did you get it?" she asked. Not what, exactly. Damn, she hated having to talk around stuff like they both didn't know what he was doing.

"Maggie did."

"Maggie?" Audrey didn't have to feign surprise. Maggie had warned her that dream weaver training was top secret, so the boys couldn't know they were being spied on, but she didn't realize that's where Maggie had gone.

"The woman's a crack shot, I'll give her that." After one last squeeze, Damien put her down. "What smells so good?"

Audrey sank on to her couch. "Spaghetti. The pasta's cooking now, and the sauce is hot, so dinner will be done soon." It all felt so nice and domestic. She wanted to wrap the scene up and keep it somewhere safe, keep *him* somewhere safe. She'd encountered were-bats before and knew how cruel and ruthless they could be. She shuddered to think—

No, she couldn't think about what would happen to Damien if the were-bat or some other nightmare creature were to get him before he and Charlie could get it. What it would be like to get a knock on the door or a phone call that would shatter her life like it had when the officer had told her mother about her father? She thought she'd gotten over it and accepted Damien had a sometimes dangerous job, but when something didn't go quite right, the old panic snapped into place.

"You okay?" he asked and sat beside her.

She nodded. She couldn't let on that she knew he'd been in danger. And he knew better than to give her details. Not that he could, not until whoever managed his clearance did the same for her. They were working on it, Maggie said. As a dream weaver, she'd be an invaluable asset to their little team. Once she figured out how to do it.

"Hey." He put a finger under her chin and turned her face to him. "If something's bothering you, tell me. Is it my job again?"

"It's that. It's the fact that I can't seem to get a hang of the dream-weaving thing. It's that I'm useless and only get to sit here and make pasta while everyone else has adventures." Dangerous adventures. With creatures who wanted to kill them.

"You're not useless. So it's not going well?" He dropped his hand from her face and rubbed her shoulder nearest him.

She relaxed marginally. "Maybe she was wrong. Maybe I'm not a true dream weaver. Maybe it was the sleeping pill I tried that let me into the C.U., not my own talent."

"And if that's the case, that's fine."

The timer for the pasta beeped, and Audrey stood more roughly than she needed to. He looked up at her, his eyebrows lifted and his hand hanging where it had been on her shoulder.

"Dinner's ready." She walked into the kitchen, turned off the timer, and drained the pasta.

He leaned on the door frame between kitchen and living room, his arms crossed."I didn't say the right thing, did I?"

She plated the pasta, giving him a slightly larger portion and an extra meatball. "I don't know. I mean, I don't want you to lie, to say you're sure I'm doing fine and that I'll get the hang of it eventually since you can't see what I'm doing. It's just..." She sighed and picked up the bowls. He stepped back so she could carry them to the small dining area between the couch and kitchen. "I'm just feeling useless," she said again.

"It's okay. I mean—" He rubbed his face. "I can see how

you'd be frustrated. But if you decided to not be a dream weaver, to go back to your journalism, I'd be okay with that."

"Oh?" She warned him with her tone.

"I'm fine with whatever you want to do."

Somehow she doubted that was the case, but she didn't say anything. Why were relationships so hard?

5

——————

Morgan studied the island through the pair of binoculars she'd packed in her bag. The boat rose and fell with the waves, but the motion didn't bother her. The water did.

The lake lay like a mirror, the gray sky a perfect reflection on its surface. She watched the boy try to skip stones, but he wasn't coordinated enough yet, and the stones sank rather than skipped. The water absorbed the ripples before they got too far, the liquid more like quicksand. The heaviness of the humid air didn't help the sense of oppressiveness and only confirmed what she'd been thinking—she needed to escape Avalon.

Morgan blinked the memory away. The past liked to intrude when she felt unsure of the present. The trick of the water had been Merlin's, and indeed, rather than the usual tumble of waves along the shore, the sea only lapped at the edge of the sand.

Getting past that would be her first challenge.

"There's a defense spell at the shoreline." She lowered the binoculars and looked at Elric. "Remind me what's so special about...?" She inclined her head toward the island.

Elric only shrugged. "Tatiana wants him. That's all you need to know."

Morgan raised the binoculars again. She caught a glimpse of something moving in the foliage. They'd had the captain drop the anchor and shut off the engines and lights so no one would know they were there, but the tingling feeling at the back of her neck told Morgan they'd been spotted. A twin pair of red lights appeared.

"Crap, he's hungry." And there was no telling what a starving young vamp would do. But there was something strange about how he moved. He reeled, almost drunkenly, or that's how it appeared from the motion of the lights. She lowered the binoculars and shook her head. There was definitely something weird going on.

"I've inflated the raft." Elric gestured to the rubber dingy that now floated next to the boat.

"Right." Morgan put the binoculars back in her bag and walked to the rail. She dropped her bag into the flimsy-looking vessel and took a deep breath, ignoring the chemical-plastic smell. Next to still water, she hated small watercraft the most. "And I have to bring him back alive?"

"Yes." Elric's mouth had almost disappeared into a straight line, and a tiny muscle danced along his jaw. "You can't collect on a pile of ash."

"Damn." Flimsy boat, hungry vamp, secured island... What could go right?

She swung a leg over the rail, followed it with the other one, and then climbed down into the raft. The oars were inside. With a sigh, she took off toward the island.

After about ten minutes of rowing, the momentum of the surf took over, and she floated closer and closer to her target. Then the raft bumped into something that allowed the water to pass through, albeit in a muted fashion with smaller waves, but stopped her progress. An almost electric buzz hummed beneath her, and fog rolled in from both sides, obscuring her vision.

Ah, at least that felt familiar. Merlin had modernized his spell, but she guessed it was similar to what had protected Avalon. Not that Merlin had come up with that one—it had preceded him by centuries—but it hadn't taken long for him to figure it out and refine it.

Morgan whispered the Celtic phrase that had parted the mists at Avalon, but of course it didn't work. She needed a modern phrase for a modern spell. Merlin had always had an ego, so she searched her brain for phrases he would appreciate in reference to himself.

"Merlin, greatest wizard of all time." The fog rolled, but it didn't part.

"Merlin, he who must be obeyed." Okay, she didn't really think that one would work, but it was worth a shot.

"Merlin the Magnificent, advisor to kings and head of the Truth Seekers."

A keypad made of mists appeared in front of her. Aha, so she'd summoned the lock. What would Merlin use as his password? She thought about trying 1-2-3-4, but while she would've appreciated the irony, she didn't know how many shots she'd get. So she tried the one date Merlin would always cherish— the date of the coronation of Arthur, when Merlin had secured his own place of power. Calendars had changed, but Morgan had a good sense for when dates were and had been. She punched in the date, and the fog rolled away and allowed her little dinghy to proceed.

"One down," she muttered. The water guided her vessel to bump gently against the sand. She pulled a stake crossbow from her bag. She loaded it with what she called her baby stakes—non-consecrated wood and without a silver core. If the vamp charged her, she'd at least be able to slow him down without killing him. At least not before she could deliver him to Tatiana. If he died soon after, she'd at least have met her part of the bargain.

The sound of crashing in the foliage just beyond the shoreline made her duck into the boat. Then she remembered it wouldn't provide much of a shield. She jumped out and ran along the sand so she'd at least not be in direct sight of whatever it was when it emerged.

She crouched behind a fallen tree and watched. A figure stumbled out of the forest and sprawled on the sand.

"Fucking birds with your fucking berries," a male voice slurred. The creature lifted its head and looked around, the dim red of its eyes illuminating the sand around it.

Morgan's jaw dropped. A drunken vampire? How in the world could that have happened? Then something smacked her in the back of the head.

She turned to see a colorful small bird, and it seemed to be as intoxicated as the vampire, judging by how it reeled on the sand. At the sound of the bird flailing around, the vampire got to his hands and knees and crawled toward Morgan's hiding place. She grabbed the bird and tossed it out on to the sand. The vampire pounced on it in a spray of feathers and drained it. He sat back and laughed.

"Oh, fucking *Twilight* never prepared me for this." Then he started to sing, "Ninety-nine birdies of rum on the wall, ninety-nine birdies of rum..."

Morgan stifled a chuckle, finally making the connection between the birds and the berry bush she crouched next to. She pulled off a berry, squished it, and sniffed. Yep, fermented. The birds were eating the berries, and the poor vampire was feeding on the drunken birds.

Typical Merlin, sticking the poor kid—because he couldn't

have been more than twenty-five when he was turned—in an impossible and ridiculous situation. She almost felt sorry for him. But what had he done to attract Merlin's attention? And Tatiana's?

Drunk or not, he shouldn't be underestimated. But how should she approach a drunken vampire who was amusing himself by rolling around on the sand and singing?

She didn't have to. One emphatic roll took him to where her raft was beached. He staggered to his feet and scratched his dark curls.

"Huh, don't remember that being there." He turned. "Merlin, you fucking arsehole, is that you? Did you come to visit me?"

Something jolted through Morgan when he spotted her, and she stood.

"I don't mean you any harm."

He put his hands on his hips. He wore the remains of jeans that had been sawed off at the legs to make shorts that revealed a nice muscular pair of legs and a T-shirt that had frayed to threadbare in spots, showing he'd been in good shape when he'd died.

"Then why do you have a weapon? Oh, it's one of those crossbow thingies. Like Maggie's friend has. Bastard." He made a sweeping gesture and stumbled, barely catching himself. "They're all bastards. Truth Seekers and wizards and... And..." He frowned. "What was I saying?"

"I'm not a Truth Seeker." Morgan slowly approached him, the crossbow pointed at the sand but ready to come up at any moment. "Nor am I a wizard. I'm just...me."

"And what's your name?" He crossed his arms. "Pardon my manners, but I don't get many visitors." He snickered. "Or any."

"Morgan. And Maggie who?"

Could he have encountered her traitorous aunt?

"Margaret the Truth Seeker. Redhead." He shook his head. "Should've known better. Mom told me never to trust a redhead." With a sniffle, he added, "Poor Mum probably thinks I'm dead." Then he giggled. "I kind of am."

"When were you turned?" Morgan stopped what she hoped was a safe distance away, but she couldn't do much with him being between her and the raft.

"Last January." He shook his head. "Not sure how long ago that was. This fucking island doesn't have seasons."

That matched the description she'd been given, but she just couldn't believe this poor mess was who Tatiana wanted her to fetch. Was this some sort of trick? And what did her dear Aunt Maggie have to do with all this?

And worse, why was Elric hiding stuff from her? Previously he'd given her all the intel to make her jobs easier.

"Well, I need you to come with me." She gave him her most charming smile.

"Can't." He shrugged. "Merlin put a barrier around the island. I tried to swim off the first few nights I was here, and I nearly drowned when I couldn't get past it."

"I can. And I can bring you with me."

"Really?" His hopeful expression made him look all that much more pathetic.

"Really. I just need you to promise not to attack me."

He sniffed the air, and she realized she stood upwind from him. His nostrils flared, and he licked his lips. "I don't know if I can make that promise. You smell delicious. Like Maggie." He narrowed his eyes. "Morgan who?"

She sighed. Might as well give him some truthful info so he'd trust her. "Morgan le Fay. Yes, that one."

"Another legend. Lucky me." He spread his hands. "Want to knock me out? I can't promise to wake up un-hungry, but at least you'd be safe."

"I'll just tie you up, if that's okay with you." This was so not the context she thought she'd be saying those words in.

"Fine." He turned and put his hands behind him. "But come at me from downwind so I won't smell you."

She circled around him, then studied his posture and her possible escape routes should he decide she'd make a good snack after all. Her Fae blood somehow made her irresistible to vampires, hence why she had avoided them 'til now. "You're really desperate, aren't you?"

"Is it that obvious?" His shoulders slumped. "Even if you stake me, it's got to be better than this. Stupid birds."

"Right." But it had been ingenious of him. "Where did you get the idea?" She approached him slowly so she wouldn't startle him into biting but also to give her more time to assess the threat he posed.

"*Interview with the Vampire*. At least they're not rats."

"One of my favorite movies even if it's not entirely correct."

"You're telling me."

Morgan grinned, despite the anger that had been simmering and now wanted to boil over. What had the poor guy done to deserve this fate? She guessed Merlin had banked on him dying of hunger, exposure, or both. That brought up another question.

"Where have you been sleeping?" Just a few steps away now.

"I buried myself in the sand the first few nights. Then when I was digging my bed the fourth night, I found rocks, which turned out to be the entrance to a cave. No treasure, though."

She stopped behind him and tied his wrists, moving quickly. Indeed, he turned, his eyes fully ablaze, his nostrils flared.

"Sorry," she said and grabbed him in a carotid paralysis hold. His eyes rolled up and back, and he crumpled. She nudged his fall so he landed in the raft, and she adjusted him to maintain the craft's balance.

With her prisoner in tow, she rowed back to the boat. Now all she had to do was get him away from Elric and figure out what to do with him after that. She couldn't turn him over to Tatiana until she had the whole story.

6

After cleaning up, Maggie spent the night in meditation to clear her aura of whatever energy might have contaminated her from the mirror's explosion. She opened her eyes with the sunrise and waited all the next day for Merlin to be in touch with her. He'd always known when she tried to contact him. Since her obsidian mirror was now cracked and useless, she filled a black bowl of water. A crude substitute, but it would have to do.

And that drew her mind to other problems—what had Morgan been doing in a boat with Elric? Maggie had heard her niece had taken the occasional bounty hunting job—and was good at it—but the High Fae didn't get involved in their own dirty work. Had Morgan been seduced by Elric? Or had she seduced him?

Finally as dusk descended once again, the surface of the water rippled, but nothing appeared. Maggie wiped her hands on her jeans—she couldn't just sit and do nothing. She'd go back to the place where the small faerie had appeared and look around for evidence of nightmare creatures. Perhaps an all-night stakeout would reveal some answers. She hadn't done

one of those in a while. It may be fun to play real detective for once.

She'd changed into her dark clothing and tucked her hair into a black knitted hat when someone knocked on her door. She opened it to see Lieutenant Charles Allen MacKenzie wearing his black DPD polo shirt and black jeans. He carried a black cap and had a dark jacket slung over his arm.

"Yes?" she asked.

He leaned on the door frame so she could neither close the door on him nor get past him. "I've been waiting for you to contact me. I need your perspective for the report." His tone was neither friendly nor angry.

"This isn't a good time, Lieutenant."

"But it's a good time for a stakeout?" He gestured to her clothing.

"What do you mean?" She tried for wide-eyed innocence.

"Uh huh. I'm not falling for it." He ticked his points off on his fingers. "One, we encountered something strange in the woods. Two, we're both detectives of a sort. Three, I know you, as much as you don't want to admit it. You want to check out the scene, see what turns up."

Drat. She couldn't lie to him. "And how do you know it's safe?"

"I'm guessing you can tell somehow. Didn't you and your sisters have a connection to the fairies?"

"You've obviously read the legends." She shrugged to hide the fact he'd scored a hit. "What did they tell you?"

"They're inconsistent. Some speculate that you had some sort of agreement with the Fae, and others that you were part Fae, which explained the magical hold you seemed to have on the men in your lives."

She turned away from the suspicion in his gaze. "I'm no faerie, Charlie, but yes, I do understand them. And yes, I can typically tell when they're around, although that one snuck up on me yesterday, probably because I wasn't looking for it, and it was in nature. Never underestimate them."

"I know better than that." The look he gave her told her he hadn't discounted her connection with the Fae, nor her warning.

"Fine, let's go."

As much as she hated to admit it, Charlie's appearance focused her back on the problem at hand and away from the conundrum of why Merlin hadn't gotten back in touch with her. She led the way to the elevator that would take them to the parking garage, but her feet traced the familiar path automatically while her mind worked. What had the minor Fae been doing in the forest, and why had it chased them off? Now that the sky had tipped to the post-sundown side of twilight, the minor Fae would be gone, and she had just enough time before the night creatures emerged. Her biggest challenge would be to get rid of Charlie. Unfortunately she knew exactly how to do that.

Meanwhile, Charlie's silence weighted the space between them, simultaneously making the elevator seem too large and too small. Saying something may break whatever tension thrummed between them. Or make it worse. Or do nothing. In her thousand years as a Truth Seeker, Maggie had never encountered a situation that felt so out of her control. And she'd faced some gnarly situations. She turned to tell Charlie about one time when she'd been chased by trolls in the Alps but stopped herself. Sharing would create intimacy, and intimacy led to danger and grief. Would she never learn?

By the time they reached her car—a silver Chrysler Sebring —the words—any words—wanted to burst out of her. But when she asked, "Where's your car?" her nerves strangled her speech so she had to repeat herself.

"At the station," Charlie said. "I figured we could go together."

Damn. Sometimes there were disadvantages to being within walking distance of the police station.

Maggie unlocked the car, and they got in. Jazz flowed from the satellite radio, easing some of the tension. At least they had something to divert their attention. It made the drive all too short, and Maggie pulled into a small parking area where her car wouldn't be easily visible from the street.

"Well, here we are." She unlocked the doors.

With a chuckle, Charlie got out of the car, and when his door closed, the air thickened again, and this time she could smell his aftershave. She practically jumped out of her seat and took a deep breath of the autumn-sharp air to clear her head.

He donned his cap and jacket, and she zipped hers against the chill. So why did her cheeks burn under his gaze? Maybe seeing Morgan had brought her past mistakes—the big ones— to the surface of her mind, which meant guilt and shame lay only a heartbeat away. And she wouldn't hurt him. Or at least she'd try her best not to.

PHILIPPE WOKE to a pounding headache and a mouth full of bloody sand. No, scratch that, it only felt like his mouth was full of sand, it was so dry. Even on his worst hung over days after late concert nights, he'd never felt like this. A low, intense argument scraped against his ears, bringing him fully to consciousness, but he didn't move.

What had happened? He'd dreamed before of being off the island, but it had never been like this, where he wore scratchy new clothes, and the air smelled of barbecue and flowers and all sorts of other yummy things.

Crap, he'd been taken by the Fae. Now he remembered. Out of the magical cauldron, into the hellfire underneath.

"I'll take him from here," a guy's voice said. "You've

discharged your duty. The binding tattoo should fade once I get him to Tatiana."

"Not so fast. It's my last take, and I should have the honor of bringing him in." That was the young woman who had rescued him. She'd smelled mostly human but still had that irresistible edge. He squirmed. He would need to eat soon or it wouldn't matter who ended up with him. At least not if they wanted him alive.

They did want him alive, didn't they? He sat up, hitting his shoulder on the bottom of a soap dish and bounced back to his pillow. That knocked loose the booze in his stomach, and he turned, vomiting over the side of the bathtub he lay in and into a wastebasket that someone had put there.

That stopped the argument. Almost.

"He's awake," the woman said.

"It is just past sunset, so of course he is."

"He'll be hungry." Then a pause. When the woman spoke again, her tone had become seductive. "Let me take him hunting, and then I'll bring him back, and we can go to Tatiana together."

"Oh, all right."

Kissing sounds. Great. Philippe had ended up with a pair of bounty hunter lovers. Just another reminder of how he'd always be alone. That was fine with him—the first time he'd really fallen for someone, she'd rejected him hard, and he'd become a vampire.

"Go and find our nearest portal to the Fae realm. Just be careful. I think I saw another lagoon creature in the surf when we were on our way in this morning."

Lagoon creature? Those existed? Philippe snorted. Of course they did. He did, didn't he?

A door slammed. The woman unlocked and then opened the door to the room where they'd been keeping him, which turned out to be a windowless bathroom. At least they'd given him a pillow.

She wrinkled her nose. "Guess the booze didn't stick around, huh?"

"No." He didn't know what else to say to her. Questions crowded his mind with confusion, and hunger flashed through him at her scent. Now that he only saw one of her, he noticed her beauty in other senses as well. Her dark hair lay windblown around her face, and her dark blue eyes sparkled with amusement and mischief. She had been outside that day, or at least looked like she had from the color on her face. She carried a backpack and jacket slung over one arm and wore a halter top. When she moved, he saw hints of what looked like a dark tattoo that resembled a necklace of ancient symbols across her collarbones and neck.

What would it be like to taste that neck? To take just a little bite, one tiny slurp, and—

"And your eyes are glowing like mad. I need to find somewhere for you to hunt something bigger than birds."

He struggled to his knees, and she helped him out of the tub. The tiny sliver of brain that still operated held him in check, but barely.

"Take me to the back alleys," he rasped. "The poor part of town."

"Okay, but I'm not going to untie you until we get there."

"Whatever you need to do. Just try not to get too close to me."

She nodded and slung the backpack straps over her shoulders, then held the rope. "Hang on. I can only do this very occasionally, but the circumstances warrant it."

The bathroom disappeared, and the humid air of the night slammed on to his skin and made his ears pop as shabby buildings appeared around him. He could still smell her but couldn't see her. He could also smell other predators, but not of the supernatural type.

He'd always been aware of them, especially once he had become involved with the band and had to notice suspicious characters who might want to steal their stuff or harass the female band members and girlfriends. Consequently he'd mastered a version of the West Coast Stare, more challenging than the defiant look pedestrians gave motorists as they crossed in the middle of the block.

That look came back to him now as he narrowed his eyes and flared his nostrils at a man in the shadows. The metallic scent of blood and the bitter plastic tang of chemicals told him who it was—a drug dealer who had just killed someone. The reason didn't matter. He'd kill more with his tainted wares if Philippe didn't take him out.

Justification? Maybe. But he grinned, his fangs elongating, his vision going infrared.

"Hey, man, I don't have anything for you." The dealer backed up and hit the wall that had protected him from a surprise assault but trapped him in this frontal one. He dodged to the left, and Philippe caught him by the neck.

"Oh, but I think you do."

Now the funky odor of fear joined the other smells.

Not Philippe's ideal combination of tastes—he'd always been more of a pizza and beer guy—but hunger didn't care. He pounced. Just as when he'd been human and hadn't eaten for half a day, he only came into awareness of what he was consuming after he'd been eating for a minute. He reminded himself to slow down and give the soporific chemicals his fangs had injected into the guy time to work so he didn't suffer. The drug dealer slumped, and the slowing of the man's blood's pumping told Philippe he had almost killed him.

He pulled back, his fangs coming out with a pop, and let the man fall against the building. His eyes fluttered open briefly.

"Consider this your warning. Stop hurting people." Philippe turned to Morgan. "Do you have a phone on you?"

Her dark eyes widened. "Yes, why?"

"To call medical services. Whatever they are here." He waved to the buildings around him. "I didn't kill him, but I was hungry. I may have taken too much."

"What do you care? You're a vampire. A killer." She dug around in the bag she'd carried with her.

He drew in a quick breath. Was that what she saw when she looked at him? "I have to eat like everyone does. But I don't have to destroy."

"Okay." She dialed something on the phone. "Yes, a man slumped in Tin Alley. He may have been attacked. Yes, I'll hold on." She hung up. "Now let's get out of here."

"Can you do what you did back in the hotel room?"

Her stumble when she turned to leave gave him her answer before she spoke. "No. Like I said, I can only do that every so often. At least right now."

"Where are we going?" He followed just behind her, ready to catch her elbow if she needed him, but each of her steps looked stronger than the last. Soon he was stretching his legs to keep up with her.

"That's a good question. Not back to the hotel. We're not safe there."

"Because of that guy?" Philippe knew he hadn't liked the sound of him. "I can take care of him."

She stopped, and he had to hop to the side so as not to run into her. Thankfully they walked along a deserted sidewalk. When she turned to face him, her expression had hardened into a mixture of wide-eyed incredulity and fear.

"No. You. Can't." She stabbed his chest with her finger with each word. "He's one of the more powerful Fae nobles. You're a baby vampire who barely knows what to do with his fangs."

Damn. She had a good point. He caught her hand and

almost released it when an electric sensation ran through him. "Then I will have to trust you to protect me. You obviously have a lot of power."

"Not as much as I used to," she grumbled and pulled her hand back. "But yes, we're avoiding him. Something strange is going on, and I need to make sure I'm not going to be tricked out of what's due to me." She shook her head. "That would be just my luck."

A rumbling sound filled the air between them.

"It sounds like you're hungry," Philippe observed and tried not to laugh.

She closed her eyes and sighed. "Yes, I burn a lot of energy when I make those jumps. Let's find a diner, and I'll figure out our next step."

Philippe followed her, but one step behind. A sense of déjà vu prickled the back of his neck. The last time he'd trusted an immortal woman to protect him, he'd ended up changed into a vampire. Granted, part of that had been his own fault. But still... Perhaps he should start looking for an escape route.

7

——————

Morgan dragged a fry through some ketchup and tried not to roll her eyes back in pleasure when the salty-sweet crunchy-soft combination met her tongue. Dear gods, deep fried food had to rank up there along with rock music as her favorite modern invention. And she would enjoy every bite of the "conch and chips" she had ordered at the all-night beachside cafe.

Morgan and Philippe sat in a corner, blending in among the drunken tourists who'd had one too many daiquiris and who satisfied their alcohol munchies with unhealthy food. Sixties rock blared over the speakers, and she smiled when the song "Witchy Woman" came on.

"What are you grinning at?" Philippe asked. He pretended to sip on a daiquiri that they supposedly shared, but of course she drank all of it. With the thug's blood running through him, Philippe looked almost normal, although still pale among the tanned tourists.

She lowered her voice so others wouldn't overhear her. She knew he could with his supernaturally heightened senses.

"I took this as my theme back in the day." She bit into a

piece of fried conch and watched his reaction. His lips tightened for a split second before he smiled and nodded.

"It fits. I was a roadie for a female artist cover band back in my day. Well, last year."

"Oh?"

"Yeah, it was mostly eighties stuff, y'know, like Heart, but sometimes they'd do older songs. And newer, too. Like Melissa Etheridge." He hummed a couple of bars of "I Wanna Come Over."

Morgan finished the musical phrase with her own humming. "I love Melissa, but Heart is my favorite! So angsty. Her voice was gorgeous, too."

Philippe grinned for a second, but then his expression snapped back to closed. "You did some interesting stuff earlier."

"Yeah." She looked back down at her food, which had started to fill the deep hole she always felt in her energy after a major telepathic effort. "And paid the price."

Zapping from place to place, as she'd overheard a couple of Truth Seekers call it, wore her out, and since she'd carried Philippe with her, she'd become doubly tired. Thankfully he'd taken care of the thug who had eyed her with lascivious curiosity because she hadn't been able to defend herself. Poor judgment on her part to make herself so vulnerable, but she'd just needed to escape from Elric, who she knew had warded the hotel room door so he'd know if she physically walked through it. The question was, where could they go? Somewhere close enough that a flight could get them there before dawn. Their ideal destination would also have enough iron, steel, and other Fae-repellent building materials to keep Elric and the others away. She had to buy time to figure out what was going on. There was no way she was going to hand Philippe over until she knew all the conditions. Elric had lied to her, and the queen's messenger hadn't been telling the entire truth.

Philippe put a hand over hers. She snatched it back. "What?"

"You were drumming your fingers on the tabletop. People were starting to look." He leaned back and pretended to take a swig of the daiquiri. "Don't want them to think I'm being mean to you."

"Thanks." She picked a piece of fried coating off her plate and crunched it between her molars to bring herself back to the present. "I was thinking."

"I noticed." He slumped, placing his forearms on the table. "You remind me of someone. She's intense like you."

"Oh?"

"Yeah, Maggie."

"Oh." The formerly delicious bite in her mouth turned to sludge, which she swallowed. "That's not a compliment."

"You're more personable, though." He spoke quickly. "More real. I never saw her eat fried food. She hardly ate anything except..." He shook his head. "Never mind."

Poor guy, he'd fallen hard for Dear Aunt Margaret. And it looked like he'd fared as well from the encounter as Morgan had. "Truth Seekers have efficient metabolisms."

"And you don't?" He gave her a classic down-up-down look. "You seem to be in pretty good shape."

"And I'm taking the daiquiri away." She reached across the table and plucked the stemmed plastic cup from his place mat. It was lighter than the last time she'd drunk from it. "You're not supposed to be drinking that. Although since you're still within a year of changing, you can tolerate some regular food. But alcohol will go straight to your head."

"I noticed. It was automatic."

She sighed. She needed to remember he'd had no guidance and didn't know what he could and couldn't do. Despite his supernatural abilities and senses, he was as helpless as a baby chick.

Which also meant the Fae would eat him alive, maybe literally depending on their mood. But it wasn't like Tatiana to waste a big assignment on a bit of sport. Granted, fairies were capricious, but... But not many humans had had encounters with the Truth Seekers.

"How do you know my Aunt Margaret?" Morgan asked.

He bowed his head. "I got caught in some magical tunnels after some friends dared me to steal magic coffee beans. I didn't know they were magic. I also didn't know what the tunnels were—a way for Niniane to get around the restrictions that ghosts have on how far they can go from their haunting spot."

Morgan reminded herself to close her mouth. She'd swallow a fly if she wasn't careful. "Okay, so you do have some sort of special abilities. And you have met my cousin Niniane."

"Niniane's a bitch." He emphasized his words with a nod.

"I would have to agree." She gestured for him to go on.

"Your aunt rescued me. Then there was some mess about a couple of lockets, and I swallowed Niniane's, which poisoned me, and then a vampire tricked me into thinking I had a chance with your aunt, and..." He spread his hands.

Morgan blinked. "That's... Wow. I'll need to get more details from you later."

He looked away. "Thanks, but I'd rather not discuss it. I relived the whole experience—and my stupidity—repeatedly in my nightmares on that island."

"I bet." She'd had nightmares for centuries. "So... Has anyone else tried to get to you, that you know of?"

"No, Merlin had me pretty well hidden. I overheard him telling Maggie that he'd get me through the change, then put me somewhere I couldn't hurt anyone. I guess birds don't count."

Morgan crushed a fry in the ketchup, a poor substitute for the harm she'd like to inflict on Merlin. The poor boy had gotten caught up in supernatural politics, but he hadn't done anything wrong. Except maybe swallow the locket, but she needed more on that part of the story.

So he too had had negative encounters with Merlin and Margaret of Cornwall. Morgan allowed herself a small smile at finding someone who might understand her feelings about Saint Margaret, as she'd always called her aunt in her head. But first things first. She pulled out her phone.

"We'll figure out what to do," she assured Philippe. "I've got my phone checking for cheap flights out of here. I'm afraid I can't zap us far."

Her phone dinged with a text—*Morgan, where in Hades are you? The pathway is warmed up. Will need to make a transfer in Atlanta, but can be in Faerie before dawn if we hurry.*

"Crap," she muttered. "Elric is getting impatient."

"Do I need to make a run for it?" Philippe half-turned in his chair. She held up a hand to stop him.

"Let me see if I can come up with another option. Unfortunately there aren't any good flights for us, and I don't want to stay here another day. Elric would find us."

She tapped the icon for her Dark Mirror app, which she used rarely due to the in-app charges for searches. The dwarves had moved from crafting to coding, but they still liked their gold.

"Mirror mirror in my phone," she murmured. Her screen went dark, and then a swirl of smoke appeared. It coalesced into a number that was higher than she thought it would be. Someone had made a deposit into her account. She didn't have time to worry about that now. She had more than enough for a quick search. "Tell me where Truth Seeker Margaret of Cornwall is located."

The screen resolved into a map. Great, the dwarves had synched with Google Maps. But it showed her very specifically where her aunt was. The pin put her strangely near a pathway entry point about six and a half miles east of the city of Atlanta.

"Hmmm." Boy, that would be so fucking hilariously awkward if she and Philippe were to show up wherever Margaret was. But it seemed that all paths to the answers to Morgan's questions literally lay with her aunt, at least for now.

"Got anything?" Philippe asked.

"Yep." She tapped out a text for Elric to meet her at the hotel, then locked her phone and popped the last bit of fried conch in her mouth. "We're going to use a Pathway."

"What is a Pathway?" He arched an eyebrow in suspicion.

"It's a place where two dimensions meet and form a crease. It allows those who know how to travel from place to place, and realm to realm, but it requires powerful magic to open the connection. Normally only the Fae can use them, but Elric has been kind enough to open and warm one up for us."

She and Philippe threw away their trash and walked into the darkness. Once away from the crush of people, she put a finger to her lips and opened her senses, including her sixth one to find the vibration. It tickled her left ear, and she followed it, pleased it grew stronger as they went. It brought her back to the place on the beach where the queen's messenger had found her. That made sense.

"Is it in the water?" Philippe asked.

"Yes, but not too far. You shouldn't even have to hold your breath."

She grabbed his hand to lead him into the ocean, but found herself blocked by the lagoon creature from earlier.

"Mistress," it said and bowed.

"Creature of water and darkness." She returned the gesture, and Philippe did likewise. "Let us pass."

It stood aside and said something in a sibilant gurgling that was difficult to understand, but she thought it told her, "I shall guard your going from the Fae."

"Thank you, but I do not ask you to become involved in my personal business."

"It is more than your business, Mistress." It held out a hand. Paw? Flipper? "Go."

"Thank you," she said again. She wanted to question it, but her phone buzzed, and she knew Elric wouldn't be far. He could close the Pathway if he got to within a certain distance, so she opted to continue. She tucked her phone into a waterproof pocket, which she sealed. She walked into the surf.

Philippe followed her, but at the last second, he pulled away. She turned, and the lagoon creature shoved him at her. She caught him with both hands, and they tumbled into the water and the Pathway.

No matter how many times Charlie had observed the difference, the change from benign, friendly daytime woods to dark nighttime forest with potential danger behind every tree and around every bend startled him. November woods especially struck him as creepy with trees reaching their skeletal, mostly naked limbs to the full moon as they rattled their few remaining dry leaves.

Next to him, Maggie shivered. At this point, they could walk side-by-side on the trail, but soon they'd have to argue as to who went first. There was no way he'd let her go into a dangerous situation headlong, but he also didn't want her to be snatched from behind him.

"Cold?" Charlie asked in an almost whisper. "Or do you sense something else?"

"Neither." She gestured to the trees. "It always startles me how the forest can go from a healing, soul-soothing place during the day to damn creepy at night. I was just adjusting to the difference in the energy."

It didn't surprise him that they thought so similarly, but the bite of disappointment about the situation—or lack thereof—

between them deepened, so he didn't reply. The path narrowed, and she stepped in front of him. He didn't argue—at least he could keep an eye on her.

"About a hundred yards ahead, right?" She held up a hand, and a small glowing peach-colored orb appeared. It illuminated the ground and trail within a few feet of them. "Witchlight," she explained over her shoulder. "It shouldn't interfere with our night vision, and it also won't give us away until something is right on us."

"So be ready for surprises?" As if he hadn't had enough that week.

"Always." Her grin brought out his own, which he stifled, making him tuck the corners of his mouth into an awkward expression. Yep, it was a good thing she walked ahead and couldn't see him.

They progressed in as much silence as the forest floor would allow, the crackling leaves under their feet extra loud. Finally the trees thinned, and Maggie extinguished the witchlight. They stood at the edge of the clearing, and he did his best to direct his mind to the situation at hand and not wonder what other neat tricks she could do. Sure, he'd always found her magical, sometimes literally, and she always amazed him. The almost full moon gave them enough light to see most of the area around them, although it still looked damn creepy, as she'd said.

He spotted the former smelting chimney, and a movement in his peripheral vision directed his gaze to a black and white cat that cleaned itself at the edge of the clearing. Its markings made parts of it disappear and other parts stand out, and it almost looked to his brain like a small child playing with something. Maggie grabbed his arm and pointed to a large tabby cat that lolled on the other side of the chimney. Charlie frowned. It almost looked like the one that had attacked them earlier, but not tiger-sized.

"Is it the one from earlier?" he mouthed.

"I can't tell. Can't see its eyes."

At least the presence of the cats indicated that they'd taken care of the were-bat. Fae and nightmare creatures didn't mix, at least not from what he'd been told.

The moon rose higher and bathed the clearing in its silvery light. The edges of shadows became darker, and each individual blade of grass and fallen leaf stood in stark relief against the backdrop. Charlie fought the urge to smooth the tingling at the back of his neck. Maggie hadn't released his arm, and she clutched tighter.

Glowing mushrooms sprouted in the grass. Well, Charlie thought they glowed. They seemed to draw the light to them as they emerged in a clockwise circle. The cats melted into the shadows of the woods behind them—at least now he knew they'd been just ordinary cats.

Or maybe they weren't. The large tabby cat returned and walked into the circle. It rolled on its back and offered its belly to be scratched by a figure that materialized out of moonlight and mist. No, it was two figures, and they tumbled into the circle along with a wave of water that came out of nowhere. The smell of brine made Charlie's nose twitch. With a cry, the feline rolled to its feet, dashed out of the circle, and disappeared into the shadows, only pausing to lick at some of the salt water it had been doused with.

The word Maggie muttered sounded Celtic, but Charlie didn't need to know the language to recognize the tone of a curse.

"Who is it?" He didn't know if she heard his question—he spoke quietly so they wouldn't be detected. The two figures in the middle of the circle panted, and the smaller one struggled to sit.

Maggie squeezed his arm, and her words came straight into

his head. *"I can't tell. Their energy is familiar, but something is masking them. Or keeping them from coming all the way through."*

She glanced over her shoulder and tugged him farther off the trail and into the woods.

"What did you see?" He tried the telepathy thing.

They stopped about a quarter of the way around the clearing. Charlie's leg muscles twinged in protest when he squatted again, this time behind a shrubbery. He focused on the soreness so he wouldn't imagine any of the inappropriate things he'd thought about doing with Maggie. While useful, the mental link could get him in trouble.

"No more trouble than you're already in." Her mind voice held a trill of amusement.

The mushrooms went dark, and a young woman stood halfway, her hands on knees. Her pale skin almost glowed under the moonlight, and her face had a classic beauty under straight-cut dark bangs. She wore some sort of midriff-baring dark top, dark pants, and a long leather jacket straight out of the *Matrix* movie costuming department.

Maggie stiffened.

"Someone you know?"

She nodded but didn't look away from the girl. *"My niece, Morgan."*

Morgan held out a hand to help the other person to his feet, and now Charlie's curse joined Maggie's. The last time Charlie had seen the young man had been just after he'd been turned into a vampire, and Charlie had tried to kill him.

8

Oh, gods, what is Philippe doing here? And with Morgan? Maggie didn't know whose appearance gave her more of a sinking feeling—the niece she'd betrayed or the vampire she'd failed to save. She pinched her leg through her jeans to see if she may be in the middle of a nightmare.

The mushrooms glowed again, and a tall gentleman dressed in jeans and a long-sleeved gray T-shirt appeared. His human resemblance ended with his clothing, which sheathed limbs too long and slender. Maggie recognized the pale skin that could have been made from moonlight, hair as dark as the deepest of shadows, and haughty expression. This was a high Fae, one who attended the queen in the Seelie Court, and therefore one of the last ones she wanted to see.

The being looked down his long, narrow nose at the soggy Morgan and Philippe.

"Who is that?" Charlie had quickly picked up the telepathy trick, which he'd only be able to do when they touched, and she still blushed at some of the thoughts that had come through before he'd figured out how to only direct what he wanted.

"That's Prince Elric. He's one of the queen's consorts. Whenever she sends one of her closest boy toys, it means trouble. Big trouble."

Charlie nodded. *"No high Fae goes anywhere in this realm unless they expect a welcoming committee. It goes with their ego. I thought I heard something behind us."*

"They don't look very welcoming." Maggie tensed in case she needed to intervene, but she didn't want to reveal herself—and bring up old family drama—unless it was necessary.

Morgan shoved Philippe behind her. Maggie ignored the spike of possessive worry. She'd released Philippe into Merlin's custody, which made his appearance doubly disturbing. Where was Merlin?

"How did you get past the lagoon creature?" Morgan asked.

Elric smiled. His face glowed golden-peach, and although his expression hadn't wavered, he appeared more friendly and approachable. Charlie started to rise.

Maggie dug into his arm with her nails. *"Don't succumb to the glamour."*

Morgan didn't appear to fall for it, either. She waved her hand, and his light went out with the soft suddenness of a firefly. "You can charm them, but you can't fool me."

"But apparently you can fool *me*. What were you thinking, taking the vampire through the Pathway? Did you not think I would follow?"

"I'm not going with you." Philippe stepped out from behind Morgan. "I choose to stay with her."

"You don't have a choice, nightmare scum." Elric's expression turned cold, and Philippe shivered. "Come here."

"No!" Morgan flung herself in front of Philippe again.

The Fae moved—fast—and wrapped one arm around Morgan. He used the other to pull her hair back to expose her neck. She struggled but couldn't move.

"Oh, so you've decided you like neck-biters? I'll let him drain you, you worthless bitch. Come on, Vampy."

Philippe's expression glazed over, and his irises glowed red.

Maggie hadn't used her Fae-given powers in a long time—wasn't sure she even still had them—but the energy coming off Elric thrummed through her, and she slammed her own resistance against the glamour while holding Charlie back. Maggie moved as fast as Elric had and in what felt like one move, tripped Charlie to incapacitate him, jumped from the bushes, and put a steel knife to Elric's throat. It wasn't as good as a pure iron one, but it got his attention.

"Drop her, Elric. Stand down, Philippe." The vibration in the air cleared.

Philippe's eyes returned to their normal color, and he shook his head.

Elric slowly released Morgan, who rubbed the back of her head but looked annoyed, not relieved.

Philippe moved to her, but didn't look away from Maggie. "Margaret?"

"Aunt Margaret?" Morgan asked without a hint of surprise. "Long time, no see."

Of course there was no thank you for saving her. Maggie held in a resigned sigh. In truth, she hadn't expected any gratitude. And maybe she didn't deserve it after everything that had happened in the past. But there was no time to think about that now—she had a pissed-off high Fae to deal with.

Elric held his hands up. "So sorry to interrupt this touching family reunion, but could I be released, please?"

Maggie kept her grip on the knife steady despite the sweat that slicked its surface. "Not until you tell me what you're doing here."

"Queen's business, Love." He shrugged his shoulders, the gesture still elegant despite his informal attire. "I like my hide, so I'm not going to tell you."

"If it's in my realm, it's my business."

With another shrug, he disappeared in a puff of smoke,

presumably back into the Pathway. He couldn't stay in the area for long with its abundance of buried metal.

But—and the thought made a chill run down Maggie's spine—the other Fae had. She suspected she would be seeing Elric again.

Her thoughts whirring, Maggie lowered the knife and sheathed it back in her boot. If it had been pure iron, she could have kept him there.

Morgan put her hands on her hips."What were you doing? I had him right where I wanted him."

Maggie bit back a laugh. "What? Like hell you did. He was about to let Philippe rip your throat out."

"So you do know him." Morgan crossed her arms and looked from one to the other. Uncertainty flitted across her face before being replaced by annoyance.

"She's got a point." Philippe scratched the back of his head. The color of his skin told Maggie he'd recently fed. On Morgan? Were they a thing?

Maggie rubbed her temples. The situation grew more and more complicated.

Morgan undid the back of her halter top and lowered it— but not to an indecent level—to reveal a binding tattoo, a thin, dark string of letters that looked like words intermingled with barbed wire, around her neck. "I'm on the queen's business as well, and you just messed it up." She sighed—overly dramatically, but that's how Morgan worked—and refastened her top. She opened her mouth to say something else, then stopped, her eyes wide and her mouth open. Philippe scowled.

Maggie turned to see Charlie had emerged from the bushes and watched them with a smirk.

"Who's the hot stuff?" Morgan walked around him and nodded approvingly. "Well, hel-lo, handsome. Care to introduce me, Auntie?"

"Down, Morgan." Maggie couldn't believe it. How had the

girl supposedly aged for centuries and still managed to be a brat where men were concerned? But—and the thought came with a poke of guilt—it wasn't like she'd been taught otherwise. "This is Lieutenant Charles MacKenzie. He's an investigator with the Decatur Police Department." She didn't add that that was mostly a cover for his secret but truer job as a special investigator for the Truth Seekers. "Lieutenant, this is my niece, Morgan le Fay. And Philippe Ormandie."

"We've met," Philippe grumbled. Right, the night he'd been turned, Charlie had almost killed him. Thankfully Philippe didn't move toward them.

"Ooh, a cop." Morgan held out her hands. "Care to arrest me, Lieutenant? I've been a bad girl."

Maggie hoped Charlie's speechlessness came from shock, not from attraction.

"Nice to meet you," he said but didn't touch her. Smart man. "Do you know what that Fae gentleman was doing here?"

Morgan shook her head with a pout. "No. What were you two doing in the bushes?" She put her hands over her mouth. "Oh! Did I interrupt a tryst?"

"No." Maggie sighed. The girl's lie had turned the air at the back of Maggie's throat sour. She wanted to truth-spell her niece and get every shred of information out of her, but she had some decency. She'd at least give Morgan the chance to come clean on her own.

Maggie didn't expect a straight answer, so she was surprised when Morgan seemed to respond to her next question at least half-truthfully. "What are you doing here?"

"Oh, I just felt like I was overdue for a family visit." Morgan turned toward the trail. "So let's get something to eat, and we can catch up."

Maggie glanced at Philippe, who shrugged and said, "I just want some dry clothes."

Charlie looked annoyingly bemused. With a sigh, Maggie

followed Morgan and Philippe down the trail, Charlie behind her. She guessed he'd have some questions for Morgan, but this wasn't the time to answer them. Meanwhile, it looked like Maggie would be returning to her least favorite activity from her time as a royal aunt—babysitting.

MORGAN AND PHILIPPE piled into the backseat of Maggie's car. It smelled of lavender and some sort of savory herb—sage, perhaps—indicating her aunt kept the space both physically and energetically clean. And then when Maggie started the engine, soft jazz came through the speakers.

While she could appreciate the neatness and the sense of coming into a protected, calm space, the tension in Morgan's shoulders increased into a sharp pain just above her right shoulder blade. She rolled her shoulders back, but she couldn't allow herself to relax. Her heart beat a reminder—betrayed, betrayed, betrayed—and she couldn't help but catch the tension from Philippe as well. He hadn't taken his gaze from Maggie, his expression intense, although Morgan couldn't tell whether he felt attracted, angry, or a combination of the two. Or maybe his wet clothing made him miserable.

Morgan ignored her soggy attire. She had to focus too hard on the role she played—bratty niece. When dealing with her family, she'd found a variation of the "under promise and over deliver" business strategy worked well—over-act and under-disappoint. That way none of them knew what she really thought or felt. Or what to expect.

"Is it far?" she asked. "I've really got to pee." Not a lie, although her bladder had the strength of centuries.

"No." Maggie fiddled with a knob on the console. "Is the temperature okay? I've got the heat on for you two."

Philippe's words came out with a snap. "It's fine."

Morgan raised her eyebrows at his tone. She guessed he was more angry than happy to see her aunt.

"I've got some clothes in my car that may fit him if you don't have anything," the blond cop—Charlie?—offered. Morgan had missed his name as her mind whirred with how to act toward him.

"That won't be necessary." Maggie glanced back at Philippe, then returned her attention to the road. "I've got some stuff from...before."

Morgan lowered her voice to a purr. "That's very kind of you, Lieutenant." Not that she was attracted to blond guys as a rule. Not since her brother, Arthur... And she wouldn't allow her memories to go in that direction. Being around Maggie made them veer enough toward their mutually uncomfortable past. Would Elric's actions and words—which hurt her more than she would let herself admit—make her swear off dark-haired men as well?

She couldn't help but glance at Philippe, who now looked out of the window at the passing buildings. They seemed to be in some sort of small town with shops and restaurants in brick buildings along busy streets. Philippe's dark hair, which must have been slightly too long when he'd been turned, curled in its dampness. The clothing Elric had gotten for him at one of the beach shops looked ridiculous here in autumn-cold Atlanta, where people walked around in warm attire, but he didn't shiver. Vampires didn't feel cold, but the wet clothing could chafe.

Worthless bitch. The words not so much floated as stung Morgan's heart. And that after they'd spent two amazing nights together. She blinked, swearing the stinging in her eyes came from the salt water that had splashed in her face.

Maggie pulled into a little parking lot behind a police station. Morgan looked around frantically—had her aunt betrayed her again? Were human and supernatural authorities waiting for her? She didn't think she had done anything illegal, but some people and beings had it out for bounty hunters.

"Here you go," Maggie said to Charlie. "Thank you for your help."

"No, thank *you* for allowing me to tag along. That was...educational."

Morgan had the sense that they no longer attended to her and Philippe. They both sat silently as Maggie and Charlie said goodbye. Or she tried to, but he kept the conversation going, much to Morgan's amusement.

"Have a good rest of your night," Maggie said. "I hope it's not too late for you to get some sleep."

"I'll be fine. I'm good on five hours. But I need you to come give a statement tomorrow." He shrugged and grinned. "Some of us have paperwork, you know."

"Oh, I'm aware. I'll drop by tomorrow." She unlocked the doors.

"What time do you think it will be? So I can make sure to be here."

Morgan almost snickered at the annoyance of Maggie's next exhale. "I'm not sure," Maggie told him. "I'll give you a call." He opened his mouth, but she cut him off. "I have your number. Good night, Charlie."

"Good night, Margaret."

The look they gave each other had all the intimacy of a good night kiss, but they didn't move toward each other. After a long five seconds, Charlie nodded and got out of the car. When his door closed behind him, Morgan fanned herself with her hand.

"Wow," she said. "I haven't seen so much unrequited lust since Lancelot and Guinevere. I hope it ends up better for you two."

"Shut up, Morgan," Maggie snapped.

Morgan grinned. Score one for her. *Take that, bitch. You're not the only one with boy problems.* She tried to catch Philippe's eye so they could share a grin, but he scowled at Maggie, and Morgan quickly looked away. *Okay, then.* She should have felt like she'd gotten an advantage, but a smidge of guilt bloomed in her chest.

She sat in uncomfortable silence until Maggie pulled into a parking deck and a "Residents Only" spot.

"Here we are." Maggie's tone sounded cheerfully forced.

Morgan didn't say anything—she'd been snapped at enough for one evening, thank you very much—and followed Maggie into the building, up three floors on an elevator, and into a condo.

Maggie spoke without looking at them. "Uh, Philippe, you know where everything is. I'm going to put you in the guest room closet since it's the one completely enclosed space with the most room."

She led them through a living room space with an open kitchen and to a door that opened to a room behind it. Morgan wrinkled her nose at the acrid tang of obsidian smoke. What had happened in here?

"What's that smell?"

Maggie waved her hand. "Had a little accident with my obsidian mirror. I've cleaned up the shards, but I haven't had the chance to deal with the smoke stains. I'm sorry."

Morgan didn't think Truth Seekers could lie, but she could tell Maggie hadn't told them the whole truth. It took more than a "little accident" to break an obsidian mirror.

Maggie opened the closet door, and the smell grew stronger. Sure enough, a shattered obsidian mirror sat on an altar, the top of which had been destroyed, and smoke marks stained the ceilings down to a line about three feet from the floor. There were definite blast marks and scratches on the walls as well.

What the hell had happened? Morgan glanced at Philippe,

who stood with arms crossed and his eyebrows drawn down in a frown.

"You want me to sleep in there?" he asked.

"Yes, I'm afraid it's the best I've got right now." Maggie's grin looked like more of a grimace. "I'm so sorry."

Philippe relaxed slightly, and Morgan had the sense her aunt apologized for more than the sleeping space.

"I'll be fine." Philippe's tone returned to normal. "I'll just grab a pillow and some blankets off the bed. The carpeted floor will feel luxurious compared to where I've been sleeping. No sand."

"I'm glad." Maggie's smile appeared more genuine, and she gestured for them to precede her out of the closet. "Morgan, you can take the couch if you like."

"No, I'll sleep in here." There was no way she'd leave Philippe unguarded, no matter how many fancy magical wards her aunt had on the place.

"All right." Maggie shrugged. "You're adults."

The awkward realization made Morgan cover her mouth so as not to laugh—her aunt thought she and Philippe were a couple. She thought about correcting her, but as nothing had been stated directly, she decided not to say anything.

After Maggie showed Philippe where to find some fresh clothes—and the level of awkwardness had returned—she left the two of them alone. Morgan turned to Philippe and blurted out, "What the heck happened between the two of you?"

9

———

P hilippe rubbed his eyes. Of course Morgan would ask what had happened. Anyone with half a brain could tell there was some old tension. And being back here in the bedroom where he'd spent his last night as a human, or at least his last partial night, made the memories flood in. Of lying on the ground looking at the moon. Of Maggie running after the imp that had stolen the token that could have made her vulnerable, even though she'd vanquished the witch wielding it. Of her not letting Charlie kill him but allowing Merlin to take him to a place that was more uncomfortable than death.

What would Morgan think about what an idiot he'd been?

"I need a shower."

She stepped aside. "Be my guest."

Philippe grabbed the pajamas from the top drawer of the dresser, just as he had on that fateful night when they thought everything would work out and that they'd do a little ritual, get the poisonous magical locket out of his stomach, and send him home to his old life. And he thought there could be something between them, and he'd help her get rid of her curse.

The thoughts and memories swirled through his mind as he showered. The water felt good and warmed his skin from the outside-in, joining the heat from the blood he'd ingested until he felt almost like a human again. But only almost. He lay his forehead against the cool tile. He'd been such a dolt.

After finishing up and putting on the fresh clothes Maggie had saved for him—which felt like a step backward—he emerged from the bathroom.

"Feel better?" Morgan looked up from the magazine she'd been reading. She sat cross legged with her back against the pillow she'd pushed against the headboard. She looked human, although he'd figured out that she, like him, was only almost human. Her book bag sat open beside the bed, and her coat hung on a hanger over the back of the closet door. She gestured to it.

"I'll move my coat to the bathroom now that you're done. Or we can use it to block any light that may go through that space at the bottom of the door."

"I'm sure I'll be fine," Philippe told her. But would he? A tearful pressure welled from his chest at her wanting to take care of him. Then he remembered—she was taking him to the Fae, so she needed him to be in good condition.

So why had they detoured? And how had he ended up in this place again?

And could the delay mean there was some hope for him to escape and live his own undead life?

She might have questions, but so did he. Their mutual curiosity burned in the space between them.

"Are you going to take a shower?" he asked. The thought of her naked, her long hair clinging to her lithe body, came to him unbidden, and he hoped she couldn't see evidence of this different kind of hunger filling the front of the pajama bottoms. It had been so long.

"Maybe after you go to sleep."

Right, she didn't want him to escape.

"Are you going to stay awake all night?" he asked.

She shrugged. "I don't need much sleep these days."

He'd forgotten. She was part Fae. That's what her name meant, right? Morgan le Fay. So her loyalty lay with them no matter how nice she was to him. That thought threw cold water on his arousal, and he found himself able to walk to the other side of the bed and sit. She turned to face him.

"So, you and my aunt...?" she prompted.

"Nope," he said. "Not until you tell me what you're going to do with me."

She dropped her gaze. "I don't know. I'm contracted to bring you to Faerie, but I don't want to until I know exactly what's going on."

Okay, that was something. "What do you mean? I don't want to go to Faerie."

"Unfortunately, you probably don't have a choice. If I don't bring you in, Elric or someone else will. But I'm questioning whether it's a good idea."

"Questioning is good." Think strategically, he reminded himself. But the long night was catching up with him. "What's wrong? Not that I'm in support of this plan, but it's only fair for me to know what I'm being forced into."

She gave him a long, measuring look. "Fair enough. I'd want the same." Then she stood and paced as she spoke. "This was supposed to be a straightforward job—I grab you, bring you to Faerie, and I get my powers back. But I'm getting different orders from different Fae, and I have the gut feeling I'm missing a part of it. A big part." She stopped and faced the window, which was covered by a set of blinds and a curtain. Philippe could feel the slow burn of the distant sunrise, even though no evidence of it yet touched the sky, and he yawned. He tried to digest what she told him, but threads of lethargy crept into his brain.

"What does your aunt have to do with this?" he asked. And there was something about powers. What had she said? He was so tired.

"That's what I'm hoping you'll tell me." She sat on the bed beside him and put a hand to his cheek. "What happened with you two?"

When he pulled her fingers from his face, heat spread into his hand. He disengaged her touch from his skin as soon as he could. "She rescued me from the tunnels. The coffee tunnels." He blinked. He knew his words didn't make sense. "And then I swallowed Niniane's locket. And I thought I could win her heart if I had enough time, but the gray man turned me into a vampire." There. That was the whole story. But... "Did that make sense?"

"Sort of." She frowned and checked her watch, then her phone. "Right, sunrise is only an hour away. You must be exhausted. We'll talk more tonight."

She grabbed the pillow she'd been leaning on and the folded blanket from the foot of the bed and disappeared into the closet. He sat and blinked at the open door, listening to her. His thoughts floated through his mind like lazy summer clouds. Should he follow her? Should he wait for her to give him orders? But what if he was tired of other people telling him what to do?

Okay, he was just tired.

When she emerged, she said, "I made it as comfortable as I could in there for you. I'll tuck a towel under the door to keep any light from coming through, but you may want to wrap yourself in the blanket just in case."

"Because you can't deliver damaged goods?" He couldn't help the bitterness that bubbled up to give him a spike of awareness.

"No, because I don't want you to be hurt anymore." She grabbed his hands and tugged him to his feet, then steered him to the closet. He followed because he was too exhausted to fight her. He'd figure out how to escape after he got some rest. No matter how much he wanted to know more about this mysterious and conflicted Morgan le Fay.

THE SOUND of the bedroom doorknob turning startled Morgan, and she reached with her bottom hand under her pillow for the knife she'd stashed there.

"Morgan?" It was Margaret, her whisper barely audible over the hum of the A.C. "Are you awake?"

"Go away. I've barely slept." She didn't have to try too hard to make her tone plaintive. Her statement was true—she'd only allowed herself a light doze, and every little noise had disrupted her half-sleep. Considering Margaret lived in a city, there had been a lot of sounds, different from the ones she was used to. But none from the closet. As expected, Philippe slumbered like the undead—silently.

"I need to talk to you."

Morgan released the knife and rolled to face her aunt. "Give me five minutes to get ready."

Margaret—she went by Maggie now, Morgan had noticed—nodded and closed the door as quietly as she'd opened it. Morgan frowned. Surely she wasn't afraid of waking the vampire. Or maybe that's what her Truth Seeker training had told her to do.

Morgan snorted and rolled out of the bed. Her muscles ached—right, going through the Faerie portals sapped the energy of all who weren't Fae. Morgan tolerated it like she could because of her mixed heritage. She guessed Philippe had since he'd just fed, but it had taken some of his vitality, too. The poor guy had been exhausted by the time he'd hit the closet.

Not guy, she reminded herself and walked into the bathroom. *Vampire. He's a vampire. A loathsome nightmare creature.* But the description held all the weight of a rote teaching that had lost its actual meaning. He'd been and still was stuck in a tough situation. And it seemed his predicament, like hers, could be traced back to her aunt.

After her morning routine, which took all of ten minutes, Morgan pulled her hair back in a ponytail, put on her spare set of clothing, and walked into the living room. Sunlight blazed through the windows, which looked over a street, a small strip of shops and restaurants, and naked trees.

"Wow, it's bare and depressing here." Again, a genuine sentiment. After the green of southern Louisiana and then the islands she'd been on, the energy of this place felt constricted and tired. Kind of like her heart.

"It's almost winter." Maggie stood in the kitchen, which was open to the living room and a small dining area. "Coffee or tea?"

"I don't suppose you have any coffee with chicory." Morgan stalked to the kitchen and sat on one of the stools on the other side of the counter.

"No, 'fraid I don't."

In the bright morning sunlight, Margaret looked fresh and rested, although if Morgan looked closely enough, she could see a very fine web of wrinkles under her aunt's eyes. Like Morgan's, Maggie's face didn't look near what her age must be.

"I'll take regular coffee, then." Morgan lifted her chin. "With lots of cream." She pushed away the questions that flooded her brain, like did Maggie ever get tired of having to pretend she was something she wasn't?

"How about coconut milk creamer?" Maggie shrugged. "I find as I get older that my stomach gets less and less tolerant of cow dairy."

Morgan cataloged Maggie's admission of weakness. "If that's all you've got... Can't you conjure a cow or something?"

"No, I didn't pay the large animal pet deposit."

Maggie pulled one of those ceramic cow creamer pitchers out of the fridge, and Morgan smiled at the irony before she caught herself. She allowed the fake cow to vomit fake milk into her hopefully real coffee and stirred it with the spoon Maggie offered. Then she put the spoon down and looked at her aunt.

Morgan and Maggie faced each other over the island that had sink and counter space on one side, eating area on the other, and questions thick in the air over it. Morgan sipped her coffee, waiting for Maggie to say something. She'd learned long ago that allowing the enemy the first word could be useful.

"So about that vampire in my spare room closet..." Maggie raised her eyebrows and inclined her head to the left toward the bedrooms.

"Mmmhmm?" Morgan mimicked the eyebrow raise. "What about him?"

"How did you meet him?"

Morgan shrugged. "In the islands." Then with an innocent look. "You?"

Maggie wiped her hands on a dishtowel. She hadn't washed them or gotten them wet. Morgan smiled behind her cup.

"On a job." Maggie picked up her coffee and leaned against the stove behind her.

Fine, the verbal ball had returned to Morgan's court. "Old friend?" she speculated.

"You could say that. What is he to you?"

Morgan could practically hear the *thwack* of the questions being hit back and forth. "An acquaintance. I haven't known him that long."

"I figured." Maggie pinched the bridge of her nose. "Look, Morgan, I sense you're in some sort of trouble, but I can't help you if you won't be honest with me."

Morgan blinked away the memory of her mother, Igraine, making the same exasperated gesture with her. *"Look, Morgan, I can't help you if you won't let me. I know you don't like that I'm going to Uther's palace and that your baby brother is being sent away. And I know you don't like having to go to Avalon, but your Aunt Maggie and cousin Niniane will take good care of you."*

Morgan snorted. Maggie and Niniane had taken good care of her all right. As in they'd used her and then banished her without her child when she'd tried to escape.

"Like you helped me in the past?" Morgan snapped. "As I recall, that didn't work out so well."

Maggie lowered her gaze, her cheeks pink. "I did the best I could. Many things were beyond my control. Niniane..." She took a deep, shuddering breath. "She was already being corrupted. I see that now."

"Wait, what?" Morgan wanted Maggie to look at her again, but her aunt shook her head, lost in memory. Or like someone who finally had the pieces to an old puzzle.

Maggie spoke so quietly Morgan almost couldn't hear her. "How could I have been so blind? Of course it was him."

"Him who? And where is Niniane?" Morgan glanced over her shoulder. "Not here, I hope. I never want to see that bitch again."

"I'm sure you don't." Maggie emerged from her thoughts, her expression determined. "She allied herself with the nightmare creatures and has since been banished to a realm beyond Faerie and the Collective Unconscious."

"What, couldn't you kill her?" Morgan tried to look angry to cover the firework of fear that had just bloomed in her stomach. What if her aunt found out the nightmare creatures had a strange fascination with her? Morgan had never allied with them, well, not until Philippe, if that's what their connection could be called, but she'd heard the Truth Seekers didn't always dig too hard for the truth they supposedly sought.

"No." Maggie shook her head again. "I couldn't bring myself to. Plus she had something that limited my power. I got it back," she added, too quickly.

What, did she think Morgan would want to try to find it and take the advantage? Rude.

And disappointing. "You may want me to trust you." Morgan stood. "But until you show that you trust me, I'm not going to tell you anything."

"Wait."

But it was too late. Morgan was already half-running, half-walking back to her room, and she slammed the door more loudly than she intended. She winced, looking at the closet, before remembering that noise wouldn't wake Philippe. She almost grinned at the thought she might have acted in an immature way, but at least she hadn't slammed the door hard enough to wake the dead.

A knock on the door preceded Maggie saying the last thing Morgan expected to hear from her. "You have every right to be angry with me. I would like to talk things out and apologize for where I went wrong. Both to you and Philippe. Think about it. I need to go to work, but I'll be back around lunchtime. The apartment is warded, so you should both be safe."

Then footsteps, and the soft click-whoosh-thud of the front door opening and closing. And silence.

"Couldn't you at least pretend to breathe or snore or something?" Morgan asked Philippe just to break the thick quiet.

Yes, the lack of human noise in the apartment would drive her nuts before too long. It left way too much space for her thoughts to crowd in.

10

———

Audrey woke and stretched after a passionate night in the Collective Unconscious with Damien. Last night, their room had looked over a moonlit ocean. It was different every night, and she had no trouble manipulating the environment they made love in. So why couldn't she accomplish even the basic stuff Maggie was trying to train her to do?

And today would be the day they could bring their love-making into the waking world. She grabbed her phone and checked her calendar, and then the email reminder, for the umpteenth time. Yes, at 2:00 she'd be meeting with the specialist who had been treating her collarbone injury to get cleared for activity.

Her phone dinged with a text as she was holding it. Damien.

Can't wait to go to the real beach with you. Good luck at dr appt today!

Audrey smiled and texted back a heart. It always amazed her that they could meet like that, although she shouldn't be surprised. Atlanta businessman and overall sleazeball, Lyle Ames, had tried to build a brothel in the Collective Unconscious, after all. She'd been involved in stopping him, which had led to the hairline fracture in her collarbone. And the persistent feeling that something wasn't quite right, that it wasn't over, even beyond her and Damien struggling to come to terms with the other's vulnerability to what they each feared most.

But those thoughts were for another day. She'd focus on how her abilities somehow worked fine in that limited environment, so maybe she wasn't as bad at manipulating the C.U. as she'd thought. She rolled over, noticing how she still moved carefully even though she hadn't had the electric pain radiating down her left arm for weeks. She pushed herself upright using that arm and exhaled with relief. It was still noticeably weaker than the other arm, but again, no pain or even a tender feeling.

Another text. The ID said J.J., and she deliberately had to stretch the tension from the corners of her mouth. That was another complicated situation.

Good luck at doc today. I have a feeling you'll get good news. :-)

Although she wanted to grin at the confirmation of her own suspicions that she was better, she couldn't. Each time she thought she'd come to terms with the fact her beloved older stepbrother wasn't who she'd thought, that flash of grief through the middle of her chest knocked her backward into feelings of betrayal.

Thanks. She texted back, wondering who would get the text —her stepbrother, or his alternate identity Emergency Room physician Arthur Rizzo. Or maybe he hung out in his apartment as his true self, some sort of protective being.*"Kind of like a guardian angel,"* he'd told her. *"But unfortunately not a very good one. Hence why I'm here."* And then hadn't elaborated.

After feeding her cat, Athena, and otherwise doing her morning routine, she ate breakfast, brushed her teeth, and gave the cat a scratch on the head. "Be a good girl. Don't let those silly squirrels make you mad. Is that why you're not on your regular morning window perch?"

Athena just blinked her golden eyes and yawned. Audrey caught herself yet again studying the pattern on Athena's calico coat for any sign that she could be the goddess herself. It would be just her luck. But the patches of black and brown seemed random, not implying a skull helmet or other image that would be associated with the goddess. She'd asked Maggie one day when the shop was quiet if her cat could be a goddess in disguise, but Maggie had shaken her head and made a comment that it was unlikely, although she could see how Audrey would be suspicious. After all, cats had never forgotten that some cultures treated them as gods.

Still... Enough strange stuff had happened to her. And Athena had a knack for knowing who should be trusted.

"I'm just being paranoid," Audrey muttered as she locked the door.

"It's not paranoia if they are out to get you." The lilting voice of her duplex neighbor Madame Lucia startled Audrey out of her thoughts. "Thinking about your cat again?"

"Oh, good morning, Lucia. It's a chilly day to take your morning coffee outside."

The psychic sat on her Adirondack chair on the other side of their shared porch and raised her mug. "I wanted to wish you luck for your appointment today. I can imagine the limitations of your healing time have been frustrating for you."

Audrey couldn't help the heat that flushed her cheeks, although she guessed Lucia meant general limitations, not bedroom ones. "Thank you. I'm ready to get back to my regular exercise routine."

"And other things." Lucia grinned as she took a sip of her coffee, then asked, "How is Officer Lewis?"

"He's doing fine. We're doing fine."

"Good. Have a good day."

"You too." Audrey shook her head at herself as she walked into Decatur. She'd gotten a text from Maggie to please open the shop since she might be late. She didn't mind. It got her out of the house and gave her a break from her freelance work. And obsessing about what sort of danger Damien might be in.

She stopped into Java Lemur to grab a cup of coffee. The events of the previous month seemed like a distant dream, but she still checked for supernatural creatures. Nope, it was the usual mix of businesspeople, college students, and others there for their morning fix. And—there was that warmth in her cheeks again—Damien. He stood with Charlie and two of the patrol officers near the coffee condiments. They wore their khaki pants, black shirts, and lanyards with tags, but beyond their uniforms and athletic builds, their appearances made for a nice contrast. Damien—dark, intense, with gray bedroom eyes. Charlie—blond, blue-eyed, jovial...and exhausted-looking.

Had he been up thinking about Maggie? It was none of her business, but Audrey couldn't help but wonder. She got her coffee, greeted the group, and then gave Damien a good morning kiss. He tasted of coffee and pastry, and he smelled like he'd just come out of the shower.

"Are you opening up the shop today?" Charlie asked.

"Yep, Maggie asked me to. She said she'd be late." She cocked her head at Charlie.

"Yeah, she has family in town," he said.

Audrey raised her eyebrows. They all knew who Maggie was—the lost aunt of King Arthur—so what family could she possibly have visiting?

"Who?" she asked.

Charlie gave her his trademark teasing grin. "You'll have to find out from Maggie. Trust me, it's good."

"But you need to be extra careful," Damien told her. "Officers Speed and Jameson were telling us that there have been complaints of a Peeping Tom in your neighborhood."

"Really? Is he dangerous?" A chill went down Audrey's back. Was that why Athena hadn't been watching the wildlife? Had she seen something she didn't like?

"We don't know yet, ma'am," the shorter of the two patrol officers said. "But please call in if you see anything suspicious."

"Thanks, I definitely will." She checked her watch. "Crap, I'm late. Bye, y'all." She kissed Damien again, but when she stepped into the day, it seemed less bright than previously, even with the heavy clouds.

She wasn't a psychic like Lucia, but when Damien had said "Peeping Tom," she had almost felt an eddy in the spiritual current that she'd been able to pick up since she'd been traveling more in the Collective Unconscious. It had felt like a ripple of cold water in a warm stream, and on some level, she'd felt she was the target.

By the time Maggie left to open the shop, she had a headache that spread from her back teeth up through her temples and down into her neck. She almost hoped the Fae would come retrieve Morgan and take the girl—and the memories she provoked—off her hands, and not just because her presence brought up Maggie's deepest regrets. Morgan practically hummed with Fae magic, which made Maggie's own abilities unpredictable. In other words, she might have been able to conjure a rat-sized cow, and she might have taken pleasure in watching Morgan try to milk it. Going to work would get her out of temptation's way to see what she could do that she shouldn't. And give Morgan space to sort out her own thoughts.

And then there was the suspicion, quickly growing into certainty, at the back of her mind that Morgan was putting on some sort of act to divert her from the truth. But what that could be, she had no idea.

Maggie took the elevator down to the ground floor and walked into the cool, foggy autumn morning. Something about the atmosphere made her pause, a sense of deep familiarity like she'd lived a day similar to this one before, but an important event had happened.

Don't be silly, you've lived thousands of days, and they've all been important.

Sometimes the weight of her immortality slowed her, but she didn't allow it to make her steps sluggish this morning. She only hoped Morgan wouldn't get into too much mischief. Perhaps her niece's unplanned visit had prompted the déjà vu. She hoped so.

When she arrived at The Crystal Cave, her magic and crystal store, Maggie found Audrey had already arrived and was filing the receipts from the previous day. At least someone in her life did what she was asked without any complaints.

"Morning. You're low on amethysts," Audrey said. "Want me to order more?"

Maggie avoided the question, which was about more than the amethysts. Ordering more would mean she was staying. But she couldn't know until she heard from Merlin, who was still missing.

"Thanks for covering for me yesterday afternoon." Maggie checked the shelves—there were just enough of the purple crystals to last them through the next few days if previous days' sales were any indication. In a town known for its alcohol consumption, the supposedly hangover-preventing stones tended to sell reliably. As for whether she should order more... "Let's hold off for now."

"No problem. Oh, I ran into Damien and Charlie and a couple of the patrol guys at Java Lemur this morning. Charlie looked tired." She raised her eyebrows with an unspoken question.

"Oh?" Maggie wasn't touching that one, although she guessed if Audrey looked closely, she'd see similar fatigue on Maggie's face. Was it as hard for Charlie to work with Maggie as it was for her to be in regular contact with him?

"Was it the fairies again? How did they get inside the Perimeter?"

Of course Damien had shared with Audrey the results of their mission from two days before. Maggie tried to drown the spike of jealousy in her gut with a big swig of coffee but ended up with some going the wrong way, which led to a coughing fit.

"I didn't realize they were such a sore subject," Audrey said once Maggie had recovered her composure. But in spite of her joke, her expression remained serious.

"They're always trouble. And I honestly don't know how they're getting in. They shouldn't be." Maggie glanced at the clear glass shelves that held an assortment of small fairy statues. Something seemed different, but like with the sense of familiarity, she couldn't specify exactly what caused the feeling.

"Do you know what they want?"

Maggie looked back at Audrey, who pressed her hands tightly together, her green eyes wide with concern. Maggie didn't need a mental link to guess the source of Audrey's distress. The goddess archetype Aphrodite had warned Audrey and Damien that trouble was coming, but they'd all assumed it would be from the Greek gods, who had caused enough chaos in the weeks before Halloween to last Maggie several lifetimes. She reminded herself how intense this must all feel to the mortals, especially to Audrey with her frustration about her training.

"Has something happened to make you feel threatened?"

"Damien said something about a Peeping Tom. We get them

here occasionally, but he's in my neighborhood, and I feel like it's got something to do with me."

Maggie couldn't help but think the line between caution and paranoia grew thin these days, and she didn't know what side they stood on now. "Did you see something?"

"No." Audrey stacked the receipts she'd been entering. "But Athena wasn't in her usual window perch this morning. I wondered if something spooked her. Are you sure...?"

"I haven't seen the real Athena for a while, but I doubt she's your cat. She always hated eating the same thing day after day." Maggie straightened one of the fairy statues. They looked like something heavy had run through the shop and turned them all in one direction. "Did you rearrange these?"

"No. I haven't touched them." She frowned. "And I'm pretty sure they were all facing straight when I left yesterday. I would've noticed if they hadn't been."

The bell over the door tinkled, and since they'd just been talking about fairies, Maggie shouldn't have been surprised to see Morgan. Wearing Maggie's favorite pair of boots and a condescending expression.

11

Morgan fixed herself a toaster waffle for breakfast and another cup of coffee—her aunt had left one for her. Somehow this kind gesture irked her. Now Margaret—er, Maggie—wanted to take care of her? What about all those years ago on Avalon and after, when Maggie had been doing the "noble" work of Avalon, and Morgan had been forced into a loveless marriage? And then, when her husband died under mysterious circumstances, Morgan had no choice but to move into the itinerant and dangerous life of a solitary fortune-teller.

No, Maggie hadn't taken care of her when it mattered, so it was too late now.

"I'm going to go nuts if I stay here." The words bounced off the walls. She tried turning on the television, but it was the same crappy morning programming she got at home. What did her aunt think she was? She was a do-er, not a wait-er. And she needed to figure out what the Fae queen wanted with a neophyte vampire and what that vampire had to do with Maggie.

And why Elric, after all these centuries, had turned on her.

The sting from his betrayal added to Morgan's pain from older wounds. No matter how long she wore them in her soul, they never grew more comfortable. And made it hard for her to sit still. She blinked herself out of her memories and looked down. She no longer sat on the couch, but stood at the stove and cleaned what few fingerprints there were off the shiny surface.

Morgan threw the sponge in the sink. She had to focus before she found herself doing something dangerous. Plus she wasn't Margaret's maid. No, she obviously wasn't going to get anything from Philippe today, so she might as well shadow her aunt and see what she could find out. A glance at the calendar confirmed she only had a few days left before her deadline. She shoved away the thought that she didn't really want to bring Philippe to Tatiana. He wasn't her problem.

Morgan's boots were still wet from the splash they'd gotten coming out of the Pathway, and the sandals she'd worn in the islands wouldn't be appropriate for the weather, so she went to her aunt's bedroom to see what she could find. She hesitated at the door—would it be warded? She tentatively held out a hand, and when nothing pushed back against her, she walked in.

Huh. Maybe she does trust me. The room was a mirror image of the one she'd slept in, so she found the closet, this one vampire-free and without any magical apparatus. What it did contain was a wardrobe, mostly black, and an assortment of shoes, including a darling pair of pointed-toe ankle boots with leather ties on the sides. When Morgan tried them on, they fit perfectly.

After finishing getting ready for the day, she grabbed her backpack and the spare key and headed out. She added her own wards to the door after she'd passed through her aunt's. Not that she worried about anyone getting to Philippe through them, or him leaving until he woke at sunset, but she'd learned never to be too careful. The Fae liked to leave traps in the most unexpected of places, sometimes in the most protected ones.

Once she reached the sidewalk, she breathed in the smells of this place. The sharp, dusty odor of dried leaves and twigs, and rain not too far in the future. A slight breeze brought the scent of salt water, but when Morgan glanced around, she couldn't see any, not even a puddle. The breeze changed direction, carrying the odor away, but it left a chill behind that clung to her neck and a familiar sense that things were about to go very wrong.

Morgan couldn't see any obvious threat, so she pulled out her phone and opened her Dark Mirror app. She hadn't asked her aunt where she was going, but she'd said she would be back by lunch, so she shouldn't be far. The technology to find other beings was technically illegal, but she'd theoretically gotten a bounty hunter exception.

Sure enough, the map popped up and showed her where to find her aunt—in a place called The Crystal Cave, about six blocks away.

Huh, cute. She tried putting in Elric, but as she suspected, it didn't work for him. It showed a flickering dot that appeared and disappeared in random places, points of Fae energy that, truth be told, shouldn't be here in the middle of a big city. She shrugged, put her phone in her pocket, and walked to The Crystal Cave.

A bell over the door chimed when she entered the cozy shop. The walls, a medium purple, sparkled with something in the paint, and shelves lined the walls and area behind the windows. She thought she recognized some of the Collective Unconscious' more notorious characters like a vegetarian dragon named Zinfandel, whom she'd never met but had heard enough about to know he worked with the Truth Seekers. She smiled at her aunt and the young woman who sat behind the computer, the latter of whom had some Fae blood in her, or Morgan would eat her aunt's boots.

"Oh, hi, Auntie. So this is where you work."

Maggie didn't look happy to see her. Too bad. "Morgan. What are you doing here?"

Morgan waved the question away. "Almost a thousand channels, and nothing on. It was too quiet. Plus, I wanted to see where you work. I thought people like you didn't have to be tied to a boring old job." She didn't have to pretend—she was genuinely curious about what a Truth Seeker was doing with a regular gig. Was it some sort of cover?

Maggie pursed her lips before answering. "Sometimes the boring jobs are the best ones. But this one is interesting enough since I—"

Since Maggie obviously wouldn't give Morgan the straight answer, Morgan cut her aunt off and went straight to the girl behind the computer that must also serve as a register. "Oh, hello little mortal." She held out a hand. "I'm Morgan le Fay. Who are you?"

The girl didn't back down, just looked at Morgan with frank curiosity, which seemed to intensify once Morgan gave her legendary name. And then, to Morgan's delight, answered. "Oh, hello, silly immortal, I'm Audrey Aurora Sonoma. It's nice to meet you."

She shook Morgan's hand, and Morgan grinned when she picked up some of the girl's dominant memories. Yes, this one was special. No wonder her aunt had found her.

"Ah, so you're the one who faced down Zeus. That was epic enough that word of it reached Faerie." And beyond, but she didn't say so. Elric had sent her a link to an article about it— Zeus Caught in His Own Trap—to one of the magical gossip papers that immortals and non-humans read. Of course Cupid, the little attention whore, had given interviews everywhere he could. Elric had added a comment to the email—*"This is pretty epic."* She'd had to agree. It was always nice to see the Arche-types get their comeuppances, especially the Greek ones, who lorded humanity's continued fascination with them over everyone else.

Audrey shrugged and looked away. "It had to be done."

Morgan moved a step closer, just hovering outside the girl's space. "No, seriously, that was amazing. Not everyone comes away from an encounter with the Greek chief unscathed." Then something tickled the back of her mind. "Actually, no one does."

But Audrey looked fine. Still... Was this a piece of her puzzle?

"I haven't noticed any effects. Feeling fine." Audrey kept her eyes on the computer screen, but Morgan didn't move.

"Are you sure? No tingling, changes of vision, having visions? Trouble doing stuff that should come easily?"

Maggie and Audrey exchanged a glance. Then Maggie looked at the shelves against the back wall that held the fairy statues—some of whom looked familiar—and frowned. She walked to the other side of the store.

"Um, Audrey, could you come here a moment?"

Audrey did, and Morgan put a hand over her mouth. The statues moved so slowly that it would be almost imperceptible to human eyes, but they rotated to follow Audrey across the space.

"Do you see that?" Audrey sounded more intrigued than afraid. Good for her—fear didn't help anyone.

"Yes." Maggie grabbed Audrey by the arm, and they slowly backed toward the front of the store. Morgan didn't move. She watched the statues, waiting for them to do something, but they remained still as though they knew they were being observed.

"Morgan, are you doing this?" Maggie asked.

"No." The question, although logical, hurt. "I have nothing to do with this."

The bell over the door chimed again, and the statues snapped into straight-ahead display orientation.

MAGGIE TURNED with a forced smile at the bell heralded the arrival of a customer. Then a real smile when she saw it wasn't a customer, but Damien. He wore tan pants and a black polo shirt with the Decatur Police Department shield on the chest.

"Hi!" Audrey threw her arms around him. Maggie turned away from their greeting, wanting to give them some privacy and to make sure Morgan behaved. She also checked on the statues. Had a couple of them moved slightly?

"Who's that?" Morgan asked.

"Damien Lewis. Audrey's boyfriend. He works with Lieutenant MacKenzie."

"Is he the one who was with her in the C.U. when she took on Zeus?"

Maggie moved toward the register and gestured for Morgan to follow.

"We're going outside for a second." Audrey led Damien by the hand to the door, and with a tinkle, they'd gone. Maggie didn't blame her. The morning had suddenly gotten creepy.

"Yes, and thank you for not hitting on him." Maggie checked the numbers in the computer. It looked like Audrey had done everything correctly. No surprise there. She shoved away the thought that Audrey would make a great Truth Seeker. It would be fairer to allow the girl to have a normal life.

"Of course I didn't hit on him. He's obviously very attached. Give me some credit, Auntie." Morgan fiddled with the silver bead on a leather thong tied around her wrist.

"Sorry." Maggie ignored the stab of disappointment that Charlie was so obviously non-attached that Morgan had attempted to flirt with him. She'd rejected him, so it made no sense. Damn, she hated when her feelings got in the way. "So what do you know about Audrey's encounter with Zeus in the Collective Unconscious?"

"Gods, you're so formal." Morgan straightened her shoulders. "You have to realize it was all over the alternate realms within a day. Cupid is such a gossip. Of course the way he told it, he was the one who rescued himself, but everyone knows better."

"Right." Maggie had attempted damage control, but there was no such thing with the god of love involved. There was only damage minimization. She had hoped the humans' names would be left out of the story. That would explain the fairies' interest—they and the Greek gods had a mutual hate-fascination relationship.

"So you were there," Morgan pressed. "What really happened?" She leaned in, her eyes wide. "Did someone really stab Zeus in the foot with one of Cupid's arrows and force him to make a promise?"

Maggie blinked away the images of the temple and breathed against the pressure of the close call memory. Was that why she had gotten stuck here watching Charlie? As punishment for allowing the situation to become dramatic? Her supervisors preferred clean and subtle, and the stream of events had not been that. But that's what happened when Aphrodite and Cupid were involved—drama and trauma.

"I can't give you all the details. That's classified."

"Of course." Morgan huffed. "I should've figured you'd choose work over family. You always have."

Remembered panic dissolved like tissue paper in a flare of anger. "That's not fair. I've always done what I've had to do."

"Truer words have never been spoken." Morgan plucked Maggie's hands off the keyboard and forced Maggie to meet her eyes. "Auntie, it's a good thing I'm here. You need to have a little fun."

Maggie tugged, but Morgan didn't let go of her fingers. "I have fun. I enjoy my work. And when I close the store for my lunch break, I'm going to really enjoy packing those fairy statues up and moving them into the back." She lowered her voice. "If we've managed to gather their interest, I don't want to give them a chance to spy on me."

To Maggie's surprise, Morgan shuddered. "Me, neither. I'll help you."

Maggie raised her eyebrows. "You're offering to help me?" She filed away the kernel of truth—something had scared Morgan.

"Yes. There have been rumors of the queen being up to something. Well, more than usual." And there was another half-truth.

A crash startled them, and Maggie retrieved her hands. They tingled from where Morgan had touched her. She walked to where the noise had come from and bent to retrieve the pieces of the broken statue of a dark-haired fairy prince and similarly colored princess. It had been a lovely piece with the two bent toward each other in an almost kiss, their half-furled wings in the shape of a heart. Now that Maggie looked closer, their little faces resembled Elric and Morgan.

Was this a warning? She noticed that despite Morgan's offer of help, she hadn't moved. In fact, she leaned against the counter, her already fair skin as pale as the porcelain of the statue. She clutched her fists together beneath her breasts above her diaphragm.

"Are you all right?" Maggie asked.

"I think something's happened to Elric."

12

———

O nce the tinkle of the bell indicated the door had closed behind them, Audrey felt like she'd exhaled for the first time since Morgan had walked into the shop. She didn't claim to be psychic like Lucia or whatever Maggie was, but the girl kicked off some strange energy.

They walked down Church Street toward the Presbyterian church, which always soothed Audrey with its Gothic brick architecture, and turned left on to a quieter road. A shady spot off the main sidewalk and near the church gave them some privacy. Plus, wasn't there something about the protection of sacred ground?

"So who was that?" Damien asked. "The girl in the shop."

Audrey hardly believed it, but at this point, she couldn't dismiss strangeness, no matter how much she might want to. "Maggie's niece. Morgan le Fay."

"Morgan le Fay?" Damien asked. "As in from the King Arthur legends." He shook his head. "Charlie told me, but I didn't know whether to believe him."

"I can hardly believe it." Audrey crossed her arms. She'd forgotten her jacket in her rush to leave the shop. Damien put an arm around her, and she grinned up at him. "Why don't you ever get cold?"

"You never give me the chance to be. I always have to warm you up." He tugged her closer until she felt his heat against her entire right side. His handcuffs case dug into her waist, but she didn't care. She put her arms around him, careful to position her hands well above his holster. She remembered her father lecturing her and J.J. to always keep their hands well away from a policeman's weapon because they were trained to protect it and might have unpredictable—and dangerous—reflexes.

Despite their cozy pose, which would normally have soothed her, Audrey's chest thrummed with anxiety, both at what had happened and at how to tell him without freaking him out. "What do you think her being here means?"

"Charlie said she appeared yesterday with some vampire and a fairy prince, and Maggie scooped them up." The bitterness in Damien's voice didn't surprise Audrey—he liked the adventurous parts of working with Charlie like hunting down the were-bats, but he generally didn't like the supernatural beings.

"A fairy prince? That's interesting." Again she sighed to loosen the area around her heart. "Not a Greek god, then."

"No." His exhale spoke of his own relief.

"Or not yet. Dammit, I wish Aphrodite had been more specific with her warning so I knew what to look for."

He squeezed her. "But if you did, you may end up missing something you didn't expect."

She heard what he didn't tell her—that he would protect her no matter what came at them. Warmth and dread fought in a weird hot-cold mix in her middle. Gods, she loved him, but she also knew his job had deadly risks, and he could be gone in a moment. Like her father.

A hot tear squeezed out from her left eye before she could stop it.

"Are you okay?" Damien asked. He loosened his grip and turned her to face him.

She nodded, her throat strangling her words.

"Is it your collarbone? I didn't mean to squeeze you so hard."

She shook her head. "No, it's just been a strange morning."

He bent to kiss her, and it made her tingle from head to toe. She shoved away thoughts of the impermanence of the situation. She would enjoy him while she had him.

The wind ruffled her hair like caressing fingers, and the sickly sweet odor of gardenia floated on the breeze. Now warmth crept around them, and when Audrey opened her eyes, she caught a golden glow that faded in an instant. He opened his eyes just after.

"Something's here," she said. She'd been so relieved to get out of the shop she'd almost forgotten to tell him.

"What?" The softness of his embrace vanished into muscle taut and ready for action.

She stepped back so she could look at him fully. "The statues of the fairies in the store. They followed me so they'd always be looking at me. They turned so slowly it was hard to tell, but..." She realized how crazy that must sound. Then she had to grab him as he stepped forward.

"I'll smash every single one of them."

"No, wait." She held on to his arm, thankful he'd stopped because she couldn't compete with his strength, especially not when he went into determined protector mode.

His chest heaved, but he relaxed the muscles in his jaw slightly, and she knew he'd gotten control of himself. That was the good thing about dating a cop—they could be controlled. Sometimes to a fault.

"What do you want me to do?" He ran a hand through his dark, curly hair.

"Just leave it for a while and trust me."

Now he caressed her cheek and ended by tucking a stray

strand behind one ear. "I do trust you. I just don't trust them." The set of his jaw said he didn't like her request. But didn't he realize he was in danger, too?

"I trust Maggie. She'll know what to do."

He nodded, but he looked away. They walked back to the store hand-in-hand but didn't say anything. Audrey didn't know what had just happened while they kissed, but she'd remember his words—it was best to be alert for any strangeness, not just the kind she had learned to expect.

Damien got a call on his phone, and when he hung up, he said, "I'm sorry, but there's been a new development on the Peeping Tom case. I've got to talk to Charlie."

"That's okay. I won't be hanging around here long."

"Good." He tilted her chin up so she looked him in the eye. "It would kill me if anything were to happen to you."

"Likewise."

He kissed her, and then when his phone beeped, he sighed. "I'll let you know what I find out. Be careful."

"You too." She watched him walk down the street, her arms crossed in front of her against the chill. As always, she said a prayer to whatever deity might be listening for his safety. Then she returned to her own weirdness.

But when she got back to the store, the Closed sign faced outward.

MORGAN DIDN'T JUST THINK something had happened to Elric. She knew because he stood in the corner, trying to talk to her. And she could see the door to the storage room through him. Morgan clutched the edge of the counter, for once not caring if she left fingerprints on its glossy surface, and her heart pounded against the denial that filled her chest.

"No..." If his shade stood in front of her, it meant he'd been killed. Stinging tears filled her eyes. She'd been angry, yes, and hurt, but she hadn't wished harm to come to him.

Her aunt straightened from the broken statue, walked to the door, and flipped the Open sign to Closed. Then she stood beside Morgan. "What do you see?"

"Elric. His shade." Morgan covered her mouth just before a sob erupted from her gut. "He's dead. Oh, gods, he's dead." Centuries of memories piled on to her, of conversations and intimate moments. He'd never make her laugh or touch her again. And their last conversation... How could they have left things like that?

"I'm so sorry, Morgan." Maggie stroked Morgan's hair, a familiar gesture of comfort from when she'd been upset as a little girl. She didn't jerk away. "Is his *doppelganger* trying to tell you something? Is that why he's here?"

"I can't tell what he's saying." She moved to approach him, but he held out his hands and looked like he tried to yell something. He moved his mouth too quickly for her to catch what he was trying to say. She'd always sucked at lip-reading. "I think he's trying to warn me."

He disappeared in a puff of smoke like he had previously, but this time Morgan knew she'd never see him again. Still, she had to ask, "Is there some way we can bring him back? So I can see him again, tell him I'm sorry for speaking so harshly to him the last time—" She pressed the back of her hand into her lips. Her skin smelled of the coffee they'd drunk earlier before the day had gone to Hades. The last time she'd seen him. She thought he'd betrayed her. But had he been trying to protect her without giving away Tatiana's secrets?

Maggie shook her head. "You know as well as I that it will take a thousand years for him to be able to return, if he does at all. The Fae have always been secretive about their afterlife, only that they have some sort of reincarnation and that it takes a millennium."

Morgan turned to her aunt and sobbed into her shoulder. At that moment, she didn't care about the past or that her aunt still stroked her hair, and she should be angry because Maggie had stopped being a comfort when Morgan had become a young woman and had hurt her badly. Could she have meant what she said about wanting to apologize and talk things out? Morgan couldn't think about that now. Not with every fun, happy, sad, sweet, annoying memory with Elric playing in her head, teasing her with sorrow over what she'd never experience again.

And then terror. Tatiana would be furious. Elric had been a favorite of hers, and the queen didn't grieve. She got even.

Morgan straightened and stepped back. "I have to figure out what's going on."

"Does it have something to do with Philippe?"

Morgan bristled at the brusque tone her aunt's voice had taken. Once a Truth Seeker... "Maybe. I don't know." And there was another lie. But they came so easily in the name of self-preservation.

Maggie reached for her lenses, and Morgan tensed. Was her aunt seriously about to truth-spell her?

No. Maggie dropped her hand. "Look, I really want to help you, but can't you see? This situation is bigger than your concerns, and I need to know what's going on."

"Can't. Client confidentiality. Bounty hunter's code." That wasn't entirely untrue. Tatiana—through Elric, damn those tears that built up in her throat again—had made her sign a nondisclosure agreement, so it had become her code. But were all bets off now? Would Tatiana be coming after her next?

No, Tatiana still held the key to Morgan getting her full range of powers back, whatever those were. She'd been stifled for so long she couldn't remember, only that she'd had the most potential of anyone on Avalon. Even now, at half-strength, she was a powerful sorceress, one of the most feared in the world, she'd guess. But she wasn't powerful enough to resist a truth-spelling. And she needed information that Maggie held to fill in the blanks in her knowledge. Like what had really happened with Philippe?

Maggie studied Morgan with a quizzical look, and Morgan realized she'd slipped and revealed why she was traveling with Philippe. Shards of bloody sharp crystal! The shock of Elric's death had made her careless. She crossed her arms and lifted her chin but didn't feel the false confidence she tried to portray.

"So Philippe is a bounty?" Maggie frowned. "For whom? Right, you can't tell me. But someone powerful if your Fae lover has been killed. I'm sorry, but don't look so shocked—the energy between the two of you was palpable. Him pulling a knife on you was a nice try to put me off, by the way."

"I don't think that was an act." But what had it been? What had made him so angry? "The only time I've seen him so pissed is when something challenged the sanctity of the Fae realm."

The channel of trust and communication that had opened between them shut when Audrey let herself in with her key.

"Stay back!" Maggie moved too quickly for a human and kept Audrey from entering the store beyond a few steps. "It could be dangerous."

"Sorry." Audrey looked between Morgan and Maggie. "I need my purse and my jacket. Then I'll leave."

Morgan glanced at the fairy statues. Yep, they had moved again. "You really shouldn't be here," she said. "Where's your stuff?"

"In the back. Purple leather purse and black leather jacket."

Morgan managed a slight smile. "I like your taste." She walked into the storeroom, disappointed at the lack of residual energy shadow from Elric's shade in front of it. But what had she been hoping for? Something to hold on to? She couldn't cling to a shadow.

She found Audrey's things and walked back to the front of the store.

"I don't know what it was," Audrey was saying. "Only that there was a warm breeze and the smell of something really sweet and flowery. Gardenia, maybe?"

Morgan stilled. Tatiana wore gardenia essence, and what was subtle in the sensory overload of Faerie would be overpowering in the human realms.

"But you didn't see anything?" Maggie asked.

"No. And it was over really quickly."

Morgan handed Audrey her purse and jacket. "Here's your stuff."

"Thanks. Well, I've got my appointment this afternoon, but I'll be available this evening if you decide to open up again."

"Not until we can make sure everything is safe." Maggie held the door open. "You may want to lie low for a bit."

"No worries." Audrey grinned. "I've got plans tonight anyway." She walked out, and Morgan and Maggie looked at each other. Morgan still couldn't believe the day had taken such an awful turn.

Maggie spoke first. "I want to know why that statue jumped off the shelf. Are you up for a ritual?"

Morgan raised her eyebrows. "You'd trust me in a ritual?"

Maggie's response didn't make her feel better. "I don't feel like I have a choice."

13

———

Charlie sat in his office on the second floor of the Decatur Police Station and checked over Damien's report. He'd sighed when he put on his polo shirt and khakis rather than his hunting gear. It sucked that paperwork days—plural—inevitably followed the excitement of being in the field. At least now he had a trainee to do the police department reports, and all he had to do was edit them and then copy and paste them to the Truth Seeker system and then add the supernatural details for his superior, who had been strangely quiet as of late. He'd never responded to Charlie's query about the orders for the were-bat being messed up.

Charlie grinned at the report—Damien had a knack for giving just enough information for the event to sound plausible to humans but not so many as to prompt questions.

Even better, Damien was always willing to fetch coffee. Charlie suspected he'd walked up to Java Lemur to grab it since that would take him past The Crystal Cave, and if he recalled correctly, Audrey and Maggie worked together on Thursday mornings doing inventory. What was it like to be so into someone you couldn't get enough of them? He'd never had a relationship like that, at least not one that had lasted more than a week. He admired Damien and Audrey for keeping that magic alive for a full month.

A knock on the door startled him, and he waved whoever it was in after he minimized the TS system screen. He would have preferred to do his paperwork in the bunker beneath the station, but he had to keep up the appearance of being an investigator, and besides, Damien didn't have access to it since he hadn't been cleared yet.

"Morning, MacKenzie." The operations lieutenant walked in carrying a file. "Got the witness statement on that Peeping Tom."

Charlie took the file the other man handed him. "What is it?" He opened it to see a report from a patrol officer and a sketch of a man with a thin face. He looked vaguely familiar.

"Got another complaint about a Peeping Tom this morning. Sounds like the same guy as last night."

Charlie closed the file, his mind half-occupied with chasing the memory of a face with those narrow lines. "What do you need me for?"

"The officer who took the reports said there was something strange about the guy, at least from what the women told him. Said he moved quickly, and one swore he vanished like smoke. 'Like, literally.'" He mimicked the witness, which might have been funny when the officer who had taken the statements had originally done it, but secondhand imitation never did the original justice. Still, Charlie got the idea since Elric had done just that.

Elric.

Charlie opened the file to look at the sketch again. It could have been Elric, but then, it could have not been. The man wore a knit cap that covered the tips of his ears. Charlie would have to show the sketch to Maggie and Morgan. "Who did this?"

"One of the women. She's an art student." He sighed. "Literally."

Charlie chuckled. Then he saw the addresses of the complaints—both on Sycamore near Audrey's duplex. "Thanks, I'll look into it. Are the officers still around?"

"They've both left."

Charlie nodded. "I'll talk to the victims myself, then. With Lewis."

"What about me?" Damien walked into the office and gave the lieutenant a respectful nod. He handed one of the coffees he carried to Charlie. "Good morning, Lieutenant Davis."

"Good morning, Officer Lewis. How are you liking investigations?"

"I'm enjoying it a lot, Sir."

Charlie grinned behind his coffee cup. Damien enjoyed the hunting and chasing as much as he did. And detested the paperwork.

"Good. The paperwork for your promotion is on the chief's desk ready to be signed. I'll let you know as soon as it's official."

"Thank you, Sir."

Lieutenant Davis wished them both a good day and left, and Damien closed the door behind him.

MORGAN WATCHED as Maggie gathered up as much of the busted statue as she could, even to the point of sweeping up the shards from the floor, and put it all in a cardboard box. Then she followed her aunt out of the store and back to the condo complex.

"I'm going to check on Philippe." Morgan took a few moments in the bedroom to close her eyes and slow her heart rate, then peeked into the closet.

As she'd advised, Philippe had rolled himself up in the

blanket so he looked even more corpse-like, wrapped up like a body ready for burial. His unnatural stillness didn't help. She shoved aside the comparison, but the question still surfaced—what had happened to Elric? Was he lying somewhere just as still, but not just corpse-like?

She backed out of the closet and shut the door. Whatever happened, she wouldn't let Philippe be punished for someone else's mistakes. She'd seen too much misdirected revenge in her long lifetime already.

When Morgan emerged from the spare bedroom, she saw Maggie had set up a makeshift altar on her dining room table. A classic setup, it included a dagger and cup as well as symbols of the four cardinal directions and candles spread out on a black velvet cloth.

Maggie gestured to the spread. "Luckily my travel set was not in the spare bedroom when the obsidian mirror broke."

"What happened with that, anyway? It's tough to destroy one of those."

Maggie gave her a strange look. "You don't know?"

"Why would I?" Morgan returned her aunt's bewildered gaze.

"Because it happened when I saw you and Elric through it."

Morgan blinked back tears. "When was that?"

"A few nights ago. You were in a boat."

Morgan frowned. Could that have been when she and Elric had been riding out to the island where Philippe was being kept? Elric had waved a hand at something. Again, she felt sorry for having deceived him.

"I remember him swatting at something, but I didn't know it was you through your mirror."

Maggie took off her glasses and rubbed her eyes. "That's all right. I'm starting to think that you're as clueless in all this as I am."

"Finally," Morgan muttered. Then said aloud, "What are we doing?"

"We're going to analyze the statue to see who or what put a spell on it. The shop is warded. Nothing should have been able to get in to manipulate the behavior of the statues."

"What do you think Audrey has to do with it?" Morgan didn't like to think of the girl as being in danger, but she obviously had attracted the attention of something that didn't wish her well. But what could the Fae want with her? Was it the same mysterious thing Tatiana wanted with the fledgling vampire?

"I wish I knew."

Previously Morgan would have grinned, maybe even laughed, at her aunt's discomfort, but she felt just as confused, and therefore uncomfortable. And she liked Audrey, feeling for some reason that they were kindred spirits. Maybe it was that Audrey had faced down Zeus and won. Or so they had all thought. Morgan sensed some sort of unfinished business there. But what could it have to do with the Fae?

"So we're going to magically analyze the statue?" The face of the male fairy looked at Morgan, or seemed to, with pleading eyes.

"As much as we're able. Their legs and most of the base is intact, so we'll focus our energies there."

"Is that safe?"

"I don't know." Maggie frowned at her. "Is it? Do you sense something?"

Morgan looked at the porcelain fragments. "No, not really."

"Okay, then we'll start there." Maggie chanted to herself as she lit the candles in a clockwise motion, beginning with the one at the northern point of the altar.

A damp sweat covered Morgan's skin, and she recognized the ritual opening as what Maggie—then Margaret—had traditionally done on Avalon when Niniane hadn't felt up to leading the ritual, for whatever reason. She breathed against the panic and tried not to hear the gentle lapping of the waves of the lake or the calls of the water birds at dawn on the island.

An echo of Morgan's former powers washed through her, a tingle that spread from the crown of her head through her center and to her extremities. Then it faded, leaving the familiar ache of regret and grief in the hollow they'd carved in her chest. Now she remembered why she avoided rituals—they brought back too many memories. And why she needed to get this one—and this job—right.

Maggie handed her the cup, which was filled with water, and Morgan poured some over the statue. The words came back to her, a plea to the goddess to watch over them and give them the answers they sought. The statue darkened with dampness, and steam rose from its surface.

Not steam, something else. Something worse.

"Fae-fire!" Morgan grabbed Maggie and pulled her beneath the table just before the statue exploded in a plume of flame, the reflection of which she saw in the windows. Thick smoke filled the apartment and Morgan's lungs, and she coughed and wheezed. Gentle hands helped her to stand, and Maggie guided her out of the apartment and into the hallway.

Oh, gods, would Maggie think this had been her fault? And what about Philippe?

Damien and Charlie spoke simultaneously.

"Something's up at Maggie's store."

"There was another sighting of the Peeping Tom in Audrey's neighborhood."

"Wait, what?"

Charlie held a hand up. "Whoa, okay, you go first. What's happening at the store?"

Damien took a deep breath, whatever good that would do. He'd hoped the half mile walk from the store to the station would have calmed him, but instead he found himself more bothered. Even the good news from Lieutenant Davis about his promotion couldn't calm the thrum of worry around his heart. And now some creep was wandering around his girlfriend's neighborhood...

Right, deep breath.

"You know how Maggie has those shelves of ceramic statues, mostly of fairies? They were acting strange."

He waited for Charlie to scoff, but his friend only nodded. "Strange?"

"She said they slowly turned to follow Audrey's movements around the store. Like they're watching her."

Charlie nodded. "Maybe in more ways than one." He handed the case folder he'd been holding to Damien. "The witnesses said there was something strange about this guy. As in, he seemed to vanish like smoke."

"Can fairies do that?" Damien opened the file and looked at a crude drawing of a guy with features he could only describe as snotty and aristocratic. They looked out of place under the knit cap.

"I saw one do it last night."

Damien looked up from the file. "When?"

"When Maggie's niece arrived. Come on, we need to talk to them. They may know this guy. Give me a minute to shut everything down here."

While Charlie logged out of everything and turned off the computer, Damien studied the case file. There had been two separate reports, both of a white male looking into windows and vanishing when caught. That was an interesting term—vanishing. Not running or hiding or slinking. Just vanishing. The addresses were one street over from Audrey's duplex, though. The same chill that had stolen over him when Audrey mentioned the statues returned.

Once they were outside and out of earshot, Damien asked, "What do you know about Maggie's niece? Is she connected to all of this?"

"I wish I knew."

When they arrived at the Crystal Cave, the sign on the door had been turned to Closed. Damien attempted to peer in, but Maggie had lowered the shades that covered the windows at night. He knocked anyway, and Charlie pulled out his phone.

"What are you doing?"

"Texting her."

No noise came from inside the store, so Damien texted Audrey. She responded with—*Maggie told me to go home. Said something happened with one of the fairy statues.* She ended the text with a shrugging emoji.

"Audrey went home," he said. Then he texted, *Meet for lunch in a few?*

Can't. About to leave for doctor - have to go early for x-rays. Will send news when I have it.

Good luck!

She sent back a heart, and he smiled. Then caught Charlie frowning at him and tried to bend his cheeks and lips back into a serious expression.

"You've got it bad, dude." Charlie walked down Church Street and crossed to go left on Ponce. Damien followed him.

"What?"

"You're in love. We're going to Maggie's, by the way. She and Morgan are doing some sort of ritual to attempt to see what's going on with the statue."

"Witchy stuff?" Damien's steps slowed without his brain telling them to. Rituals reminded him too much of his grandmother's odd hobbies, and those hadn't ended well for her. He had to constantly remind himself that the supernatural exposure hadn't driven her over the edge. Lack of people who understood it and could help balance her had.

"I don't know. It's a side of Maggie I haven't seen before."

Damien rolled his eyes and forced his legs to keep moving. "You sound both terrified and excited. And how many sides have you seen of her?"

Charlie flashed him a grin. "Not nearly enough."

"Uh huh. Who has what bad?"

They rang the bell, and Maggie buzzed them in. They got off the elevator on her floor, and Damien nearly stumbled into the wall. Smoke filled the hall, but the alarms were silent. Charlie found one and pulled, as did Damien. A loud, rhythmic buzzing filled the hall.

"Which one is her apartment?" Damien yelled over the din.

"This way."

They tried to run and keep close to the ground, but smoke choked them. The wail of sirens from outside joined the alarm inside. They reached the apartment door. Black smoke that smelled both sulfurous and plant-based billowed from underneath, and Charlie raised his leg to kick the door in. Damien stopped him.

"They're steel-reinforced," he coughed out. "You'll break your leg."

"But they're in there. She's in there."

Damien put a hand on the door. It wasn't hot. It swung inward, and Maggie and Morgan stumbled out, coughing. Charlie grabbed Maggie, and Damien Morgan, and they raced toward the stairs.

14

———————

Strong hands guided Maggie to the stairwell. Once the fire door clanged to a close behind them, she took her first full breath of the relatively fresher air. A fit of coughing followed, and Charlie rubbed her back in circles until she could breathe normally.

"What. The hell. Happened?" The smoke made Charlie's voice raspy, deep, and comforting, and Maggie blinked against the stinging in her eyes so she wouldn't cry with relief. The fire alarm strobe lit the stairwell in a surreal pattern.

She tried to say, "I don't know," but she coughed again. He held her until the spasms in her lungs ceased. She looked at Morgan, who seemed mostly unaffected. She maintained at least a foot's distance from Damien and leaned against the wall with crossed arms. Why wasn't she coughing her lungs out?

"You need medical attention." Damien pointed to her and Charlie. "Both of you. Can you make it down the stairs?"

They both nodded, and Damien moved to help, but Charlie waved him off. He didn't release Maggie's waist until they'd reached the bottom floor and stumbled into the watery sunshine. A paramedic spotted them and made them separate.

He guided Maggie to sit on a stretcher, and after a quick exam, put an oxygen mask over her face.

The sun broke through a crack in the clouds, and once its light touched her, Maggie healed from the outside in. She gestured to the medic to remove the oxygen mask.

"Are you sure, Miss?"

"Yes." Her voice sounded husky and hollowed, but that wouldn't last long. He helped her to sit, then checked her vitals.

"All normal. You're lucky. Anyone else who'd inhaled as much smoke as it looks like you did would've been much worse off."

"Thank you for your help." She didn't feel like putting too much effort into evading his questions. Telling him the truth—that she was an immortal human with certain privileges—was obviously out of the question.

But then there was Charlie, who was just a regular guy who—and she had to stop and lean against a brick wall for a second—had risked his life to save hers. No, he was more than just a regular guy. And gods, she'd been so stupid. She should've figured the statuette would have been booby-trapped to explode in a shower of razor-sharp shards and fae-fire, which burned hotter and longer than normal flames. Her apartment would be toast. But she didn't have time to think about that. Or about the fact that Morgan had somehow known and saved her.

Where had her niece disappeared to? Maggie spotted Damien looking on worriedly as two paramedics administered oxygen and monitored Charlie, who lay on a stretcher inside an ambulance. Morgan was nowhere to be seen. Her absence created a wisp of doubt in Maggie's mind. Had she left now that she'd fulfilled her purpose? Had she gone back to check on the vampire—her bounty? Philippe, being in a dead sleep state, shouldn't be harmed. Maggie trusted the wards she'd put around her apartment, and especially around her ritual closet, would keep first responders from finding him.

"How is he?" Maggie asked, gesturing to Charlie.

Damien shook his head. "He collapsed as soon as they took you away. He never told me he had asthma."

"Asthma?" Maggie's lungs tightened in sympathy, her heart in fear.

"That's what they said it looked like. Apparently he had it as a kid." He ran one hand through his hair, spiking the dark waves. "I didn't know until they pulled it out of one of his pockets that he still carried an inhaler."

Maggie's forehead tightened in surprise. If anyone would have known about Charlie's asthma, it would have been his best friend. "What exactly happened?"

He shot her a quizzical glance, but they'd worked together long enough for him to not ask questions. Not that he could with those naive to the supernatural forces at work in their midst all around them.

"As I said, he collapsed. He put his hands to his throat and seemed to have trouble breathing. He was wheezing, but not like any wheeze I've ever heard on any emergency call." He stopped and swallowed, and his fear flickered across his face before he regained control.

Maggie wanted to put a hand on his arm to comfort him but didn't want to overstep her bounds. She'd known he and Charlie had a close working relationship, but Damien's expression hadn't been fear for a colleague—he was terrified for his friend. And with them being in the open, she couldn't say that's what the smoke from fae-fire would do...to its target. At least he had been in the position to get help quickly.

"We need to take him to the E.R.," one of the men said. They put the stretcher into the vehicle, closed the door, and Damien pulled Maggie away so they wouldn't run over her. She didn't realize she'd reached toward it until he gently lowered her arm.

"I can't get you into my car if you're stretched out like that," he said, the curve of his lips sympathy rather than amusement. "It's at the station. Come on, can you make it?"

"Yes. I'm fine now."

Once they reached his car—and he wouldn't move fast enough for her, insisting that he couldn't take both her and Charlie collapsing on him—and the doors were closed, she explained.

"That was fae-fire, not regular fire." The memory of its burning peat smell came back to her. "It burns hotter and longer than the combustion humans are typically used to. It also has a magical component that can be activated to do extra damage to those it's targeted at."

Damien's hands tightened on the wheel, making his knuckles white. "And it was aimed at Charlie?"

A lump had formed in Maggie's throat, and she knew it had nothing to do with the flames. She had to force her words out around it. "And me. That's why Morgan was relatively unhurt. They set a trap inside a statuette that would be triggered when it was subjected to a ritual."

"So someone knew you'd be doing that. And that Charlie would be close by."

"Or come to rescue me." She looked at her hands. Would she have been able to forgive herself if his blood had ended up on them? But why were they trying to get at her? She was a Truth Seeker in limbo waiting on her next assignment. While she had made plenty of enemies, there was no reason for someone to be coming after her now.

To his credit, Damien didn't chastise her or tell her she should have anticipated what would happen, a relief since she'd been beating up on herself enough since she recognized the trap had been for Charlie.

"And will they know what to do at the hospital?" he asked.

"Does fae-fire smoke damage require a different intervention than regular smoke inhalation?"

Of course. Another thing she should have thought about. "Not necessarily. At least not as far as I know."

"That's not comforting, Maggie."

"I know." She balled her hands, one inside the other. "Hopefully your friend Arthur Rizzo is on duty. He'll know what to do."

Damien glanced at her, then back at the road, the muscles around his gray eyes tight. "I suspect he will be. I think he's appointed himself guardian spirit to us all."

"Let's hope we don't all need one." But she suspected they might if she couldn't figure it all out soon.

But where was Morgan? Maggie pulled out her phone, which had been in her pocket, and sent a text, but got no answer.

MORGAN HUNG BACK WHEN MAGGIE, Charlie, and Damien staggered out of the building. She wedged herself into the corner of the stairwell and counted to ten in three different languages. When no one returned for her, she ran up the stairs back to the fifth floor, thankful she'd managed to stay in such good shape. She guessed the firefighters would be searching for the source of the smoke, and she hoped she wasn't too late. It wouldn't go well for her aunt for them to find Philippe, an apparent dead body, in her closet. Nor would it end well for Philippe should they drag him into the sunlit room, even if they kept the blinds closed.

Maggie's defensive wards wrapped icy doubt around Morgan's heart that she should even be entering the apartment, and the impulse to run away made her close her eyes and grit her teeth. She pushed against the uncomfortable emotions and whispered, "I'm Morgan le Fay, niece of Margaret of Cornwall. She invited me in. You felt us leave together—you know I belong." With those words, they eased, and she entered. She didn't know how well they would work against a determined fireman or policeman who'd been trained to push past fear, but maybe if they'd developed good gut sense, they could be fooled into thinking their own intuition warned them off.

She shook her head. She needed to develop better gut sense. She still couldn't believe she'd been so mean to Elric when he'd only been trying to protect her.

Or had he? Gods, she hated not having all the information. She hated even more that she'd jumped to the conclusion that he'd betrayed her. And now this. Something was definitely up, and the statue's resemblance to her and Elric told her that the Fae had possibly used her in some sort of trap. Had they counted on her being killed or seriously hurt?

Morgan looked around for clues to their motivations. There was nothing left of the statue aside from barely perceptible fragments lodged in the walls and the surface of the dining room table. Maggie's velvet cloth still smoldered somewhat, but the smoke from the fae-fire had at least dissipated. Morgan knelt under the table, where something white caught her attention. It was the face of the guy fairy, the one who looked kind of like Elric. And whose expression now seemed accusatory rather than affectionate. Or maybe that was her interpretation.

"I'd raise you and kick your ass if I could," she muttered and stuck the piece in the pocket of her hoodie. "And then kiss you, you silly Fae." A wave of grief overtook her from her gut, and she paused and leaned against the door frame between the spare bedroom and living room.

A flash came to her, a place memory, of a human Philippe standing there, looking angry.

"You don't trust me."

And then it was gone. What had happened between him

and Margaret? They must have been more than acquaintances if questions of trust were coming up.

She blinked to adjust her vision to the gloom of the bedroom, where she'd left both the blinds and the curtains drawn. A heavy knocking on the front door of the condo made her slip into the closet, where she sat with her hand on the doorknob in case someone should try to open it. Not that they should, but just in case.

The door swung open with a crash, and voices drifted through the thin walls—two men.

"This is where it started?"

"Yep, looks like some sort of witchy ritual gone bad. Look at that cloth."

"Not enough to cause the smoke inhalation injuries we saw."

Morgan raised her eyebrows. Injuries? Sure, her aunt and the blond cop had been coughing, but they seemed to be mostly fine. At least okay enough to make it down the stairs. Had someone else been hurt?

"Look, this is giving me the creeps. Looks all clear to me."

"Yeah, let's go."

Good, so the wards were working, sort of. But...

"Wait, we should at least check the bedrooms, make sure no one's passed out in there. I bet there were drugs involved. Looks like something exploded."

"Right. But it doesn't smell like meth."

"Nope."

Morgan could feel the wards screaming at the men to leave, and she covered one of her ears, not that it helped. The screaming was all energetic, and she added her mental chant to it, *Leave now, leave now, leave now...*

Heavy footsteps clomped through the apartment, but they didn't make it too far into the bedroom. Still, she tightened her hold on the door knob and tried not to make any noise. She also turned her phone to Do Not Disturb so it wouldn't buzz.

The footfalls indicated the two men entered the bedroom, checked the bathroom, did the same in the other one, and then left. She wondered what their report would say—pagan drug ritual gone wrong. When she loosened her grip on the door knob, her hand came away slicked with sweat, which she wiped on her jeans.

"They're not going to burn me at the stake. Not anymore." She spoke softly and hoped the men were truly gone. But hearing the words in the air around her was the only thing that comforted her. Damn Inquisition. It had given her Posttraumatic Stress Disorder before PTSD was a thing, at least one that was recognized in women. And she had never stopped feeling inadequately prepared to defend herself since losing her powers.

She cracked the door open and peeked out, but the apartment was empty. She crawled out of the closet to the door of the bedroom and confirmed that the firemen had shut the door behind them. Still, it felt too open, so she returned to the closet and sat by Philippe. His head lay on the pillow in front of the dresser that still held the obsidian mirror, and he had covered himself in the blanket. He looked like a dead dude, but Morgan wedged herself beside him and put a hand on his head. The rough texture of the knitted material felt comforting and real to her fingers, and soon she was able to slow her heart down.

Crap, heartbeat. The vampire would be hungry when he woke. She folded her hands in her lap, leaned back, and looked at him.

"Well, we're in a pickle, aren't we?" She didn't know when fermented vegetables had become synonymous with difficult situations, but she liked the expression. She leaned her head back against the wall of the closet, and her eyelids drooped. *Crap, I forgot what fae-fire does to me.* It had been so long, at least five centuries, since she'd last encountered it. And then she had slept for a whole day after Elric had dragged her out of the temple that was being burned by enemies of the Fae for disrespecting them. The arsonist had been the bounty that time, and Morgan had eventually gotten her. She wondered what had happened to the poor human.

She fought to stay awake, but the fatigue from the smoke made the world turn gray, although she didn't allow herself to sleep completely. The sensation of a rubber band snapping through her middle made her open her eyes in a small house.

A calico cat sat on the couch and preened itself, and it blinked golden eyes at her. Then a voice in Morgan's head said, *"Watch and listen. She needs you."*

15

The bullies were holding him down again. Charlie tried to breathe against the cotton T-shirt they held against his nose and mouth, its fibers drying out his tongue and the insides of his cheek such that he wouldn't be able to spit in their faces when they released him. He thought he'd grown out of fearing them, but he knew they'd find him eventually. No matter how much he worked out or how many were-bats and other creatures he saved the world from, they'd appear to show him the fraud he was. He'd always be the new boy with asthma who couldn't stand up to them and who couldn't always charm the adults into protecting him.

But he didn't remember the burning all the way through his nose, mouth, throat, and lungs, like he'd drunk bad whiskey that had gone down the wrong way. His lungs loosened ever so slightly, allowing in the cool air to relieve the heat. Each breath came easier, and he floated away from the bullies toward the orange light that must be the backs of his eyelids. He couldn't resist turning, or imagining doing so, to give the bullies he moved away from a double middle-fingered salute.

"'Til next time, assholes."

But instead of the two older boys who had tormented him on that base in Texas, he saw the sneering face of Elric. "Well, fuck you, too, Fae."

He awoke to find his hands clenched in the same defiantly rude gesture. The amused face of a doctor with round spectacles and wild gray hair and beard looked down at him.

"I think he'll be all right," Doctor Arthur Rizzo said with a laugh. "You can go now, Casey, Lainey."

Charlie turned to see two nurses, one guy and one girl, standing in the background. The nurse snickered and walked out of the room, her hand over her mouth. When they were alone, Rizzo checked Charlie's pulse and made a note in the chart.

"What the hell did you get into, Lieutenant MacKenzie?" he asked. "Oh, right." After another glance at the monitor, he removed the oxygen mask. "Your O2 sat is good now, but let me know if you feel short of breath or have any tightness in your chest."

Charlie took a couple of breaths unassisted, and Rizzo raised the bed so Charlie semi-reclined.

"I didn't realize you were my guardian angel, too," Charlie said once he found confidence in his ability to breathe.

Rizzo made a motion for him to keep his voice down. "I didn't, either. You're lucky I'm the one who got your case—the others wouldn't have known how to modify treatment for fae-fire."

"For what?" Charlie struggled to sit more upright. "Are Maggie and Damien all right? And Morgan?"

Rizzo pushed him back, and to Charlie's dismay, he couldn't resist.

"None of the others have been brought in, but I suspect they'll be here soon to see you. Morgan?"

Charlie picked at the thin hospital blanket. "Maggie's niece."

"Oh?" Rizzo's eyebrows crawled upward. "What have you

four gotten yourselves into now? I thought you were supposed to be cleaning up the mess left by the Greeks."

"That's what we thought, too. Is anyone where they could hear? Oh, and do you have someone else to take care of?"

Rizzo checked the hallway. "It's a nice quiet day in the ER, so I'm not needed, and we're alone. What's going on? Is Audrey involved?"

Charlie filled him in on what he could remember, including the Peeping Tom. As he talked, his strength returned, and by the end of the story, his voice sounded normal again.

Rizzo listened and only asked for a few points of clarification. "The Fae are definitely up to something, then. That's concerning. I was afraid the situation with the Greeks wouldn't be resolved so easily."

Hearing Rizzo say it cemented the suspicion that had been growing in Charlie's mind. "You think they're connected? How?"

"I don't know. I'll have to do my own digging. You wouldn't perhaps know if the illustrious Madame Lucia has been consulted yet, would you?"

Now Charlie had to hide a laugh. "No, this all just came up over the past twenty-four hours."

"All right. Well, I'm going to let you rest."

"Can you ask them to bring Maggie and Damien back when they get here?"

Rizzo stroked his beard. "You know you can't have visitors in the E.R., but I'll see what I can do. Margaret is a force of nature I'd rather not tangle with."

"I wouldn't mind a good tangle with her," Charlie murmured. He wasn't sure if he'd said it out loud, though. Rizzo dimmed the lights, and Charlie's eyelids ignored his wish that they remain open. He was almost asleep when he remembered that Casey was the name of one of the bullies from Texas, and he would be about the same age as the nurse. Was his past about to haunt him as much as his present?

He got his answer as soon as he drifted off and found himself in the schoolyard in Texas in his dream.

"So we meet again, Charlie MacKenzie."

"I DON'T KNOW how you managed to heal so quickly." The orthopedic doctor, a slim woman with a mass of blonde curls shook her head at the x-ray, which showed no damage. "Most of these breaks heal in four to eight weeks, but after seeing yours, I figured it would be on the longer end."

Audrey appreciated the doctor's honesty, but she didn't like others pointing out how she was different. It brought back too many memories of returning to school and being the kid whose father had been killed.

"So that means I'm cleared for activity?" Her cheeks warmed at the thought of what kind of activity she would be doing with Damien, finally in the waking world.

The woman turned from the screen, and her puzzled expression cleared into a knowing one. "And what kind of activity would that be?"

If Audrey's face heated any more, it would catch fire. "I have a, er, new boyfriend." She guessed she could call him the b-word. They hadn't discussed anything, but she wasn't dating anyone else, and she knew he wasn't.

The doctor shook her head. "And I thought you meant running."

"Well, that too."

The doctor scribbled something on a pad. "Take whatever you do easy. Here's a prescription for something that's essentially high strength ibuprofen in case you do overdo it and the area hurts. Physical therapy will help, too, so I'll have the front desk set you up."

Audrey took the script and said goodbye but missed whatever else she said. Finally, she and Damien could make love in the waking world! She'd been ready weeks ago, but he hadn't wanted to accidentally hurt her. She appreciated his caution, but still. A girl had needs.

She checked the time when she left the office, physical therapy referral in hand—just about two. She wondered where her guardian angel, also known as J.J. and sometimes as Dr. Rizzo was. Not angel, he'd pointed out. Spirit. The angels were much better at what they did than he was.

She shook her head—if someone had told her a year ago she'd be involved in supernatural adventures, she would have said they were crazy. Now sometimes she wondered if she was.

The sweet smell of gardenia wafted on the breeze when she emerged from the professional building, and the hairs across her neck and upper back raised. She checked behind her, but she didn't see anyone.

Yep, going to see Rizzo seemed like a grand idea. In fact, she had to remind herself to pause and look both ways before crossing the driveway between the main hospital and the professional buildings. She hesitated before walking into the emergency room entrance. J.J. had told her to come any time and ask for him in his alternate form, especially if she felt endangered, but she still felt weird doing so. Besides, shouldn't he know when she was in trouble? Well, whatever he was, she needed to check in with him about the morning's strangeness.

When she entered the waiting area, the two people who turned away from the desk toward her were the two she least expected—Maggie and Damien.

"What are y'all doing here?" Then dread settled in her stomach when she realized if they were there... "Where's Charlie? What happened?"

"There was a fire," Maggie said. She cocked her head toward the receptionist, and Audrey got the hint—she couldn't share all the details in front of a mundane. Then Maggie continued,

"And Charlie and Damien came to rescue us, but Charlie inhaled more smoke."

"Are you okay?" Audrey asked both but looked at Damien.

"I'm fine." He opened his arms to her, and she walked into them, glad he was safe. He smelled of his usual soap and a manly smell she couldn't define, but he also had a smoky odor, like something unpleasant had been barbecued.

She pulled away. The smell repelled her, although she wanted to make sure he was safe and solid and unharmed. Now the anxiety buzzed in her gut—what if he'd been hurt? Or worse? Could she handle the stabbing uncertainty every time he walked out of the door to go to work?

"They won't let us go see him," Damien told her, and now guilt joined the other feelings. Charlie was his best friend. She shouldn't be thinking about herself.

"I'll see about that. Is Doctor Rizzo in?" Audrey asked the receptionist.

"He's at lunch."

"Would you page him and tell him his niece is here to see him?" She cocked her head at Maggie. "And where's *your* niece?"

Maggie sighed. "Your guess is as good as mine. She vanished after the fire."

With a sigh and a shrug, the receptionist did as Audrey asked. She guessed that since none of them were bleeding, they weren't that interesting. The receptionist picked up the phone, and with a glare, nodded at whatever the person on the other side was saying.

"He says to come on in. He'll meet you at the other side of the doors."

"Thank you." She led Damien and Maggie through the automatic doors and into the emergency department. Small rooms lined the hallway, and she tried not to look at the ones that were occupied. She wanted to know where Charlie was, but it seemed an invasion of privacy to peek at the other patients.

Arthur Rizzo, who looked like an older, grizzled version of the man she'd grown up knowing as J.J.—her older stepbrother —met them in the hall.

"I'm guessing you're not here to see me," he said after giving Audrey a squeeze on her shoulder and shaking Damien's hand.

"Is Charlie all right?" Maggie asked.

When Rizzo looked at Maggie, it wasn't with kindness. "He's resting. It's my day off, but I'm filling in for one of the other docs who's sick. Good thing I am, too." The normally jovial doctor's face went grim, and he gestured for them to follow him. "Whatever are you playing at to get him exposed to fae-fire?"

Audrey reminded herself that his glare pointed at Maggie, not her. Still, she didn't refuse Damien's hand when he offered it. They held back to allow the two older beings their space to discuss.

"I don't know," Maggie didn't sound intimidated. "I was hoping you'd heard something. The fae are getting through the city's perimeter barrier."

"What?" His eyebrows seemed to crawl up his forehead. "That's not possible. Are they sneaking through the C.U. or some other parallel?"

"Again, I don't know. I don't have all the answers, Arthur."

"I'm guessing it's not the first time you've said that," Rizzo grumbled. He stopped in front of one of the rooms. "One peek, but no more. He's sleeping."

"Low blow." Maggie peered into the dim room, and she put a hand over her mouth. "Oh. Oh! He's not sleeping, he's battling." She shoved her way past Rizzo and went to stand by Charlie's bed.

"Come on," she said and caressed his hair. "It's okay. You can come back now."

~

"WHAT DO YOU WANT, you skinny fae bastard?" Charlie planted his feet and clenched his fists, ready to throw a punch at whoever came at him next. He'd be damned if Elric or Casey or the other two boys who circled him would knock him down. Never mind that his nose dripped blood and snot into his mouth and the ribs on his left side felt bruised, forcing him to take short, shallow breaths.

"Your fortitude is admirable." Elric wore black jeans and a long leather jacket that looked out of place in the muggy Texas summer.

Wait, it *was* out of place. Charlie blinked, and the sweat stung his eyes. Why was there a skinny guy with pointed ears and leather in the schoolyard? Was he a pedophile? Shouldn't someone be calling the police?

Oh, right, Charlie was the police. But then why was he fighting these boys? He should be big enough to kick their little bully asses. Not that he would hurt a child, especially not now as a grown man.

"Stop." The scene froze. Casey, a little bruiser with curly light brown hair, had his right fist reared back for a punch. His two friends, the blond Smith boys, stood one on either side and a little behind him, their mouths open in silent jeers. Charlie found himself kneeling, his inhaler in the light brown dust by his right knee, and when he stood, the three boys vanished. Elric remained, but not suspended in time. He only took in the surroundings. His slightly wrinkled aristocratic nose and thinned lips told Charlie he was not impressed.

"Why are you in my dream?" Charlie asked and looked around. Yes, it was his elementary school playground. He shuddered. Being the new kid with asthma had not been easy. And since his father had been military and moved them around a lot... Well, his childhood had sucked. So why was he back there?

"Am I in your dream, or are you in mine?" Elric looked around at the dull gray and browns of the playground they stood in. Everything had been faded into an almost monochromatic landscape by the sun. "Hmmm, no, my dream would be more colorful."

Then it came back to him—he'd rescued Maggie and Morgan from a fire. So was he dead or only dreaming? Or...

"Like the fae-fire in the trap you set for me?" Charlie shoved Elric in the shoulder.

Elric looked down like Charlie had just smeared him with excrement. "Touch me again, human, and you'll regret it."

Charlie took a deep breath, his lungs no longer constricted by a hundred metal bands, and spoke through a clenched jaw. "Answer my damn question, and I won't kick your ass."

"Fine." Elric sniffed, and Charlie waited. And waited. And balled his fists.

"And...?"

Elric straightened the cuffs of his long-sleeved black T-shirt under his leather jacket. "I am in your dream. And this may be the Collective Unconscious seeing that you and I are both here."

Charlie closed his eyes. Right. Fae. Tricky bastards. "That's not the question I meant. You'd already answered that one."

"You didn't specify."

Charlie cocked his fist again, but then he recalled who he was and where he was. And that he hated violence. Fine, he would play the game and ask the kind of questions he would get reasonable answers to. "What are you doing here?"

"What do you think? You're connected, you and I, but you don't know how yet."

"Do you?"

Now Elric's face lost some of its haughty expression. "No. In fact, I do not know what has happened to me. I must have sought you out since you are associated with the Truth Seeker. Morgan's aunt." He frowned. "That's it—I came to you because I need to warn her. But of what?"

Charlie would have laughed at the confusion on Elric's face. One didn't often get to see a high Fae, well, ever, but definitely not a disoriented one.

"Was it something to do with the statue? And the explosion."

Elric rubbed his temples. The human gesture almost made Charlie forget he spoke with a creature of pure selfishness. Almost.

"Perhaps. Or whoever separated my spirit from my body set the trap for you and Margaret. The game is much bigger than any of you realize."

Something caressed Charlie's hair, and the wind whispered, *"Come back to me. You're safe now."*

Charlie batted the invisible hand away. "Why would you seek me out?"

"Because you're brave or stupid enough to take on were-bats. And your destiny is linked with ours." Elric stiffened, his gaze straight ahead, and spouted as though it had been drilled into him, "Come to Faerie, and you will lack for nothing."

"No way, dude. I've got too much going on here."

Elric clutched his shoulder and fell to his knees. Charlie rushed to him. "What is it?"

Elric grabbed Charlie's arm with his other hand. "Please tell Morgan to be careful. She is in grave danger, and all the power in the world isn't worth her life. Enough Faustian bargains have been made already." Then, with a scream like an injured hawk, he disappeared.

This time when Charlie felt a hand run over his hair, he attempted to follow it to consciousness.

16

Charlie's eyelids fluttered open above the oxygen mask. Maggie snatched her hand back from his head and cursed the tears that stung her eyes. She couldn't cry in front of him. That would only make him feel protective and more attached to her. And there was no reason to give him false hope that she could ever give him what he wanted.

But she couldn't help the hiccup of relief that escaped from her or the tears that leaked from her eyes. She'd stood by many a fallen warrior, but none who had made her feel like this one. Or who she would mourn like him if he did die.

He lifted a hand to brush a droplet from her cheek. He couldn't speak, but his eyes said, "It's okay. I'm here. I'm alive."

"I'm not crying." She batted his hand away, but he caught it. Rizzo gently moved her aside so he could remove the oxygen mask. After a quick exam, he stepped back.

"You can have five minutes."

Maggie nodded, the lump in her throat too big to speak around.

Charlie grinned at her, but it was a faded version of his normal teasing smile, and took her hand. "If you're not crying,

I'm not lying here in a hospital bed looking up at the prettiest darn sight a guy could hope to wake up to."

"Flatterer." She pulled her hand out of his before he could press her fingers to his lips. She stepped back from the hospital bed and wiped the traitorous tears from her face with her hands. When she stirred the air, she caught an odd scent and stilled.

"What is it?" Rizzo asked. Then he sniffed too. "Oh. I'll be right back." He walked out of the room.

"What?" Audrey looked from one to the other, her hand firmly in Damien's. "What do you see?"

Maggie took a deep breath. There it was, just the faintest hint, and panic washed the almost-grief from her chest. "Not see, smell. Like sour crushed gardenia petals."

"Gardenia?" Audrey's freckles stood out against her newly pale cheeks. "I've been smelling it off and on all day. What does it mean?"

Charlie raised the head of the bed. "I saw Elric. In my dream. He said we were connected somehow."

The uncertainty in his eyes brought Maggie back to his side, but she kept her thumbs hooked in her pockets so she wouldn't give in to her urge to touch him. "The high Fae lie like humans breathe. Did he seem desperate?"

"Yes." Charlie relaxed back into the pillow. "Quite. He seemed frightened of something." He drew his blond brows together. "Where's Morgan?"

Damien stepped forward. "She disappeared after the fire."

"Oh." Charlie flopped back on the bed. "Elric said I had to warn her. That she's in danger. That whoever set the trap in the statue is the same that killed him."

Maggie put her hand to her chest, like it could stop the cloud of guilt that spread there. And she had thought Morgan had something to do with the explosion. But the Fae did lie...

Damien went to stand by the bed. "Don't worry about that

stuff now. How are you feeling? And how could you not tell me you have asthma?"

"It's been controlled until now. I only have the inhaler with me for emergencies but haven't needed it in decades."

Maggie backed away to stand beside Audrey and give the friends a moment together. Audrey sent her a look that seemed to mix pity and understanding, which only pissed Maggie off more. She wanted to leave the room, but something tethered her to Charlie, even now that she knew he was okay. It was like an invisible rope tied her to him, and if she stepped away, it would tug her heart out of her chest.

Nice. I could compete with Morgan for melodrama.

Audrey cleared her throat. "Um, Charlie, I'm glad you're okay. But I need to go. I have to take care of something."

"Are you sure it's safe?" Damien asked and reached out to her. "If they're smelling the same thing you did earlier..."

She stepped back, and annoyance flashed over her face. "Safer than going into a building full of smoke. I'll see you later."

"Okay."

She didn't lean away when Damien kissed her, but she didn't relax into it, either. Maggie looked away. They were too freaking cute, but she could see how the circumstances strained the new relationship.

"I'll catch you later, okay?" Damien asked. "I want to know how it went with the doctor."

"It was good news. I'm completely healed. We'll catch up later." But Audrey didn't sound happy, and Damien scowled as she left.

Maggie made a mental note to tell Charlie not to keep Damien too late that night. He and Audrey obviously had some stuff to talk through. And celebrate.

Maggie wasn't jealous at all. Nope. It wasn't like it had been ages since she'd had anyone she could really talk to. Just a couple of centuries. Give or take. But she needed to find Morgan. If the girl truly was in danger, she needed to know. If she didn't already. It was time for a heart-to-heart.

Damien and Charlie clasped hands, and Damien gestured for Maggie to join him at Charlie's bedside.

"I'm going to go to the station, do my report, and see if the fire department has cleared your place to go back yet," Damien said.

"What about you?" Charlie asked. He lifted the hand closest to her, but it flopped back on the bed. Maggie should have felt relief, but instead found herself disappointed that he hadn't reached for her.

"She's going to go home and let you have some rest," Rizzo said. "I'm going to admit you overnight for observation." He looked at Maggie. "I'll text you when he's in a room."

"Thanks." She did give into the urge to squeeze Charlie's hand. "Sleep now. But no more scary dreams."

"Yes, ma'am."

Rizzo ushered her out, but instead of turning back at the entrance to the E.R., he followed her into the lobby. Damien waved goodbye to both of them.

"I'm on a break now. Come to my office. There are things we need to discuss."

AUDREY LAY on the couch with a purring Athena on her lap. She couldn't get the image of Charlie out of her head. She thought of him as a ball of energy, invincible and indestructible. And seeing him lying in the hospital bed, his face half-covered by the oxygen mask... What if that had been Damien? What if he'd breathed in too much smoke and lay in the hospital balanced between life and death? She blinked the tears from her eyes.

"I don't know if I can handle it, Athena." She scratched the soft fur on and around Athena's ears. The cat purred and kneaded Audrey's sweater.

A chill breeze made Audrey sit up. She'd opened the windows to help herself cool off, figuratively and literally—but her comfort level had fallen with the darkness of the evening, which had come quickly due to the heavy clouds. Athena gave her a dirty look when Audrey chased her off the final windowsill. She'd been intent on something out there that Audrey couldn't see. Rather than amusing Audrey, the cat's behavior had freaked her out more.

When she moved to close that window, the feeling of not rightness intensified to the point all the hair on her arms, neck, and legs stood on end, and she moved to the side so as not to be seen. The breeze carried the barest hint of gardenia, but it was enough to choke her with fear. She slammed the window shut and closed the curtain.

Her phone buzzed with a text, and she moved across the room to pick it up from her nightstand, where it charged. But there wasn't anything either on the lock screen or when she opened the app.

She glanced back at the window and saw she must not have gotten the curtain closed all the way, or the window—she could still see an inch of the dark screen. But hadn't she closed it? Had the text come before she could let it down all the way? Sometimes the frame stuck.

She could almost convince herself her mind was playing tricks on her, but she knew better than to ignore warnings like the one she'd just received. She called Damien, who, oddly, picked up on the first ring.

"Hey, beautiful," he said, and she closed her eyes and almost fell over before she remembered she couldn't physically lean into his warm strength through the phone.

"Hey, can I ask you a weird favor?" She reminded herself

that they both had an expanded definition of weird so she could override the part of her brain that still insisted all of this was ridiculous.

"Anything. Are you okay?"

She looked over her shoulder, sure she would see something peering in at her. She confirmed Athena was no longer in the bedroom, walked into the living room, and closed the door.

"I am now." She added, "It's probably nothing. My mind is playing tricks on me."

"I'll be right there. I'm close."

She almost said, "I'll wait for you outside," but whatever watched her was out there. The cat paced the room and twined around her legs, but when Audrey reached down to pet her, Athena moved away.

"Okay, please hurry."

MAGGIE'S CHILDHOOD had occurred long before the invention of principals, or even offices, but as she followed Rizzo to his office in the administrative wing of the hospital, she couldn't help but feel that she was in trouble. She recognized she should attempt to find Morgan, but she also knew Morgan wouldn't be found unless she wanted to be. Anyone who'd been a bounty hunter for the Fae queen for a millennium would probably have some serious skills. That made the idea of her being in danger even more troubling.

But more immediately, she hoped she'd be able to satisfy her curiosity about some things at least.

"It looks much better than the last time I was here," she said. It was true—she could see the floor. The last time Maggie had been to Rizzo's office, it had been trashed by were-bats looking for papers linking Atlanta millionaire Lyle Ames to Zeus. Rizzo hadn't been involved in the investigation of Ames, but Zeus had thought he might be since Rizzo was one of the few guardian spirits in the area, and Persephone had ended up in the psych ward at the hospital. Now the office seemed to be in a state of arrested chaos, sort of like the being that inhabited it.

"It took some doing, but I got it straightened up. Such as it is." His round glasses magnified his blink, and he pulled a pile of books and papers from a chair in front of the desk and put them on a table by a window. He gestured for Maggie to sit. "Please."

She perched on the chair, and Rizzo walked around his desk and sank into the plush office chair behind it. "I shouldn't be so exhausted, but I am."

"Even guardian spirits need a day off," Maggie observed. "Especially those stuck in fleshy bodies." She left the invitation open for him to explain how he'd ended up that way.

Instead, he grinned, and before her eyes, he turned younger, his scraggly dark beard shrinking into a close-cropped light brown one, and his thinning salt and pepper-colored hair thickening and shortening into a modern hairstyle of the same color as his beard. His clothing, skin, and glasses also morphed, and Maggie found herself sitting across from a young man who could be related to Audrey if she didn't know better.

"That's better," he said. "Ah, the energy of youth."

"Right." Maggie stood. "I'm pretty tired as well."

"Even if your kind hardly needs to sleep? Really, sit. I'll be serious."

She lowered herself into the chair but kept her weight shifted forward in case she needed to leave quickly. "What did you need to speak with me about?"

"Your curse."

Maggie stilled. She'd only told a few people about it, and she trusted their discretion. He couldn't have talked to Philippe, could he? "How did you know?"

"I can sense things that are a danger to my charges. In this case, your curse, and the effects it is already having on Lieutenant MacKenzie, could hurt them emotionally. How do you think Damien will react to losing his best friend?"

"But Charlie will heal from the fae-fire." She paused, a horrible idea crossing her mind. "Won't he?"

"Yes, thankfully he is young and healthy, and his asthma is actually a non-issue. But he's not going to give up on you. He's not the first, I wager."

Maggie looked at her hands. "Like Philippe."

Rizzo, now J.J., waved the vampire's name away. "No, he was simply unlucky. You didn't—don't—have feelings for him. That's what the Oracle said, wasn't it? That he had to fall for you, and you him."

"I..." She sighed. "I cared for Philippe, but only as a friend. There was no possibility of romance there."

"And Charlie?"

Maggie didn't want to admit it, as though not saying it would protect him even though she couldn't deny it any longer.

"The longer you put off acknowledging your feelings, the more danger he'll be in, Margaret."

She closed her eyes and shook her head. "I can't."

"But you must."

"Fine." When she opened her eyes, his form was blurred by her tears. "I've fallen in love with him. I didn't want to, but I did. And now he's doomed."

"Maybe." He sat back and steepled his fingers. The gesture, which she'd always associated with sage individuals, looked odd on such a young form.

"What do you mean?"

"Have you ever looked into breaking the curse?"

Maggie nodded. It had been one of her worst trips into the C.U., one that had started with hope and had ended in despair. "Yes. I tried asking the Oracle, but she only said I wasn't ready for the answer. I figured she meant that it was impossible." And then Philippe had said something... But she'd dismissed it as the ravings of a newly turned vampire.

"Perhaps. Or maybe she meant that you weren't yet ready to try." He leaned forward, and the old spirit looked out through the young man's eyes. "It won't be easy."

She opened her mouth to protest that he must be mistaken —she had known the Oracle for centuries, so she knew what it had meant. But his pager beeped, and in less than the time it took Maggie to blink, he turned back into his older self. "And that would be the nurse paging me." He stood. "Seriously, Margaret. Think about what I said. All hope may not be lost for young Charles MacKenzie, but you need to have the courage to pursue the truth." His lips twisted into a sardonic grin. "Ironically."

She stood as well. "Your accusations of irony work better when you're in your hipster form."

He brushed a tear from her cheek. "I can't make any promises, but do look into it again."

"Are you sure you're only Damien's and Audrey's guardian spirit?"

"Yes." He rolled his eyes. "I can't handle any more assignments. Now come along, I'm sure Lieutenant MacKenzie would love to see you."

17

———

A knock on the door startled her, and Athena jumped down. Audrey stood, and the cat resumed her perch on the arm of the couch and seemed to be looking at something across the room. Strange cat. Audrey didn't see anything, so maybe Athena was just being a cat. Audrey hoped.

When Audrey peeked through the window of her front door, she saw Damien. She closed her eyes and sighed. She was happy to see him, but she wished she had tried to handle the situation on her own.

"Hey," he said when she opened the door. "I just took a look outside. Everything seems okay..."

"Thank you. Maybe I'm just jumpy after what happened with Charlie." She stood aside to allow him to enter, and he gave her a peck on the cheek. For a moment, she just looked at him. His gray eyes had a particular intensity about them, and his hair stood up like he'd been running his fingers through it—not a surprise, since he no doubt worried about Charlie. And her. They didn't know what was going to happen or why she was being stalked by a gardenia-scented breeze.

But did he worry about himself?

"What?" he asked and caught her hand. He brought it to her lips, and it reminded her of Charlie trying to do the same with Maggie.

Audrey wouldn't have pulled away, and she didn't now, but the energy of her anxiety raced through her limbs, making her blurt, "I'm afraid you're going to be so caught up in running around and saving everyone that you're not careful, that you take stupid risks." She blinked. "That you'll end up in a hospital bed like Charlie, or worse."

He released her hand but tucked a curl behind her ear. "It's my job, Audrey, to risk my life for others. But not all the time."

She turned and walked farther into her apartment. She couldn't think with him touching her. "It feels like all the time lately. First the were-bat. Now the fire." She turned back to him. "What happened to helping little old ladies cross the street or catching cell phone snatchers on the square?"

He shrugged. "Have you met the little old ladies here? They're an independent bunch. And I'm not a patrol officer anymore."

"Right. Being a special investigator is supposed to be safer." She waved a hand at his khaki pants and black polo shirt.

"But I still wear a badge. And you knew what I was getting into when I joined up with Charlie."

"Did I?" She threw up her hands and admitted to herself how overly dramatic she was being, but the lid was off the Pandora's box of her feelings.

Oh, gods, was Pandora real, too?

"Did *you*?" she asked.

He walked over to her, gently pushed her arms down, and folded her into a hug. "No, but I don't regret it. I'm sorry, but I can't. This is the most exciting thing I've ever been a part of."

"I thought you hated the supernatural." His shirt muffled her words.

"Only when it endangers you." He held her away from him,

and now his concern showed in his expression. "Please just stay here this evening. I know we had plans, but I don't want you out and about. Or in the C.U. At least not until we can figure out what's going on."

His worry for her should have touched her, but now a scratchy sense of irritation buzzed and swirled around the electricity of her anxiety. "No way. You can't go out and risk yourself to figure out what's going on and expect me to just stay here and wait for y'all to tell me. And if I can help by dream-weaving, then dammit, that's what I'm going to do."

His eyes flashed dark. "I couldn't take it if I walked in here and found you in a coma like the last time you got stuck there."

"And I couldn't take it if I got the call that you were in the hospital." Her next breath came out ragged, almost a sob. "Or worse."

He dropped his hands, leaving cold spots on her shoulders. "Then we seem to be at an impasse."

She nodded, her throat tight with the words that fought to escape, half of them wanting to yell at him to be reasonable and the other half wanting to beg him not to leave her.

He didn't have any such problem, and he continued in an annoyingly reasonable tone, "Look, just stay in tonight. Please. Open a bottle of wine to celebrate the good news from the doctor. We'll talk tomorrow."

"But will things be different tomorrow?" She crossed her arms.

He turned, his movements stiff. She wondered if he fought the same battle she did between her desire for him to be happy and her need for him to be safe. But what would they do if they couldn't figure it out?

"I'll see you tomorrow." The door clicked closed behind him, and she threw a pillow at it. And then added anger at herself for being childish to her already unpleasant mix of feelings.

She sat on the couch, and after stretching, Athena climbed

down from the arm to come sit on her lap. Audrey wondered why the cat hadn't run when things got intense.

"You're not an ordinary kitty, are you?" she asked and scratched Athena on the head. Athena curled up with her paws on Audrey's chest and purred against her entire torso. Audrey leaned back and allowed the gentle rumbling to soothe the emotions out of her, leaving only a few residual swirls in her gut.

Like hell she would just sit there and do nothing. She closed her eyes and practiced the visualization Maggie had taught her to put herself to sleep. She trusted that her subconscious would lead where she needed to be.

She opened the door she visualized to find her living room, but Morgan sat on the couch with an open bottle of wine and two glasses.

"Wow, that was intense." Morgan beckoned for Audrey to come in. "You look like you could use some wine."

AUDREY HESITATED at the door of the dream pathway, and Morgan put on her friendliest smile.

"It's okay. Come on, have some wine." Morgan held up the bottle. "It's a, um, well, whatever you want it to be. You're the dream weaver, after all."

Of course the cat came through the door with Audrey. Morgan frowned at the creature. Whatever it was, it hid its identity well. As if to spite her, it jumped on the couch and noisily started licking its butthole right next to her. "Classy," she said.

"That's Athena." Audrey smiled. "Her timing is impeccable."

"I'm sure." Huh, so the cat had the name of a goddess. But goddesses wouldn't clean their asses in front of humans. Or would they? Morgan shook her head. She thought she knew the rules, but they kept changing.

Audrey sat on the armchair at the head of the coffee table. "I think tonight we'll have Merlot. It's a wine of sadness. Ever seen *Sideways*?"

Okay, good, so Audrey had decided to play along. The label shifted under Morgan's hand with the sensation of a slithering snake, and it took all her self control not to drop the bottle, which now held an opaque dark purple liquid.

"A few years ago. Movies kind of run together for me." Morgan poured two glasses and handed one to her. "Here's to the men we love but hate dealing with." Not that she had anyone who fit the description at the moment. Well, not anymore. But had she really loved Elric?

Audrey raised her glass. "It's a little early to be talking about love, but yes, he's hard to deal with." Then she narrowed her eyes. "How much of that did you overhear?"

Morgan looked down at Athena, who had snuggled up next to her leg and now yawned, showing all her teeth.

She couldn't exactly come out and say, *"Well, your cat fetched me from my aunt's closet, where I was keeping watch over a slumbering vampire, to overhear the fight you were having with your boyfriend where you were both being ridiculously stubborn."* So she simply said, "Enough."

"How?" Audrey asked and leaned forward. "Are you a dream weaver, too?"

Morgan shook her head. "No, I'm just a simple sorceress with a few talents. I can move through the parts of the Collective Unconscious that mirror different worlds to watch people, but I can't manipulate it."

"So parts of the C.U. are reflections of reality?" Audrey looked around at the mirror image of her apartment. "Huh. That's interesting. Are those parts easier to access? No, wait, why were you spying on me?"

"I had a feeling there was trouble." Morgan shrugged. "Trust me, I'm good at finding trouble, especially if it's going to involve me."

"I believe you, but I'm not sure I trust you." Audrey flopped back and held the base of the wine glass in one hand, allowing the liquid to swirl slowly in the bowl. "But you're here, so there must be a reason. Did Maggie send you?"

Morgan snorted. "No, she doesn't know where I am."

"Well, where are you?" Audrey sipped. Morgan did likewise. She decided to trust Audrey with a little bit of information.

"I'm sitting in the closet of the spare bedroom at my aunt's place watching over a vampire who may be so hungry he kills and eats me when he wakes."

Audrey stopped swirling. "Damn. And I thought I had boy problems."

Morgan laughed. "Yeah, I had better be awake by dark, or I'll be in a world of trouble. But you don't have boy problems. He just wants to protect you."

With a sigh, Audrey said, "I know. It's just frustrating. My dad was a cop, and he was killed in the line of duty. And that was a month after my stepbrother almost drowned." She frowned. "Or maybe he did. He was different after." She shook her head. "The thought of Damien running into a burning building... Even if it was to go after you and Maggie. It makes the center of my chest cramp, like my heart is about to be ripped out."

"So what are you going to do?" Morgan leaned forward. "Are you going to stay at this impasse?"

"No." Audrey sighed with her entire body. "No, I like him too much. Love him, even. Whatever I feel, I can't just shove him out of my life."

"Even after he told you what you could and couldn't do?" Morgan had left men for thinking they could control her.

"He knows I'm going to do what I want." She gestured

around the room. "He didn't want me coming here, and yet here I am."

"So you're sure he's going to come back tomorrow?" Morgan asked. "Even after all that?" Not that she would know what a healthy relationship looked like.

"He said he would, so I believe him." Audrey put her glass on the table. "But thank you for helping me remember why I'm dealing with all of this. I still have work to do—and so does he —but we'll work it out."

"Right." Morgan studied her own wine. Audrey and Damien were already attached more than she'd ever been, even to the man she'd been forced to marry or to Elric, who she mourned. But now that she had the clarity of being separated from her body and its messy emotions, she could admit that he had been a friend and fuck buddy, but nothing more. She'd of course been aware that people could work on their differences in relationships, but she'd been betrayed too many times to bother putting in the effort. But could it be worth it? When she looked up, she found Audrey studying her.

"So what do I need to do to help you manage that vampire?"

The images that came into Morgan's mind had more to do with the sexy kind of vampire activity, not subduing a hungry one. She dragged her thoughts back to practicalities.

"Maybe get Maggie. I don't want anyone to be injured." Including Philippe. With a jolt, she realized she cared more for his welfare than, well, she should. That could complicate the situation. Well, more than it already was. Athena dug her claws into Morgan's leg, Morgan yelped, and her cell phone ring brought her out of her trance—and the waking dream. But she didn't answer.

The walls of the closet reflected the red light that ringed the irises of a very hungry vampire.

18

———————

Maggie followed Rizzo back through the administrative wing and into the hospital itself. She tried not to smell the antiseptic or hear the moaning of people in distress. The hospital-related sensations brought back too many memories of places of supposed healing she'd been in before and how, until very recently in her long timeline, they'd more often been places of death.

Rizzo led her on to a ward and introduced her to the nurses.

"This is Mrs. MacKenzie. She'll be staying with her husband tonight."

Maggie struggled to not look surprised and instead smiled at the nurses, making note of their nametags. "Thank you for taking such good care of him."

One of them, a young woman with dark curly hair, snorted. "Well, he just got here, but we'll do our best."

"What was that?" she asked Rizzo after they were out of earshot.

"This is a step-down unit. Only family is allowed here. I can only pull so many strings, Margaret." He put a hand on the small of her back to steer her to the correct room. "And he'll need someone to bring him clothes for when he's discharged tomorrow."

"Right, thank you."

She didn't know what she was expecting, but Charlie looked just as fragile in his new surroundings. An oxygen tube under his nose had replaced the mask, and he fiddled with the remote in one hand and with the hospital blanket fisted in the other. She hung back so Rizzo could go in first and do his doctor thing.

"I don't think I need to be here," Charlie complained to Rizzo. "Why can't I go home?"

Maggie clenched her fists. Didn't he see how sick he was?

"Your oxygen numbers are still a little low for comfort. We'll see how you do tonight, and then we can talk about discharge in the morning."

"Don't be ridiculous, I have a case." Charlie pushed the button to raise the head of the bed.

"I'm not being ridiculous, and I have someone here to help me make sure you behave." Rizzo gestured for Maggie to come in.

"Hey," she said.

"Oh. Hey." He started to reach for her, then dropped his hand. Again. But now that she knew her feelings, she could act differently.

"It's okay," she told him and came to stand beside the bed. She took his hand. "We need to talk about some stuff."

"This isn't the old, 'we need to talk, it's not you it's me' speech, is it?" He didn't even try to smile with his joke, which cracked her heart even more.

"No, it's sort of the opposite." She looked at Rizzo. "Would you mind?"

"Not at all. My shift has been over for an hour. Just don't excite him too much. If those monitors get out of a certain range, the nurses will come running and wreck your privacy." With a wink, he left.

Maggie turned back to Charlie. They looked at each other, the weight of the words that had gone unsaid for too long hanging in the air between them.

"Pull up a chair," he finally said with a hint of his usual humor. "I'd offer you a drink, but the nurses won't bring me a beer fridge."

"They probably don't want you getting too comfortable." She squeezed his hand, let go, and pulled a chair over from by the small table in the corner of the room.

He reached a hand over the bed rail, and she took it. He lowered the bed so they sat at eye level with each other. "What did you need to tell me?" he asked.

She looked away. "I've doomed you." With the words out, the last of the reserve she'd had broke open, and a well of sorrow bubbled up in her chest.

"How?" He gestured to himself. "I don't blame you for this. I chose to go in after you."

"Yes, but..." She took a deep breath so her voice wouldn't crack under the weight of her tears. "But it made me realize it—it would kill me if you died."

"Maggie, what are you saying? Or trying to say without saying?" He caressed her hand with his thumb. "I'm a detective, but sometimes I don't get things exactly right."

She attempted a smile. His directness was one of the things she—oh, gods. "Charles Allen MacKenzie, I think I may love you."

The monitor over his head showed his heart rate sped up. She hoped in a happy way.

"Well, Margaret of Cornwall, that suits me fine since I've been in love with you since I met you and you took out two were-bats and two vampires in one fight."

She grinned at the memory of their first encounter. "I had help."

"Nah, you could've done it on your own. Like you always do."

Right, like she always did. She'd been on her own for so long. "But there's the curse." She looked away again, but a tug on her hand brought her attention back to his face.

"There are no guarantees in our lives, Maggie. Especially in our line of work."

"Yes, but I hate to shorten your life." She tried to make her breath reach into her belly. "I *have* to figure out how to break this curse. I can't go to the Oracle—she's made it clear she can't or won't give me the answer to this problem."

"Maybe I can go."

She looked up at him. "Charlie... I don't even know if you can get there."

"But it's worth a shot." He took her hand in both of his. "I'm willing to do whatever it takes to give us a chance to be happy together."

Her eyes filled with tears again, but this time they were mostly joyful ones. She noticed that when he blinked, his eyelids stayed shut longer and longer.

"I should go," she said and stood. "I need to check on Morgan. And you need to rest."

"Yes, ma'am. But please come back."

"I'll return in the morning." She leaned over and brushed his lips with hers, careful not to dislodge the oxygen tube. When she did, her entire body filled with electric tingles, and something loosened in her gut.

"I'm not sure what just happened," she said after she straightened, "but I'm feeling more optimistic than I have in a long time."

"It's that MacKenzie magic." Now he achieved a full Charlie grin. "Hurry back, Red."

"Get some sleep, Charlie." She squeezed his hand one more time and left. When she walked into the hall and past the nurse's station, she noticed the dark-haired one smiling at her.

"I'm guessing that was you making his heart rate go up?" she asked.

"Guilty," Maggie said but didn't stop to chat. Once she stepped into the gloom of the evening, she stopped, the events of the day that had been crowded out in her concern for Charlie returning.

Evening.

Vampire.

"Oh, gods." She pulled out her phone and called Morgan. No matter where the girl was, Maggie would need her at the condo to subdue Philippe until they could take him somewhere to feed.

MORGAN FROZE. She knew Philippe could see her, and worse, smell the blood flowing through her veins, but maybe if she didn't move, he wouldn't pounce on her.

Right.

He gulped a breath of air, and then moaned, "So... Hungry..."

"I know you are." She slowly pushed herself to standing against the wall. "But I can't be your dinner."

The ripping sound of the blanket made her move, jumping over him and darting out of the closet. She leaned against the door, but she couldn't get enough traction to brace it. His ramming into it sent her tumbling into the spare bedroom. She executed a perfect flip and landed on her feet, spinning around to face him. He stood just outside the closet door, blinking in confusion.

The sun had set—obviously, since he was awake—and his

eyes provided the only light in the room, which gave it the creepy appearance of a horror movie scene. Morgan willed her heart to slow, since its racing would only inflame Philippe's hunger, but her system knew it shared the room with a predator and wanted her to get the hell out.

"Smell. So. Good." He licked his lips and moved toward her.

"Philippe," she breathed. "Don't hurt me. It's me, Morgan."

He stopped. The light from his eyes dimmed, then flickered when he blinked again. "Where am I?"

"We're in my Aunt Margaret's condo. In her spare room."

"Margaret?"

Morgan edged toward the bed, her main obstacle between herself and the door to the bedroom. "I believe you know her as Maggie?"

"Yesssss..." The glow brightened. "The reason I'm like this. This monster."

He charged, and she rolled across the bed and ran out of the room. The spare bedroom door was sturdier and opened in, so she held the doorknob with both hands and was able to keep it closed when he attempted to yank it open. They were engaged in a tug-of-war when Morgan heard a knock at the door of the condo.

"Morgan?" It was Audrey's voice. "Is everything all right in there?"

Morgan couldn't yell too loudly—she spent every ounce of energy keeping the bedroom door closed—but called out. "Audrey? Get Maggie."

Then her aunt's voice. "I'm here." The door opened, and Maggie and Audrey dashed in.

"Philippe?" Maggie asked.

Morgan inclined her head to the bedroom door. Her teeth chattered with every shoulder-stretching pull. Then the door-knob squished out of her sweat-soaked hands, and she tumbled backwards. In less than a second, Philippe was on her when the image of the lagoon monster flashed through Morgan's mind.

"Philippe, I command you to freeze!"

And he did, his fangs just at her neck.

Maggie pulled him back by the collar and threw him against the wall. He shook his head, dazed, then charged her. Morgan scrambled to her feet in case she needed to help, but Maggie neatly sidestepped him and tripped him. When he landed on his stomach, she planted a knee in his lower back and pulled his hands behind him.

"Morgan, there are some ropes in the bottom of the coat closet. Please grab some for me."

"But rope won't hold him." Should she freeze him again? Could she?

Maggie spoke patiently in the tone Morgan remembered from her childhood. "These are old religious habit belts. Yes, they will."

Morgan's face heated. Of course. She should know her aunt would be prepared. She grabbed the ropes as instructed and helped Maggie tie Philippe's hands behind his back and then his arms to his side. Once he was bound by the ropes, the red light around his irises faded, and he blinked again, this time like he was just waking up. Audrey handed Morgan a cool washcloth.

"For your neck," she said. "He got you with one of his fangs."

Morgan held the cool cloth to the side of her neck. Sure enough, a small spot stung.

"You're not going to turn into one, are you?" Audrey asked.

"No, only if he almost drains me and then feeds me his blood."

Philippe lay on the floor, looking up at them. "Maggie? Morgan?" His eyes widened. "Did I hurt you?"

He sounded so upset that Morgan couldn't stay mad at him.

She still had plenty of frustration with herself for ending up in such a vulnerable position—seriously, had she learned nothing over the last ten centuries?

Then Philippe licked his lips. "I'm so hungry. I taste blood, and it's like dark red wine and dark chocolate."

Morgan couldn't help a small smile. She'd always wondered what she tasted like to a vampire.

Maggie took charge of the situation. Or continued to. "We'll get you fed somehow." She tapped one foot. "I don't want to let you loose here, though."

"He's good at finding the bad guys and not killing them," Morgan said. "If you tell me where to take him, I'll make sure he only feeds but doesn't murder."

"There are some rough neighborhoods south of Memorial." Audrey pulled out her phone. "I can show you a map. Or I can take you."

Morgan arched an eyebrow. "I'm pretty sure that's not what Damien meant when he said he wanted you to stay in."

As if by magic, Damien appeared at the door with a patrol officer. "What's not what I meant?" He took in the scene and turned to the officer. "You're not needed here. I know these women. They're having a party."

The patrol officer looked around at the walls that still had small pits in them from the exploding statue, the burned velvet cloth on the dining room table, and the tied up young man, who thankfully hid his fangs, on the floor. "Are you sure?" And then he spotted the bloody cloth at Morgan's neck. "Are you injured, ma'am?"

"I'm fine." She spoke quickly so she wouldn't laugh at the poor boy's incredulous expression.

"I've got it from here," Damien said. "Thank you for coming up."

The officer left, and Damien rubbed his temples and looked at Audrey. "Dare I ask what you're doing here?"

"Helping?" She shrugged. "What are you doing here?"

"I was walking through the call center when a domestic dispute complaint came in. I heard the address and decided to tag along." He frowned at Philippe. "Who's he?"

"He," Maggie said with a grunt and gestured for Morgan to come assist her, "is a vampire of my acquaintance." They helped Philippe to sit, then stand.

"Oh, right, Charlie told me about him."

"And he's hungry," Audrey added. "We're going to make sure he's fed."

"You're not going anywhere," Damien told her, then added when she raised an eyebrow, "At least not without me. Just let me go grab some clothes out of my car so I can change."

"That's fine." Maggie wrinkled her nose. "I smell like the hospital. I'm going to change, too."

Damien fetched his clothes and went to change in Morgan's bathroom. Once Maggie went to do the same in her room, Morgan turned to Audrey. Something had been bugging her. "You came to help me even though you knew it would be dangerous."

Audrey cocked her head. "And you comforted me after my argument with Damien."

"But you hardly know me. And I was kind of a bitch to you earlier."

"Hey, we're in this together." Audrey smiled. "So we may as well help each other. Who knows? We may even become friends through this."

Friends? Morgan pushed away the memory of the sound of the waves lapping at the shore of Avalon, where her last female friend had turned her over to Niniane rather than helping her escape. "Thank you."

"Sure. Now let's go feed your pet vampire."

"Well, he's not really mine..."

"It doesn't matter whose he is," Maggie said as she emerged

from her room. "We need to hurry." She looked down at Philippe, whose eyes glowed again and who strained against his bonds. "I don't know how long he can wait."

ABOUT AN HOUR LATER, Philippe laid the drug dealer against the wall. The man's heart beat strongly, so Philippe hoped he hadn't taken too much. It was so difficult to tell. And the gnawing feeling still swirled through his gut, but he at least could control himself.

Oh, gods, what had he done to Morgan? He glanced behind him, where she stood with Maggie and two people who seemed familiar. Right, they'd been in the car with them, helping to hold him down. The guy looked in any direction except where Philippe stood. The girl spoke with Maggie and Morgan, and she kept glancing his way. He wanted to curl in on himself—now more people knew what a monster he'd become.

Maggie nudged Morgan, who walked over to Philippe.

"Feeling better?" she asked.

"Yes, a little." Then he couldn't help but add, "Don't worry, you won't be handing over damaged goods."

She stepped back like his words had stung her. "That's not what I was worried about."

"I'm sorry." He shrugged. "Still grumpy. I was always an ass when I needed to eat. Now I'm just a monster."

"You're not a monster." She sounded like she meant it. "And I'm sure there's more for you around here somewhere. Just please be careful."

"So I don't kill anyone?"

She tilted her face up, and there was something soft in her eyes. "So you don't get hurt. I'd never forgive myself. And that has nothing to do with the Fae." Then she turned and walked back to the group, leaving Philippe to hunt. And wonder.

"Hey, man, what are you doing here? This is my territory."

Philippe turned toward the sound of the gruff voice, another human. Another criminal. Another meal.

19

After Philippe had semi-drained three drug dealers and a pimp, they'd brought him back to Maggie's apartment. Once the door shut behind them, Morgan breathed a sigh of relief. Daylight Savings Time had ended, so they'd had an extra hour before people would be out and about, but still...

While Philippe showered, Damien pulled up a picture on his phone.

"This is the sketch that a woman in the neighborhood made of the Peeping Tom," he said and showed them a photo of a pencil sketch. "Does he look familiar to any of you? By the way, this neighbor lives directly behind you." He gave Audrey a pointed look, which Morgan ignored. Worry exhausted her, and she'd expended enough mental energy for one night. Every time Philippe had gone for new prey, she'd held her breath, afraid he'd get hurt or go too far with his victims, whom she knew he wanted to leave alive.

Audrey looked at the phone first and shrugged. "Never seen him." She passed it to Morgan.

Morgan cocked her head. He looked sort of familiar. "I

guess it could be Elric." She handed the phone to Maggie. "What do you think?"

Maggie barely glanced at the picture before returning the phone to Damien. "If it's him, he likely had some sort of obfuscation charm going on to keep someone from recognizing him."

Philippe emerged from the spare bedroom, looking clean and sated, his face ruddy from the shower and his meals. Morgan could see what Tatiana saw in him, if she intended to add Philippe to her collection of lovers. He certainly was handsome enough, and he definitely had that bad boy look both Tatiana and Morgan found attractive, but without the intensity that would turn Morgan off.

And he had a sort of innocence she couldn't help but be drawn to.

"Thank you, everyone, for your help." He glanced down, seemingly shy. "I hope to not trouble you too much longer. Morgan, can you come help me cover up?"

"Sure."

Audrey and Damien also rose.

"We're going to head out," Audrey said. "Damien has to be up and at work in a few hours."

They said goodnight, and Morgan followed Philippe into the spare bedroom. Instead of going into the closet, he sat on the bed and gestured for her to join him. She sat beside him, their legs almost touching.

"You didn't have to do that," he said. "I could have found food on my own." He shook his head. "Especially since you had such a rough day. And I'm sorry about this." He brushed a finger along her neck where his tooth had grazed her, leaving a trail of electric tingles in its wake. "You're lucky I'm not a werewolf."

Morgan laughed. "I'm lucky overall." And for the first time in a very long time, she felt it.

He rubbed the back of his neck. "Thank you. I just wanted to be sure to say that..."

"Before...?"

"Whatever else happens." He lowered his gaze to his hands, which now lay on his lap. "I seem to attract trouble." Then he smiled at her. "But at least the trouble I found this time is attractive. And doesn't think that drunken birds are a decent diet."

Morgan's face heated. Several men had told her she was beautiful, but they'd all wanted something from her, and she felt Philippe's sentiments were genuine. Like him. "I... I'm not used to being thanked."

He smiled and leaned closer. "You're cute when you're flustered."

Morgan leaned toward him without thinking, his guileless-ness a magnet and balance for the cynicism she'd built up over centuries. What would it be like to kiss someone without a hidden agenda? She suspected he had the same desires any guy in his twenties would, but she could handle those.

But kissing him would risk her one chance at getting her powers back.

She hesitated too long, and he closed the distance. His lips met hers in a perfect fit, and she closed her eyes, losing herself in the sensations, her thoughts sliding through her mind but not gaining purchase until the final one—he'd once loved Maggie. Did that mean Morgan was a substitute for her aunt?

Morgan pulled back, and their mouths separated with a pop. "You need to go to bed."

He smiled. "Want to cuddle?"

"No." She stood and pulled him to his feet. "You need to get covered up."

"Fine." But the grin he gave her told her he had enjoyed their kiss as much as she had.

Oh, gods, it was going to be tough to hand him over if she determined the Fae would keep their part of their bargain.

MORGAN MADE sure Philippe was fully covered and walked into the living room. She was too wired to sleep, and strange sensations filled her chest—the warmth of gratitude and something else she wasn't ready to name yet. She wondered how Audrey and Damien were getting along and hoped they'd get some sleep. Even with everything going on between them, they'd chosen to help her and Maggie manage the starving fledgling vampire. Morgan couldn't think of the last time someone had made her a priority.

Maggie stood by one of her open windows and looked out at the branches of the trees across the street. The orange glow of the streetlight made each branch distinct and emphasized the starkness. Morgan couldn't help but feel the impending dawn. Two more days. She had until the midnight between Sunday and Monday to bring Philippe to Tatiana, and she'd get her full powers back. Morgan wondered if she'd have been able to handle his blood lust herself, although she did have that strange ability to command the nightmare creatures. Not that she liked to use it. Each time she did, she risked someone thinking she was one of them.

He was a nightmare creature. Right. Maybe he was attracted to her because of whatever strange draw she had on them. But she recognized her thoughts for what they were—mere rationalizations.

"Are you going to tell me what's really going on?" Maggie pulled her purple-tinted lenses up with one hand and rubbed her eyes with the other.

Morgan stepped back. "Are you going to truth-spell me if I don't?" she asked.

Maggie replaced her glasses and shook her head. "As far as I can tell, you're not involved in anything criminal, so I'm not justified in doing so. But something strange is going on, and you're in the middle of it. Plus, you're in danger."

Morgan snorted. "I'm always in danger. That's my life."

"No, you're in real danger." Maggie turned to her. "Charlie saw Elric in a dream, and Elric said he'd been trying to warn you."

"What do you mean by real danger?" Morgan shivered, the image of Elric's shade trying to communicate to her coming unbidden into her mind.

Maggie looked at her sideways. "The kind someone else gets killed for."

Had Elric meant she'd be putting herself in danger if she brought Philippe in? Morgan needed caffeine to deal with what felt like a landscape of shifting quicksand. "Let's make some coffee. I'm not going to sleep today. Are you?"

Maggie sighed. "No. Fine, but please know you can trust me. In spite of what happened in the past."

Morgan didn't say anything, but she rubbed her arms, which had gone cold, the little hairs on them alert as though something sinister looked at her from afar.

She followed Maggie into the kitchen area. The mess from their failed ritual had been cleaned up, and only the burned spot on the coffee table and the porcelain fragment marks on the walls remained to remind her of what had almost happened. She'd thought the targets were Maggie and Charlie, but what if someone had been trying to send her a message, too? But who could possibly be threatened by her? The Fae queen essentially had her by the nuts, and Morgan had plenty of enemies, but none who could command that kind of magic. Only the Fae could wield fae-fire.

Would Maggie know? Should Morgan trust her after all that had happened?

And they weren't alone in this. Morgan bit her lip. Had she unwittingly put her aunt and her aunt's friends in danger by coming here? Something had seemed to be going on even before she arrived. That reminded her—she needed information, too.

"So what happened with you and Philippe?" Morgan asked. "He said it was your fault that he became a monster."

Maggie didn't look up from her coffee preparations. "Did he?"

"Yes, when he first woke yesterday evening, he was disoriented. Then when I told him where he was, he became angry and said that." She didn't say what he'd done before going to bed that morning. She sent her lips a stern command not to smile at the memory of their kiss.

Maggie finished making the coffee, and once she'd flicked the coffee maker to on, turned and folded her arms. "Do you remember when you were on Avalon how Niniane would sometimes get a visitor at night, a monk who wore gray robes?"

Morgan blinked. "That was a long, long time ago. Why should I remember who came and went to the island?" But a vague image teased the back of her head. "Although, now that I think about it... We used to wonder if he was Niniane's lover who came disguised as a man of God."

"He was no man of God, I can assure you." Maggie unfolded her arms and stuck her hands in the pockets of her jeans. "At least not the Christian one. I found out earlier this year that he was still alive, a vampire. He was the one responsible for turning Niniane bitter and evil and why I had to battle her. Philippe was, unfortunately, collateral damage."

"What?" Morgan tried but couldn't picture how that would happen. "What the hell kind of fight was it that caused someone to accidentally be turned into a vampire?"

"The Gray One—I still don't know his true name—tricked him. Philippe had swallowed the locket Niniane had given me when we were children. It had a lock of her hair in it and was therefore the key to banishing her. Philippe was gravely injured by both the battle and the locket, and the Gray convinced him that if he were to turn, he would have an immortal lifespan to win me and help me figure out my curse. Of course he lied." Maggie looked down. "And I will always regret that I hadn't kept a closer eye on Philippe. I should have figured out some way to protect him."

Okay, that fit with what little Philippe had told her. But... "So you two were never a thing?"

"No." Maggie shook her head emphatically. "I have certain considerations that keep me from being able to have a relationship." And then her lips curled into the shape Morgan was trying hard not to allow her own to make.

"What considerations? Does it have something to do with the curse you mentioned?"

"You're not the only one with scars from your past." The coffee maker beeped, and Maggie gave her a quick glance over the tops of her glasses. "But you're going to have to trust me before I tell you my deepest darkest secret."

AFTER THEIR CONVERSATION, Morgan left to take a walk in the sunrise and, she'd said, to clear her head. Maggie could probably use some head-clearing, too, but she headed to the hospital. She kicked herself for not bringing Charlie's keys with her so she could pick up some clothing for him. When she arrived, she found she hadn't needed to worry—Damien was there, and he'd brought a duffel bag full of clothes and toiletries for Charlie, who was in the shower.

An unfamiliar stab of jealousy spiked Maggie's chest—was a nurse in there helping him?

"Good morning, Mrs. MacKenzie," Damien teased. "Y'all should've warned me. I almost blew your cover."

Maggie's cheeks warmed. "It was Rizzo's idea."

"Whoever's it was, I'm glad." He glanced at her sideways. "Charlie is looking much better, by the way. And he says he feels fine."

Maggie smiled, but she wondered what Charlie had told his friend. Call her old-fashioned, but she didn't believe in talking about one's brand new relationship. If it could even be called that.

"Good," she said. "That's to be expected. If a fae-fire victim can survive the first thirteen hours after exposure, the effects dissipate quickly, although he'll need to take it easy for a few more days."

"Right." Damien shook his head. "He doesn't know the meaning of taking it easy."

Charlie walked out of the bathroom wearing jeans and a black T-shirt with a University of Georgia logo across the front of it, not his uniform, his feet bare and his hair damp but already drying and curling slightly. When he saw Maggie, he grinned his typical Charlie grin and said, "Hey, you." But he didn't make any moves to kiss her or otherwise show that they'd taken their relationship to a new plane.

She smiled back, this time without any reservation. Good. There was no reason for Damien to know how much more she had to lose now. She still didn't want to acknowledge it.

Damien handed Charlie a pair of socks and black boots. "Rizzo stopped by, but since you were in the shower, he said he'd come back in a few."

"Good." Charlie took his footwear and sat on the chair by the bed. "I'm ready to be out of here."

"And take the day off, right?" Maggie asked. They could grab breakfast, and then she'd drop him by his apartment while she and

Morgan continued to figure out what had happened to Elric, and Damien continued to work on the Peeping Tom case he'd been telling her about. The sketch he'd shown her could have been Elric.

Charlie looked up from tying his boot laces. "Are you kidding? There's a case that grows colder by the second." He added in his best Texas drawl, "Time's a wasting, darlin'."

Damien gave Maggie an "I told you so" look.

"Don't be ridiculous." She crossed her arms and planted her feet. "You've been exposed to fae-fire. Which targeted you. You need to rest up, recover."

"Rest is a four-letter word." He stood and spread his hands when he saw her frown. "What? It is."

"What is?" Rizzo walked into the room. "You're looking hale and hearty, Lieutenant. Have a seat and let me take a listen." He had Charlie put the oxygen probe on his finger and then had him breathe fast, slow, and in between while he listened and watched the monitor. "Everything sounds normal."

"But he needs to take it easy, right?" Maggie asked.

Rizzo chuckled. "Of course. But I suspect he won't."

Maggie's phone buzzed, and she checked it. The unfamiliar area code made her frown. She'd been around long enough she could identify most of the numerical sequences, but this one was new. She opened her text message screen.

Maggie, help. I'm in trouble. This is Morgan.

20

As soon as she was clear of Maggie's apartment, Morgan pulled out her phone and activated the bounty-finding function of the Dark Mirror app. But instead of a bounty, she imagined Elric. Yes, all indications pointed to him being dead, but she had to know for sure. Guilt tickled the back of her mind when she remembered the kiss with Philippe. Not that anything could come of it, not until she knew the nature of the situation. And she and Elric hadn't had any sort of agreement beyond that they'd be fuck buddies. But Morgan's conscience wouldn't let her move on from Elric until she had confirmation of some sort that they were truly over. Not that there had been much there to begin with.

The map on the screen of her phone zoomed in on a nearby neighborhood with a little pointy-eared face that indicated the location of the Fae she sought. He was alive? Morgan cursed, but not loud enough for any of the early morning joggers to hear. Seriously, what was this place, Healthyville? Then she caught a whiff of bacon, and her stomach growled. Nope, not that healthy.

She grabbed a fried chicken biscuit and coffee to go from

one of the local places and used the delay to imagine what she would say to Elric when she encountered him. Had he really thought it would be funny to astrally project himself into Maggie's shop and Charlie's dream? And had he had something to do with the fae-fire? How could she have been so stupid as to spend the energy mourning him?

Morgan barely tasted the biscuit and coffee, and she hardly registered when she tossed the wrapping and cup into one of the receptacles at the end of the downtown area. By the time she reached the neighborhood, she practically stomped, the rhythm of her steps echoing the question in her mind, *How dare he? How dare he? How dare he?*

She walked along a main street, and then the app told her to go into a wooded area along a stream. She shook her head. This place put parks in the weirdest spots, but she guessed no one had built there due to it likely being a flood zone. Or maybe they just liked mosquitoes.

Of course Elric would know she was coming—he always did—so she didn't bother to move quietly. The little trail petered out, and she had to shove through bushes and branches before reaching the stream bed. There she found Elric, but not as she'd expected. Even before she spotted him, the twin smells of sulfur and copper told her she'd been wrong.

He half-lay face-up in the stream bed, his empty eyes reflecting the tree branches above and the sky beyond it. She stopped, her hand over her mouth, and horror chilled the anger that had consumed her. That's when she noticed that the copper-colored scarf he wore above the neck of his T-shirt was instead the ragged remains of his throat, which had been torn out.

Morgan fell to her knees and put a hand over her mouth so she wouldn't vomit. That little spark of hope that had been ignited with her anger when she'd seen his symbol on the app winked out, and the grief rushed back in, crushing her from the inside. She sniffed and again had to quell her stomach's jumping when the smell of sulfur strengthened. Were-bat. Ugh. She hated those, now even more after it had killed Elric.

But how could a were-bat have gotten into the waking world? Was it leftover from the Zeus debacle? No, if it had been here a month, there would have been other news of it, both in the mortal and immortal papers.

The hair on the back of Morgan's neck stood so suddenly it felt as though someone pinched her, and she jumped up and spun around. The captain of the queen's guard, the same Fae who had brought her the news of Elric's original betrayal, stood in the stream, his hands on his hips.

"Tsk tsk, little witch," he said. "What have you done now?" He crossed his arms, and she wanted to slap the condescending smirk from his face. She caught a hint of the wet leaf smell that preceded a rainstorm. Ah, right, the Captain's preferred element was water. So there was no way she could defeat him as long as he stood in and drew strength from the stream.

"I haven't done anything aside from waste my time playing Fae games." She shoved her hands in her pockets so she wouldn't give away anything with an inadvertent gesture.

"But you've murdered Lord Elric, the queen's favorite." He pointed to the dead Fae at her feet. "What happened? Lover's quarrel? Everyone knew the two of you were in each other's pants."

"I did not murder Elric." She gestured to him. "Do I look like a throat-tearing witch to you?"

"No, but you can command the nightmare creatures." He shut his mouth as though he'd just said something he shouldn't have, but then continued, "I mean, you're friendly with them. You could've had a were-bat do your dirty work."

"I didn't." She forced herself not to cross her arms. That would make her look like she was hiding something. "And I'm not friendly with the nightmare creatures."

"So you say, yet you have a little love bite on your neck. Is that a vampire fang mark I see?" He shook his head. "I told the queen not to trust you. Especially with this job."

Damn damn damn. "The fang mark is a battle wound. Have you ever tried to subdue a starving vampire?"

"No, nor a horny one. The shadow of his lips is on yours." He pursed his mouth and made kissing noises. "Did Elric find out? Get angry, so you took him out?"

Morgan didn't dignify his questions with an answer. "Look, Captain, I don't know what you're playing at, but I won't allow these accusations to stand."

"Then you better work on proving your innocence. Burning at the stake is too good a fate for you." And he disappeared.

Morgan turned back to Elric. What the hell had happened? Had he done this on purpose? No, it was definitely a were-bat. But from where? And why? Typically the nightmare creatures didn't bother the Fae because they knew they were outgunned when it came to magic.

Were the nightmare creatures after Morgan, then? Had their admiration of her only been a ruse for all these centuries? That seemed like a lot of effort for beings that were, on the whole, not that smart.

Or had Maggie's old enemy, the Gray Vampire, resurfaced?

Morgan shook her head and with shaking hands texted her aunt. It looked like she was going to have to trust her whether she liked it or not.

"Excuse me." Maggie set her teeth so she wouldn't snap at Morgan out of frustration with Charlie. Did he not know how seriously he'd been hurt? She walked into the hallway and leaned against the wall so she'd be out of the way of any stretchers rushing by.

Where are you?

I went looking for Elric. I found him in a park near Sycamore. He's dead.

Maggie returned to the room and told the news to the others. "I have to go to her."

Charlie held up a hand. "Not without me you don't."

"Or me," Damien added.

"Right. We don't need too many people messing up the crime scene." Charlie stood. "Arthur, can you clear me for duty, please?"

"Let me listen to you one more time." Rizzo put his stethoscope in his ears and pressed it to Charlie's chest. Maggie tried not to look at his nicely shaped pectoral muscle, but Charlie's smirk said he'd caught her peeking.

"We don't even know there was a crime." Maggie turned her attention to the problem at hand and paced in what small area she could. "He could've met with an accident."

None of the others dignified her comment with an answer. In truth, she didn't know what sort of accident a high Fae could meet with in an urban swath of Georgia woods. And how was Morgan involved?

"All right, you can go," Arthur huffed. "But if you have even a hint of shortness of breath, you come right back here."

"Will do."

"Good. I'll send the nurse in with the paperwork." Rizzo looked back and forth between Damien and Maggie. "The two of you should probably go ahead."

"Right," Damien said. "I'll get the scene started."

"Thanks, I'll call the team."

Neither had moved, but Maggie felt she'd been pushed to the side, and she fisted her hands in her pockets. Why was no one listening to her?

Rizzo walked Damien and Maggie to the waiting area. His furry caterpillar brows conferred over the bridge of his nose.

Maggie didn't say anything so he could have time to puzzle whatever it was out. Finally he sighed.

"I don't need to tell you to be careful because there's something strange in all of this."

"Right." Maggie and Damien exchanged amused glances. Sometimes it was easy to forget Rizzo was a guardian spirit and be fooled into thinking he was a talented but quirky physician. Or e-newsletter editor—whichever form he took at the time. Since he didn't need sleep, he could do both.

"This is no laughing matter." He punctuated his words by stabbing his right index finger into his left palm and impaling Maggie with a serious look. "You, my dear, of all people know the danger the Fae pose, especially the high Fae. And now that one of their own has met a grisly end, you can only expect more of them to show up. But something tells me this is a distraction."

The sliding doors to the waiting room opened, and a warm breeze came through. Again, something about the quality of the air tickled Maggie's mind, but she couldn't tease the memory from the deep crevasses of her brain.

"I've been feeling the same." She rubbed her arms, where gooseflesh had risen, and the image of a dark, turbulent sea flashed through her brain. "Would you let me know if you come to any conclusions?"

"Of course." Rizzo's pager beeped. "And now it's time to work again."

When he left, Damien gestured for Maggie to follow him to a corner of the room where they'd have the sound of the television to mask their conversation.

"What do you know about...?" He inclined his head toward where Rizzo had just left. He shifted his weight from foot to foot and glanced at the clock. Maggie understood—the potential crime scene only grew colder the longer they waited, but would Charlie forgive them if they went without him? Or would he be happy? She'd give them five minutes and then be off. She wanted to question Morgan before they got there anyway. But first, she had to answer Damien.

"I've only encountered beings like him a few times in my years as a Truth Seeker," she admitted. She didn't want to say how many years—that would just be depressing. "Some of them much less helpful than he. But I've never run into one who was stuck in a corporeal form, guarded two people, or who had two jobs. He has a strange duality, and I don't know what to make of it." She cocked her head. "What do you think?"

"I agree it's strange." He massaged his right temple. "My grandmother talked about guardian angels, but as invisible, abstract beings or spirits. Arthur seems too literal to be one of those."

"Yes, he's not an angel in the traditional Judeo-Christian tradition. He's more limited than they are, for one thing. But again, more limited than the ones I've encountered previously, although they didn't have the breadth of power of a true angel."

Charlie emerged, and when he saw Maggie and Damien waiting for him, he smiled. "All done except the paperwork."

Maggie allowed herself to imagine embracing him, but she held back when Damien shook Charlie's hand and clapped him on the back in a manly hug. Charlie's normally tan face still looked a couple of shades pale, and the tension at the corners of his mouth kept his grin from reaching its usual wattage, but she still found him to be one of the most hand-some men she'd ever come across. And she'd encountered several.

Ugh, more reminders of my age. Thanks, brain. You have more important things to watch, like how he's doing.

"I'm going to head to the scene while you two finish up here. Charlie, I'm glad you're doing better." But she would watch him closely to make sure that didn't change.

"Thanks, Maggie." He arched an eyebrow at her as if to challenge her to say something else. She raised one hand in a wave, spun on her heel, and walked out of the hospital into watery sunlight under a sky covered in a veil of thin clouds. There had been some sort of legend about that kind of cloud cover being the wedding veil of a proud princess, but she didn't feel like digging into her memory to find it.

Time to put away the fairytales and dreams and get to work. She pulled out her phone to check to see if Morgan had texted her. Even though she tried to focus on the surroundings and plan for what she would say to Morgan, her mind raced. Gods, could she have made a more awkward exit? What must he think of her? And why did she care so much when she should be thinking about other things?

Maggie activated a small charm to deflect the attention of anyone who might try to follow her. Once she'd rescued her car, she drove to the park. And dead fairy. Her head spun with why's and what's and who's, so when she finally parked, she almost didn't see Morgan waiting for her.

A stab of pain across the top of Maggie's back made her recognize she'd tightened those muscles. She reminded herself to relax. Morgan was family and didn't require her to go into defensive mode. Or did she? She rolled her shoulders and got out of the car.

"Where is he?" she asked more harshly than she meant.

Morgan hung her head, her eyes red-rimmed. "Down the trail in the stream."

Maggie's stomach twisted. "Walk with me. We'll need to do some things on our own before the humans get here."

"We're human." Morgan followed her. "Or mostly human."

Maggie shot Morgan a look. "That's what we've always thought, and you are a half human through your father Gorlois, but there's no way to be truly human in spirit anymore after having lived for as long as we have."

"Is that what they told you at Truth Seeker school?" Morgan

pulled her hair back and secured it in a ponytail at the top of her head. "That you wouldn't be human anymore?"

"There is no Truth Seeker school." *Just lots of tough on the job training. Like Charlie is getting.* A chill that had nothing to do with the breeze that had picked up went down Maggie's spine. *And are they truly intending for him to remain a mundane operative? Or are they testing him to fully join?* And, a question that was accompanied by a stab of guilt—*Would him becoming one of us negate the curse?*

She would have to follow that train of thought later. And talk to Merlin about it. But she had more immediate problems. "Tell me how you found Elric."

"After I left your place, I went for a walk. I felt like something bad had happened to Elric in the store, remember?"

"Yes." That morning in the store seemed like a month, not a day, ago. "So you came here? Why?"

Morgan sighed. "Bounty hunter secret."

Well, at least she hadn't outright lied. Maggie and the other Truth Seekers guessed the bounty hunters had access to certain magic forbidden under the Magical Being Privacy Act of 1837.

"So you walked?"

"Yes. All the way here."

Maggie smiled at the rueful tone in her niece's voice. "It's only a couple of miles."

"When you know where you're going."

They reached the clearing, and the tips of Maggie's ears tingled, the skin across her neck and upper back tightened, and her fingertips itched as they did when she was about to encounter a major threat. The sensations added a strange note to the uneasy déjà vu feeling that had been following her all day.

"Where is he?" she asked but didn't need to. She couldn't speak at a normal volume if she tried. The scent of dead Fae— the stink of decaying organic matter with the sharpness of crushed fallen leaves—made her instinctively hush her tones lest she be reprimanded for disrespect. Not that there was anyone present who would, but memory and old training took over.

"Over there in the creek. Well, his bottom half."

Alert for any sign of threat, Maggie approached the body. He lay on his back, and his right arm was extended in a reaching position. His submerged right leg indicated he had been crawling, or trying to, when whatever had finished him off had caught him. The mushrooms beneath his left foot had been crushed. The most disturbing parts of the tableau, however, were his face and neck, which had been torn out. His handsome features twisted in a pained grimace, and Maggie wondered what he'd been reaching for or trying to get to. Or had he been interrupted mid-cross?

A faint smell of gardenia hung in the air, and she recalled Audrey's words. If that had been Elric's magic, he'd been in downtown Decatur that morning, but why would he have been following her? She guessed he'd been using his magic when he'd been killed. But by what?

"Do you know what killed him?" Morgan asked, echoing Maggie's thoughts.

"Looks like a were-bat." Maggie wrinkled her nose against the scents of copper and sulfur. "We'll have to do an autopsy to see what other injuries there may be."

Morgan shuddered. "Ugh. Here?"

"Ugh, yes." Maggie mimicked her. "We won't have much time." Her phone rang, startling them both with its mechanical sound in the middle of the forest—Charlie.

"How are you feeling?" Maggie asked.

"Fine. Are you there?"

"Yes. Morgan's right—it's Elric, and he's dead."

"Don't touch anything. I'm finally out of the hospital and on my way."

His words piqued Maggie, but she recalled her orders to step back and let him take charge. "Fine. I'll wait until you get here."

When she hung up, Morgan coughed, but it sounded like a laugh.

"What?"

"I've never known you to take orders from a man, Auntie."

"Well, there's a first time for everything." Including a nightmare creature killing a Fae. "So why did you text me you were in trouble?"

Morgan shivered and rubbed her arms. "Because the captain of Queen Tatiana's guard is trying to pin this on me." Then she said the words Maggie never thought she'd hear from her niece. "Aunt Margaret, I need your help."

21

———

Charlie hung up with Maggie and checked his watch. He wondered if he had time for one more phone call while Damien retrieved his car from the parking deck. He could see the parking deck exit, and it looked like there was quite a line for the pay booth, so he dialed the number he wouldn't ever store but which he wouldn't forget, either.

"Knight," the man on the other end answered with a clipped, self-assured inflection.

Charlie wondered how he could get that down with his own last name, which suddenly felt too long.

"Hey, Tristan, it's Charlie."

"Ah, Mackenzie. What can I do for you? Do you have another damsel in distress in a warehouse? That was great shooting, by the way. Meant to tell you."

That was a classic Tristan Knight compliment—offhand and too long after the fact to be sincere. Once again Charlie bit his tongue over the retort he wanted to make.

"I have a 48 in your territory off Sycamore." He lowered his voice in case someone overheard. "Guy named Elric. You heard of him?"

A low whistle. "The queen's gonna be pissed. She only sends her favorites on her personal business. How'd he get through the perimeter?"

"We don't know, at least not yet. How soon can you and Jennifer be there?"

"Ten minutes. Text me the coordinates."

Charlie hung up as Damien pulled up.

"Feeling okay?" Damien asked.

Charlie took a deep breath, and his lungs felt tight but didn't burn anymore. "Good as I'll be, I guess."

"Don't forget what Rizzo said. If you notice anything wrong, go back and see him."

Another deep breath, this one more comfortable. "I'm fine."

The sideways glance Damien gave him told Charlie he didn't entirely believe him, but he also knew better than to try to mother him. Would Maggie do the same now that they had a sort of understanding? One thing he'd observed about her—she liked to be in charge, which sometimes led her to micromanage those around her. He bet Morgan was a challenge for her. Speaking of whom...

"So what do you think of Morgan?" Charlie asked.

"She's interesting." Damien drummed his fingers on the steering wheel. "At first I thought the less flattering legends were true. But last night she was attacked by a vampire, and then roped us all into helping her get him fed."

Charlie held up a hand. "Don't say any more. I don't want to know if or how you violated your oath."

"Thanks." Damien shook his head. "Don't get me wrong, I don't know how much I trust her. The girl's hiding something, and I'm thinking it's trouble even beyond having a pet vampire."

Charlie watched Damien out of his peripheral vision when he asked the next question. "What does Audrey think?"

Damien didn't answer. He only said, "Hey, look at those."

Interesting. Was there trouble in paradise? He'd have to ask when they weren't on the way to a murder scene.

"I never understood Thanksgiving decorations," Charlie said when he looked out the window and found a giant inflatable turkey looking back at him.

"Doesn't your mom decorate for every holiday?"

Charlie smiled at the recollection of his mother's impressive stash of yard decorations, which took up a storage room off his parents' garage. His lower back ached at the memory of having to help her move them around at each season change. At least now she had people to do that for her. "Yeah, but that's because she never could while we moved around so much when I was a kid. She's more than made up for it." The house numbers moved into the fives, and the reports from the morning, as long ago as that felt, came to mind. "Hey, this is near where they spotted the Peeping Tom, isn't it?"

"Yep. Audrey's place is right over there."

They drove by the ranch house that had been split into a duplex.

Charlie couldn't resist floating out another comment. "Nice. Just enough room for one."

Damien rolled his eyes. "We're not to the point of moving in yet. Taking it slow."

"Oh? So you haven't...?" He bit off the crude term he'd been tempted to use. He liked Audrey and was glad Damien had finally found someone. He'd been turning into a ghost of his former self after the grandmother who had raised him died, even when he'd rotated to days.

"Not in the waking world. Waiting for her collarbone to heal."

"Oh, right. And how is it?"

Damien's grin answered before he did. "She went to the

doctor yesterday. Sounds like it's all over except the physical therapy."

"Good."

So Damien would be getting some that evening. And Charlie would likely be stuck doing paperwork. He wondered what his superiors would think about Elric's death.

By the time Morgan had finished explaining the captain's accusations, Maggie was convinced of her niece's story, but there was still some crucial piece of information she missed. She recalled the sulk storms of Morgan's younger days and had to remind herself that, although Morgan, like Maggie, retained an air of eternal youth, she was a powerful centuries-old being in her own right.

"Poor Elric," Morgan said with a glance toward the dead Fae. "Do you think he died yesterday morning when the statue fell?"

"Doubtful. The Fae don't want humans to know too much about them, so they decay quickly. My guess is that this happened this morning, but we'll have to do an autopsy." She looked at her phone to see if she'd missed a text or call from Charlie. She'd texted him and asked him to not involve the human authorities and to bring the field autopsy kit. She hoped he had. Sometimes the Truth Seekers lacked organization and foresight, but if they were testing him as an agent, he should be fully equipped.

The crunching of leaves alerted them that someone walked down the path, and Maggie turned to see not Charlie, but a different man and a woman. He carried metal poles rolled up in a tarp, and she held what looked like a tackle box. They both had backpacks slung over their shoulders.

"What are you doing here?" Maggie asked. *Ugh. Someone told the humans.*

"Got word of a dead body." The man gestured with his free hand to the corpse. "I'm guessing that's him."

Something familiar in his voice made Maggie take a closer look, and the planes of his face and bright blue eyes tickled her memory. She mentally lengthened his dark hair and added a beard. "Sir Tristan?"

His grin confirmed his identity. "Heya, Margaret. What's up? Charlie didn't tell me you'd be here."

"Wait..." Morgan squinted, and Maggie guessed she also added the hair and beard. "It *is* you."

The woman who'd accompanied him rolled her eyes and pulled her light brown hair off her neck with her free hand. The exertion of climbing down the hill with her equipment tinted her delicate features a blush color. "Can we please get through the reunion so I can set this crap down?"

"Oh, right." Tristan showed her where to put the box, which Maggie guessed was a field autopsy kit. "This is Jennifer. She's my assistant."

Maggie didn't sense anything supernatural about the woman aside from her being an old soul, so she guessed this might be another one of Merlin's recruits.

Speaking of whom, where the dickens was he? In the past, he would've shown up for a dead Fae, if only for the chance to study it.

"Who do you work for?" Maggie asked Tristan. She had a million other questions for him, but she'd start with his current situation.

"Dekalb County. You still a TS?"

"Yes." She'd forgotten his annoying tendency to only answer what was asked, but never to volunteer more. He was like the original internet search engine but less useful. She tried again. "But how did you end up there?"

He spoke while he drove the four poles into the ground in a

square outside the fairy circle. "The powers that be figured that the biggest cracks between the Collective Unconscious and Waking World are centered in this metro area thanks to Lyle Ames' less than savory activities, so they pulled a few of us out of retirement and placed us in strategic positions in the authorities."

Retirement. That was cute. Some of the legends hadn't been able to retire. "So you've worked with Charlie before."

"Yep, I run his S.W.A.T. team when needed and do other stuff. Like help with fieldwork." He gestured to Elric. "Shit's gonna hit the fan for this one. Any idea what happened?"

"Nope. And we're going to need to get the autopsy moving before he fades."

Tristan snorted. "Is that what you're calling it?"

"It seems crude to say rot."

"Right, because you're one of them."

Maggie sighed so she wouldn't get into another "am not, am so" argument.

"That's why *she's* known as le Fay. The Fairy." Tristan jerked a thumb at Morgan, who'd hung back and stared at him, uncharacteristically quiet.

"I know what it means. But you can't assume anything about our alliances."

The lift of his annoyingly graceful left eyebrow said he begged to differ, but thankfully he dropped the subject. He seemed unwilling to answer any of her other questions, though, and she felt it would be rude to pry.

Maggie wished Charlie would hurry. And that Tristan would leave her to do the autopsy on her own, but she knew she wouldn't be so lucky. Charlie and Damien finally trudged into the clearing, and Maggie held herself back from fussing over Charlie and making sure he was okay. Sometimes fae-fire took a long time to get over, even when one was treated by a guardian spirit.

Morgan held no such restraint. She threw her arms around Charlie and said, "Thank you for rescuing us yesterday!"

The stinging of her right palm told Maggie she needed to not clench her fists so hard her fingernails dug into her flesh. She loosened her hands. It didn't matter what Morgan did. Not at all.

Charlie disentangled himself from Morgan's embrace, greeted Jennifer, and shook Tristan's hand. "Thanks for coming. Yep, that's him. Guess you don't have to worry about him anymore, huh, Morgan?"

Morgan started to say something, then shook her head, her expression serious. "No, but now I'll be facing the wrath of the Fae queen. They think I did this."

"So did you kill him?" Maggie bit her tongue—she'd meant to inquire with more finesse than that. She didn't think Morgan had done him in, but she had to ask.

"What? Of course not. I don't have that kind of hold over the nightmare creatures to command them to do stuff like this." She took a shuddering breath. "And I wouldn't have anyway. Not to him."

"Right." Maggie spoke as gently as she could to try to respect Morgan's grief. "We'll have to open him up to see what else we can find." Maggie wrinkled her nose, both at the smell and the thought of the desecration they'd be committing.

Now they'd all be in trouble with the Fae queen.

22

———

Maggie listened to Charlie and Tristan chat as she and Jennifer prepared the body for a field autopsy, which basically meant rolling him on to a sheet. She wanted to know more about what Charlie's assignment was, exactly, but it wasn't like she could ask Merlin. She also wished her superiors had let her in on the knowledge that some of the Round Table knights had been brought out of retirement.

"This is turning into a freaking ballad," Maggie mumbled.

Jennifer grinned. "Weren't expecting him, were you?"

"Tristan? Nope. How do you know him?"

The young woman shrugged. "Got assigned to his team about a month ago. I was an investigator, but I kept running into weird stuff, so they put me with him. Said I'd fit in well because that's all he does. Ready?"

"Yes." They lifted Elric, who had already started to lose mass, and placed him on the sheet. Maggie held her breath, not just because she knew the stench would go from forest floor to barnyard funk as the body decayed faster than a human's, but also because she hoped he wasn't playing some sort of trick.

She didn't sense a glamour, but the high Fae had more abilities than the average one. Would he open his eyes as the wound at his throat faded or do something else to startle them?

Now that she was so close—she held his shoulders—it was easy to see why Morgan was attracted to him. She'd always been drawn to the combination of beauty and haughtiness of the high Fae.

"Do you mind if I take a look?" Maggie asked, trying not to step into command, but none of the others seemed to appreciate the urgency of the situation.

Jennifer glanced at Charlie, who said, "Let her do what she needs. She's part of the team."

Ignoring how his including her as part of the team thrilled her, Maggie accepted a pair of rubber gloves from Jennifer. Maggie donned them and knelt beside the body. Charlie also put on a pair and sank to his knees on the other side.

Damien chatted with Morgan, who stood nearby and rubbed her arms against the chill. Good. Maggie wanted to comfort her niece, but she had to take advantage of the limited time they had. Plus, having Charlie so near made Maggie's ears buzz with the things she wished he'd say to her. She almost lifted a hand to swat them away.

Instead, she said, "So this is our third Fae encounter this week." She knew she spoke in a normal volume, but it felt like the new understanding between them somehow muffled her words. The last thing he'd said to her at a previous meeting—*Some of us don't have forever*—whispered in her head and worse, in her heart with new meaning. And the echo of their kiss tingled on her lips.

He seemed to ignore her attempt at conversation, and she wondered if he was trying to maintain a professional demeanor in front of his colleagues. Or if he was hiding how sick he truly felt. She stifled the urge to pick him up and force him to lie down in the back of Damien's car.

When he looked up, the tension around his eyes told her that her second speculation was likely the more accurate one. "Do Fae versus were-bat encounters typically end like this?" His nostrils flared. "And what's that smell?"

"No, even if he'd been surprised, Elric should have been able to fend it off." She looked down at the body. "As for the odor... When they're killed in this realm, the Fae decay quickly. Or, rather, sink back into Faerie through turning into what amounts to compost."

"So that's why you're doing this here." He glanced over his shoulder. "Rather than somewhere more secure."

"Yes, motion and distance would accelerate the process. By the time they got him to the M.E.'s office, he'd be a pile of potting soil, and that, too, would dissipate until the only thing he'd left behind would be memory and a mysteriously empty bag."

So what had weakened him? It wasn't easy to eliminate a Fae, especially one of the High Fae like this one. She first looked at his entire body, at least what she could see. He wore mundane clothing—long-sleeved T-shirt, jeans, and loafers with no socks.

"Wait, he's wearing jeans," Charlie said. "Shouldn't his fingers be blistered?"

"Not necessarily." Maggie lifted the hand nearest her and forced his curled fingertips open. No blisters. "The Fae can't tolerate iron, and jeans fastenings are made from brass, copper, or zinc. But you bring up a good point—they typically avoid wearing mundane clothing because of the synthetic material, which they don't tolerate easily."

"Are they coming straight from the C.U.? Or somewhere else?"

"Faerie, their dimension, is alongside the C.U., as this one is. But I don't know." She'd wondered the same thing. And if they had something to do with the proliferation of nightmare creatures. "Please hand me the scissors. I need to get his shirt off, but I don't want to move him too much. He's going fast."

The twitch at the corner of his mouth indicated he refrained from saying something smartassed. Instead, he handed the scissors over.

She snuck a glance at Morgan again, who looked like she tried not to throw up. Poor kid. Well, not a kid. Poor woman. Morgan had gotten herself into a mess.

Maggie tried to be careful not to allow the blades to touch the body as she made slits in the soft cotton of the shirt. As expected, his skin was pale and hairless, but she found an interesting mark on his left shoulder, which looked like a purple smallpox vaccine scar. No Fae she knew, especially the High Fae, would allow themselves to be marked unless by some sort of magical tattoo that would increase their power. So what was this?

"Take a picture of that," she instructed Charlie. He rose, grabbed the digital camera from Jennifer, who hovered nearby, and took a photo of the area.

Charlie knelt beside her and leaned over her to get a closer shot. She resisted the urge to lean into his warmth and instead allowed his scent—also of the woods, but cleaner somehow—to permeate her awareness. She didn't realize she'd closed her eyes until his deep voice at her ear startled them open.

"Anything else?" His voice held a hint of laughter, like he knew the effect he had on her.

"No, we should get back to examining him. Let's look at his legs and then turn him over." She held her breath as he moved away and clenched her fists so she wouldn't reach for him.

Tristan cleared his throat. "You seem to have that handled pretty well. Mind if I grab his T-shirt and call our K-9 guy to see if we can figure out where he's been?"

"That's fine." Maggie handed over the now tattered article of clothing. "He can appear and disappear in a cloud of smoke, so you may not get very far."

"I'll do my best. Just leave the stuff here when you're done with it. Jennifer will take care of it." With a mock salute, he turned and walked out of the clearing, followed closely by his assistant. Maggie vowed to pack everything up as neatly as she could to save the girl some work.

"Ready?" Charlie had Elric by the shoulders, ready to help her turn him, but she couldn't stop looking at that spot.

"Almost. Let me get a sample from that shoulder mark. It's going fast, but perhaps I can see something about the cells under the microscope later." She grabbed a scalpel and some tweezers and carefully placed the tip of the blade into the edge of the mark. It felt like she dug through skin stuffed with sand, and when she lifted the slice out with the tweezers, it glittered like magnetic dust.

"Huh."

"What is it?"

"Something I didn't expect to ever find on a Fae, especially a high one. It looks like Elric was inoculated with some sort of metal dust."

"How well did you know him?" Damien asked.

Morgan gave him a sideways glance. Gone was the nice guy who had helped her with Philippe, and in his place stood a kind but firm detective.

But weren't detectives supposed to help you figure stuff out? The problem was, Morgan didn't think this particular kind of cop would be helpful. No, she needed to turn to the supernatural ones. Which meant...

Maggie glanced up at Morgan, but Morgan couldn't read her expression. Concern, maybe?

Damien cleared his throat, and Morgan realized she'd never answered the question.

"We worked together. I'd occasionally help the queen out, and he was my contact."

"Doing what?"

Morgan crossed her arms against the sudden chill that started at the tattoo around her neck. It warned her not to reveal anything. "Fae business. I can't say more."

He rubbed the back of his head, which meant he could feel it too. Interesting. "Can you say whether your current business would have gotten him killed? This is the guy who came through with you the other night, right?"

Ah, so Charlie had filled him in, at least a little. "Yes, that's him. And no, I can't say because I don't know." She turned to look at him and away from her aunt digging into Elric's shoulder with a scalpel. "Do you ever feel like you're doing something that should seem straightforward but actually has a much bigger, more complicated story behind it?"

To her surprise, he laughed, and she could see again why Audrey didn't want to give up on him. "All the time."

Maggie interrupted Morgan's thoughts. "Hey, Morgan, do you mind coming to look at this?"

Morgan approached the autopsy site, where they had turned Elric over. Thankfully. She couldn't not look at his throat wound, which made her feel simultaneously short of breath and nauseated every time she saw it.

Maggie had put something in a sample tube, which she handed to Morgan.

"You're closer to the Fae than anyone here. Do you know what it is?"

Morgan squinted at what looked like a piece of flesh—*don't throw up, don't throw up*—covered in black sparkle dust. "No. Do you?"

"It looks like Elric had some sort of metal inoculation. Like what they used to do with smallpox."

"Huh." Damien had also walked over to join them. "Is that how the Fae are getting through the perimeter? They've been vaccinated against metal to give them more tolerance?"

Maggie frowned. "I guess. If doing this gives them more tolerance, but even doing this should cause major injury. No, there's something else about it. Morgan, look at it *closely*. Like you were taught..."

"...on Avalon," Morgan finished. Now her stomach really did flip. That was one of the first things the novices learned, how to really look at something to see its nature. She took a deep breath and concentrated on the sample, specifically its aura, which shone dark purple. "It's nightmare magic."

"Right." Maggie frowned. "Damn, I wish we could question Elric. Or had when we had the opportunity."

Morgan looked again at the sample. Now that she thought about it, he'd hidden his shoulder from her this time. He'd insisted on the lights being off when they had sex, and he'd worn a shirt otherwise. Tricky. But it was hard to be angry with someone who had just gotten his throat torn out.

Even so, she would like to know what the hell had been going on. "If he's truly invested in giving me a warning, his spirit will still be around."

Charlie stood from where he'd been further examining the body and joined them. "You're not thinking about another ritual, are you?"

Maggie put her hands on her hips. "What if we are? And you need to be in bed. Don't think you can fool me."

Morgan covered her laugh with a cough. They must have come to some sort of agreement if Maggie was going all mother hen on him.

He didn't back down. "Need I remind you what happened during and after your last ritual?"

"But you said you encountered him in the C.U., right?" Morgan asked.

"Yes, what does that have to do with it?"

Maggie tapped her lips with one finger. "Often souls will hang out in the C.U. before crossing over completely so they can have a chance of communicating with family and friends they left behind."

"Right." Morgan sighed. She'd had promise as a dream weaver before her powers had been blocked. "I can't reach it without help, at least not with any sort of control, but I'm pretty sure Maggie can."

"Yes, no problem." Maggie put a hand on Charlie's cheek. "Please go get some rest. I'll let you know what we find as soon as I can."

Tristan and Jennifer returned, and Maggie dropped her hand. Morgan and Damien exchanged grins.

Tristan handed the T-shirt, now in a plastic bag, to Charlie. "No luck. You were right, Margaret, there was no trail to follow."

"Thanks, Tris." Charlie shook his hand. "We have a potential lead, so we'll let you finish up here. Please let us know if you find anything odd beside the mark on the shoulder."

Tristan mock saluted. "Yes, sir. Go lie down or something. You look awful."

Charlie rolled his eyes. "Is everyone ganging up on me today? Damien?"

Damien held his hands up. "I'm not going to argue with them. Do you want me to call Rizzo on you?"

Charlie sighed. "Fine. But you'll call me as soon as you have something, right, Maggie?"

Maggie nodded. Morgan's stomach pirouetted again. She was going to have to tell Maggie the whole story to give her the context, but since she'd signed the magical NDA, there was only one way Maggie was going to be able to get it out of her—to Truth Spell her.

23

———————

Charlie knew he felt like crap, or more specifically, like he was coming down with a bad cold, but...

"Before we split up, let's go by Audrey's." He shrugged when Maggie's expression snapped into exasperation, Morgan's into amusement, and Damien's into... Well, Damien had on his detective poker face. Tristan just shook his head.

"Why?" Maggie asked.

"There were complaints of a Peeping Tom. If it somehow was this guy, perhaps there's still some sort of evidence, but not something we'd be able to see without your special kind of help."

Maggie sighed. "Fine. But then you're going to bed."

"Are you going to come tuck me in?"

She didn't reply. He followed her up the trail to the parking area, where he got into the passenger seat of her car and Morgan into the back seat.

"How well do you know that crime scene tech, Jennifer?" Maggie asked. "Is she cleared?"

Charlie shoved aside his resentment that she didn't seem to

think he could trust his own people. "She and Tristan are on loan from the county. We've worked together before."

"Right, I've had contact with that department." She wrinkled her nose, and he wanted to ask what had happened, but he had to clench his jaw against the wave of protectiveness that rushed over him followed by the urge to hurt whoever had insulted her. She didn't need him to be a caveman, he reminded himself. Hell, she'd probably known a couple in her lifetime.

"You okay?" she asked.

"I think it's the moon getting to me," he said, attempting to lighten the mood, but she frowned.

"I know you're joking, but there is something strange about all this."

"More than usual?"

"Much more." She rubbed her forearms. "And familiar. I just wish I could figure out where this feeling is coming from."

Now the little hairs on his arms stood on end. Where some people had hunches, Maggie had premonitions that bore paying attention to.

"Do you remember when you felt that way before?"

"No." She looked up at the sky. "Only that it's been a very, very long time. Possibly in my previous life."

They pulled into Audrey's yard, and Audrey opened the door before they got out of the car.

"Are you okay?" she asked. "Athena has been going nuts, yowling at the back window."

"Stay inside," Charlie snapped, then, "Sorry. But if anything were to happen to you, Damien would have my head."

"Right."

"I'll stay inside with her," Morgan offered. "I want to see what's up with the cat."

"Go ahead," Maggie told her. After Morgan had accompanied Audrey inside the house, Charlie turned to Maggie.

"Don't want her messing up the evidence?" he asked.

"If there is any." She crossed her arms and cocked her head at him. "Why aren't you in bed?"

He grinned. "Because you're not there with me."

"Flirt." She shook her head, but at least she backed off. Charlie wasn't sure he wanted her to, but he did feel like a fresh batch of chocolate crap cookies, as his mom used to say. "How about we split up and take a quick look around?"

"Fine."

"See anything?" Charlie asked when they met in the back yard, where a picnic table sat on a patio. Pots surrounded it, and Charlie guessed they'd once held a patio garden. Maggie barely gave it a glance before heading to the back of the small lot, where trees and evergreen shrubbery formed a screen between that yard and the one behind it.

"No, but the clouds are making it hard to see much, and my phone flashlight isn't doing much to help."

"Mine, neither." He pulled out his flashlight and tried to flick it on, but the light sputtered and then went out.

"Let me see it," Maggie said. He handed it to her, and she flicked the switch, then blew on it. The light blazed back on. "Here."

"Care to explain?" Charlie asked, curious if something magical had interfered with his light.

"I suspect we're continuing our faerie theme of the day."

"Do you see anything?" he asked.

"Not see so much as smell," she said. She stood and brushed off her jeans. "It smells like the dead faerie we were working on before we came over."

MAGGIE WANTED to let the memories come, but she had too much to attend to in the present. Like the handsome blond man beside her. Something about the day made her want to curl up with him and read ghost stories appropriate for this time of year when the last of the leaves clung to the trees and the world seemed to be dying.

"Is there another one in there?" Charlie shone his flashlight under the bushes.

"No, and the smell is very faint. I'm guessing it's decaying along with the last of the Fae we worked on earlier. They'd be similar in their rate of disappearance." Her knowledge of what happened to them after they died in the mortal realm had not made her any friends among the Fae, who liked to be mysterious and thwart human attempts to study them.

Footsteps sounded from the front of the house and made them turn, and Charlie reached for his weapon as a young woman approached them. She put her hands up.

"Hey, watch it." Her words came out breathlessly like she'd been running. "Are you the police?"

"Yes," Charlie said. He showed his badge. "Who are you?"

"I'm the neighbor from back there." She gestured to the hedge. "I tried to call y'all about twenty minutes ago, but my landline went dead, and my cell wouldn't pick up a signal."

Maggie looked up at Charlie, who nodded. "What were you trying to report?" she asked.

"Like I said, I live back there. The chick who lives here was opening her blinds this morning, and when she did, the light caught something funny. Like a guy standing here watching her." She pointed at where Charlie and Maggie stood. "He looked like the Peeping Tom I saw the other night."

"Oh, you were one of the women who called in?" Charlie already had his phone out, taking notes.

"Yes, I'm the one who drew the sketch."

"Thanks, and was it the same guy today?"

"I don't know. It was through the bushes, so it was just a tall, narrow silhouette. Then the breeze blew, and he disappeared. I wasn't sure if I'd seen him or just some weird trick of the shadows through the leaves." She tucked her shoulder-length dark hair behind her ear, and the flush in her cheeks deepened. "That's why I waited to call. I went back and forth on if I'd seen something or not. But I know she lives alone, so I thought I'd come at least check on her."

"Thanks," Maggie said. "Do you mind if we get your contact information in case we have questions later?"

The woman nodded and handed Maggie a card. "This is the best way to get in touch with me."

After she left, Maggie and Charlie took their time walking back to the car. He went around the half of the duplex Audrey didn't live in, and Maggie retraced their steps from earlier. She kept her senses alert, but the clouds broke up and played hide and seek with the sun, which made disorienting shadows, and she found herself having to pay more attention to where she stepped. She debated taking out her pocket flashlight, but she didn't want to lose the wisps of memory just out of reach.

When she rounded the corner and looked toward where Charlie should emerge, she caught her breath. A tall blond man stood under the almost naked dogwood, but his dress and manner weren't Charlie's. In fact, they weren't modern at all, from his knee-high boots to his armored breastplate, cape, and long beard and hair. He inclined his head to her, and she felt his voice inside her head.

"Greetings, fair witch of Avalon." He placed a fist over his heart.

Maggie returned the gesture and willed her heart to stop galloping at a panicked clip. "Greetings, Uther. Long time no see."

His lips, which Maggie's sister, Igraine, had praised for their suppleness—oh, gods, why, of all things was that coming to mind at this moment?—curved, and then he spoke aloud. "Over a millennium, in fact. You recognize me."

"You're hard to forget." She glanced to the side to where she was sure Charlie would emerge, but she noticed the stillness of the air. "And you've taken us out of time."

"No, I have." A middle-aged man with salt-and-pepper hair and dressed in dark jeans and a long leather jacket appeared. He'd shaved his signature beard, but she recognized him immediately.

"Merlin?" Maggie rubbed her temples. Something about his magic had always given her a headache. "Where the hell have you been?"

"Where do you think?" Whereas Uther's smile had been charming, Merlin's mocked her. "Haven't you learned by now not to meddle with the Fae?"

She bit back the snarky response she wanted to make and instead said, "Trust me, this time wasn't by choice."

"Nor is my captivity. But listen."

"Your sisters have sent us with a warning," Uther told her. "As you've probably surmised, the Fae are up to something, but they've broken the covenant of non-interference."

"Which they claim not to be under the jurisdiction of," Maggie put in. "What have they done this time?"

Merlin and Uther glanced at each other. "They're trying to reverse the effects of the birth of Arthur, which opened the door to their downfall by allowing Christianity a firm hold in England. But we don't know how, only that they've somehow managed to overcome their inability to tolerate iron."

"But not all of them," Uther added. "And for some, it's not permanent. But it does allow a few to spend more time in this world before their shells eventually die and rot."

Maggie cursed under her breath. The thought of such powerful beings without limits scared her, but at least now she had some explanation for the events of the week.

"Thank you for the information and for the warning," she told them. "Do you have any advice?"

"Pay attention to your instincts and don't allow yourself to be distracted," Merlin said. "I've been watching you and know you sense how this evening feels familiar, but your mind is half taken by that detective." He shook his head. "After spending a thousand years trapped under a fucking tree, I feel I can warn you about the dangers of allowing heart to overrule head."

Maggie nodded, but she only pretended to agree. Merlin didn't curse unless he really wanted to emphasize his words. On the other hand, she'd lived those thousand years he'd been bound, and so had more life experience. But there was her curse to consider.

"And don't think I don't know what's going through that ginger head of yours," he admonished. "It's our destiny to be alone."

"I'm well aware of that." She thought about asking him about it, but decided against it. He'd probably just tell her to focus on the problem at hand anyway.

"Are you? You don't seem to be acting like it."

She took a deep breath of stale, time-stalled air to quell her desire to argue. "Can you give me a clue as to why this day feels as though it has happened before?"

"Me bringing Uther along isn't enough? I can't do all your thinking for you." Merlin bowed, and both men disappeared. The caress of the wind on her cheeks and the scraping of dry leaves across asphalt told Maggie that she'd been returned to the flow of time, and she gulped the fresher air. Even a wizard as powerful as Merlin couldn't take people out of it for too long. She'd heard it was like standing in a fast-moving river and trying to keep one's footing on slippery rocks. But where was he doing it from?

He'd mentioned captivity. Who was powerful enough to hold on to a wizard like Merlin?

"So Uther is a clue." She looked up at the clouds, and the sun appeared. Then the memories rushed in. Not the ones she'd sought, at least not at first. No, first there were the memories of being on Avalon with her sisters, Morgause and Igraine, and her heart swelled with grief at the loss of both her sisters and the special bond they'd shared. She could have allowed the sobs to emerge, but she rode the feeling until she accessed the other memories. Again, the three of them, but this time Morgause wove the spell that had allowed Maggie to sneak Uther in to meet Igraine on that fateful night.

"Maggie?" Charlie joined her. She hadn't heard him coming. "Are you all right? Did you see something else?"

She swallowed and brought her attention down from the moon to him. "Yes, I had a couple of visitors from my past. I really need to question Elric about what Tatiana is up to."

"How? He's dead. Really dead now."

She glanced up at him. "I'll figure something out."

24

Something about the light outside freaked Morgan out, but she attempted to appear calm when she entered Audrey's half of the duplex.

"Is it different coming in the front door?" Audrey teased.

Morgan laughed. "Sort of. But it looks just the same." Then a deep-throated growl that crescendoed into a yowl from the bedroom made every hair on her body stand up with an electric tingle. "What's that?"

"Athena." Audrey blinked, and Morgan saw the wetness of barely contained tears. "She's been like this since this morning. She'll just sit and watch for an hour, maybe ninety minutes, and then bow up, poof out, and make that noise."

Morgan walked into the bedroom and saw the cat sitting on a perch that hooked to the windowsill. Sure enough, she was bowed up and puffed out, and she put forth a rumble when Morgan approached.

"It's okay, I'm here to help." Morgan didn't know if the cat could hear her mental voice, but Athena relaxed slightly and turned to face Morgan, her yellow eyes huge in her face. *"And Truth Seeker Margaret of Cornwall is out there looking around."*

Morgan held out a hand, ready to snatch it back should Athena decide to attack, but once Athena sniffed her, she rubbed her head against Morgan's hand. Morgan caressed the soft fur between and behind her ears.

"That's a good girl."

An audible sigh of relief from behind made Morgan turn around.

"Thank goodness." Audrey leaned against the door frame. "Are you a cat whisperer or something?"

"No." Morgan smiled before she caught herself. "Just an honest to goodness Avalon witch."

"Whatever you are, thank you." Audrey approached her cat, which jumped down and twined around Audrey's legs. Audrey picked her up and sighed as she scratched Athena's head. "You're a silly floof."

Morgan stopped herself before she blurted out that she thought the cat was more than a floof. If the cat brought her into the C.U. again, she'd definitely be asking more.

Great, she was starting to think like Maggie.

"So what brought you to my yard? Well, besides the freaky events of the morning." Audrey put the cat down. "Come into the living room. I'll make some coffee."

"That would be amazing." Morgan followed Audrey into the other room. She hated to disrupt the coziness of their new and fragile friendship, but Audrey needed to know since she was somehow involved. "One of my Fae associates was found murdered near the stream that runs through the neighborhood. Maggie and Charlie thought it may have something to do with the Peeping Tom."

Audrey shuddered. "Murdered? How?"

"Were-bat."

Audrey put a hand to her throat, and Morgan nodded.

"I'm sorry for your loss," Audrey said and flipped the switch on the coffeemaker. "Did you know them well?"

"You could say that." Morgan sat back and petted Athena, who had jumped on to her lap. There was no way she could distill nine centuries of emotion—lust, confusion, trust—into an easy explanation. The mix of feelings ballooned in her chest.

"Then I'm doubly sorry. That really sucks."

"Yeah, it does." For the first time since she'd seen Elric, Morgan allowed the tears to come. Audrey came and sat on the couch and put an arm around her. Morgan cried into her shoulder as the cat purred and kneaded Morgan's right thigh.

When Morgan's sobs had subsided into sniffles, Audrey said, "I wish I could say it gets easier, but it doesn't really."

Morgan looked up. Audrey's green eyes held the kind of sadness that had been there so long it seemed like she'd been born with it.

"You sound and look like you talk from experience."

Audrey stood, and Morgan wondered if she had over-stepped her bounds. Damn, she was out of practice with the friend thing. Should she leave? Before Morgan could make up her mind to go, Audrey walked into the kitchen and brought back a tray with two cups of coffee and the usual fixings.

"I have Irish crème liqueur if you need something stronger," Audrey said with a wink.

"Thanks." Morgan fixed her coffee—with regular half and half, thank goodness—and wondered what she should say next.

"My mother," Audrey said and stirred her own coffee. "After my father was killed in the line of duty, I would make her coffee and bring it to her in bed. She said she needed the help to deal with the start of the day without him. Knowing he wasn't coming home broke her heart." She shook her head. "It was awful."

"I'm sorry to hear that," Morgan said. What else did normal people say in this situation? "That must have been really hard for you." And then the words tumbled out, "So how are you dating a cop?" She cringed at herself.

Audrey sighed. "I ask myself the same every day when we're apart, but then when he comes over, or I go to his place, and he's safe, and we're able to be two normal people..." She shrugged. "Not that cops can ever be normal, but at least it's familiar."

Morgan sipped her coffee. "This is really good. Thank you."

Audrey patted her leg. "You're welcome. You seem to be a lot like Maggie, always running around and looking into things but not taking a lot of time for yourself."

"I'm not always like that. I have a cute little magic store just outside of New Orleans, and I get plenty of quiet moments." But did she ever take them for herself outside of exercising? There was always something to do.

"Oh? That sounds interesting."

A knock on the door made the cat leap down and disappear. Audrey got up, checked the peephole, and then let Maggie and Charlie in.

"Did you find anything?"

"Not really," Maggie said. "Would you mind if Charlie were to lie down for a little while? I think he's spent."

Charlie must have been tired because he didn't argue. Guilt stabbed through Morgan. This was somehow her fault.

Audrey gestured for them to follow her into the bedroom. "Sure, he can borrow my bed."

"Thanks. I'll sleep on top of the covers."

They got Charlie settled, and Morgan poured Maggie a cup of coffee after she closed the bedroom door. Morgan didn't know what to do about creamer, but Maggie accepted the cup and took a long gulp.

"Thank you. It's a weird cool today. Not super cold, but it seeps into your bones."

Morgan refrained from commenting that some bones were

older than others. At this point, the difference in age between her and her aunt was minuscule in relation to their long life spans.

"Another were-bat, huh?" Audrey asked once they were all seated.

"Yes, and this one's still at large." Maggie studied the surface of her coffee. "And I don't know what to make of it."

"Let's do the ritual to talk to Elric," Morgan said.

Audrey looked from Morgan to Maggie. "Is that...?"

"Yes." Morgan's hands shook, so she put down the cup. "And I need to give you the context, but I've signed a magical NDA."

"And now that you are the last person to see the murder victim alive..." Maggie swallowed. "I had really hoped I wouldn't have to do this."

"It's okay, Auntie." Morgan clasped her hands together and found them covered in soft fur when Athena plopped on top of them. "Do what you have to do."

MAGGIE TOOK off her glasses and looked into Morgan's eyes. Typically when she truth-spelled someone, wherever they were took on a sepia tone, like she'd brought them into an old picture, and then there was a click of connection. This time the room dimmed into a sepia scene, but somewhere she'd tried to forget for centuries.

They stood on the shore of a lake, and the gentle lapping of the water, the place's heartbeat, beat through her entire body. The softness of the mud anchored her feet, and the earthy smell of the dirt mixed with the green smells of plants and barely moving water.

There was no click of connection, and Morgan crossed her arms, looking around with a wrinkled nose. "Why did you bring us here?"

"I didn't." Maggie smoothed the hairs on her own forearms, which showed her rising panic in spite of her efforts to appear calm. "I think you did. I hope you did."

Morgan shook her head. "I can't have. I may have once been strong enough to resist a truth-spelling, but not now. Not yet."

She put a hand over her mouth. So something was working.

"Who's working with you to help you regain them?" Maggie had put together that Morgan was some sort of bounty hunter and tied to the Fae, but what was the ultimate price?

Morgan shook her head. "I can't. It won't come out."

"So what's blocking you?" Maggie couldn't keep the exasperation from her voice.

Morgan returned her arms to their closed position. "Can't you figure it out, Auntie?" She gestured to their surroundings. "We've come back to the place of my greatest sorrow, where you and Niniane took Mordred from me and banished me from Avalon."

"Mordred made his choice." But Maggie had often wondered what had influenced the boy to run to Niniane rather than Morgan on that day. He had certainly become upset when the boat carrying Morgan and another young witch had disappeared through the mists.

Gods, she'd known something was terribly wrong. Why hadn't she acted? Or questioned?

The look Morgan gave her echoed her thoughts with its accusation. "Niniane had played a game with him, and he thought they were playing again. He told me when I found him later, when he was an adult and had been twisted by her influence."

"Oh, Morgan." Maggie put her hands to her mouth to keep the words from spilling out, stupid, inadequate words that wouldn't do anything to fix the situation. She had felt something was up, had always known she should have done something. And had always regretted that she hadn't, knowing with her whole intuition that she'd had the power to change the course of Morgan's life, and indeed of history, although she had never been able to put a firm shape on the regret. Yet another way her cousin had betrayed her. And Morgan.

And she had been so focused on her own agenda that she had missed all of it. Was it any wonder she was cursed to be alone and unhappy?

Morgan looked at the mists, her lips tight with anger and her eyes soft with longing. Maggie realized they stood on the shore, not the island.

"Do you want me to try to call the boat?"

"No." The quiet word cut through the air. "There's nothing there for me now."

Nor I. But as inadequate as the words were for the degree of the hurt she'd caused, she had to say, "I'm so very sorry."

MORGAN HAD WAITED centuries to hear her aunt say those words, for some sign that she carried the regret that mirrored Morgan's anger. Yet the sentence fell into the space between them like a twig into a koi pond, almost but not quite swallowed by the magnitude of the time that had passed and the depth of her hurt.

And she wasn't going to say it was okay. Or that she forgave her. There had been too much grief, too much loss. And now Elric's body was gone, his spirit fading.

No, they could figure this mystery out without Morgan saying what their relationship had been.

She blinked, and she found herself back in Audrey's duplex. Audrey waved her hand between Morgan and Maggie.

"Are y'all okay? I don't think that's how that's supposed to work."

Something stung Morgan's cheek, and she found tears

mixed with blood. Maggie's face was similarly stained. Audrey handed tissues to both of them. Maggie excused herself to go to the bathroom, which would take her through the bedroom, and Morgan wondered if she was taking the opportunity to check on Charlie. Or be near him.

She shivered. She'd never had an anchor like that, someone to run to for comfort. First her mother had betrayed her and her father by having an affair with Uther. And then Niniane and Maggie...

And while Morgan had held on to her secret, she now knew her aunt's. As they'd stood on the shores of Avalon in the vision, the breeze had whispered it to her, tickling her ears and her mind. Any man who loved Maggie, and who Maggie loved in return, was doomed. That was Maggie's curse.

Now another doubt wriggled into Morgan's heart and almost made her breathless with its implications. Was that why Philippe had ended up as a vampire? He'd loved Maggie? And was there still something between them? It didn't look like it, but curses didn't get activated for no reason.

"What happened?" Audrey asked. She brought Morgan a fresh cup of already fixed coffee.

"Thanks. And I don't know, exactly." Morgan tried to stifle the warmth that wanted to bloom at the thought of having someone in her life who would want to care for her, even as a friend. Friendship had always come with a side of betrayal, but Morgan also knew in a deep way she'd learned to heed that she could trust Audrey. The thought came unbidden that Audrey would be a good mom, and Morgan swallowed so she wouldn't say so. Where had that come from? Morgan didn't typically think in terms of potential parenting ability.

"What did it look like?" Morgan asked to draw herself out of her strange thoughts, which must have been muddled due to what she'd just been through.

"You just stared at each other, and then the bloody tears came."

"*Lacrima mori*," Morgan whispered. Tears of death. Something had died between her and her aunt, but she didn't know what it was. Or if it was something that should have and didn't need to be mourned. Only that it had been deep and long-lasting.

"*Lacrima* who?" Audrey asked.

"Mori. Tears of death." Morgan didn't want to tell Audrey everything. It was all still too fragile and curious and strange. "It's something that humans who have the blessing or curse of almost-immortality can do." *And how you can tell something major just happened with them.*

"Oh." Audrey cocked her head. "Are you okay? Do you need anything?"

"No, you've given me just what I needed." Morgan took a sip of coffee, and the warm, bitter liquid helped to ground her. She took a bite of one of the cookies Audrey had set out on a plate. That's one thing she always remembered—the importance of grounding herself after a powerful magical experience.

"*Lacrima mori*," Audrey said, as if trying to fit the words into her reality. "I still have so much to learn."

"We both do." Morgan sighed. Would she never get to the point where she felt prepared for what was ahead? "First thing—always ground yourself after a powerful magical experience. After any spell, really, if you're still in your first century."

Audrey laughed. "Thanks, so that's an always for me. I doubt I'll merit immortality." She frowned. "Is that why I'm having trouble in the C.U.? I'm not sufficiently grounded?"

"Maybe?" Morgan cocked her head. "Do you do any sort of preparation before dream-weaving? Anything after?"

"No, just the meditation Maggie taught me to bring me there. She's always had to run right after, so..." She frowned. "But I'm always hungry after, so I've usually eaten. And, now that I think about it, she's always fed me when our bodies have been in the same place, but she didn't say why."

"At least she did that much. It sounds like you have some instincts in place." Morgan studied Audrey. Light curly-ish brown hair, green eyes, and ears with slightly pointed tips. She looked like some Fae had made a contribution to her bloodline at some point. "Maybe having something associated with the earth like a rock or crystal would help."

Audrey smiled and curled her hands around her mug. "I've always loved crystals."

Morgan reached into her backpack and pulled out a raw amethyst the size of a large marble. Even uncut and unpolished, its clarity was apparent. She'd picked it up in the twelfth century on a job in the mountains of what would later be Brazil. It had called to her, but she'd never been able to do anything with it. Yet she hadn't been able to leave it behind because she'd had a sense it would be needed by someone in the future.

"Here," Morgan said and handed it to Audrey. When it fell into the other woman's palm, there was a sense of rightness. Audrey stared at it.

"It's lovely. Amethyst?"

"Yes, from Brazil. I found it a long time ago."

Audrey looked up, her expression incredulous. "It feels tingly."

Morgan smiled. "That means it was meant to find you. Before you dream weave, focus on it as an anchor to help ground you. And after you come back, be sure to drink and eat something to help you resettle into your body."

"Will do."

Maggie returned, her face pink like she'd just scrubbed it. "I borrowed a washcloth. I hope you don't mind."

"Not at all." Audrey handed her a cup of coffee, and Morgan tamped down her jealousy. She could share a friend.

As for Philippe... They would have to have a serious talk later.

"Thanks." Maggie patted Morgan's arm. "Are you okay?"

Morgan flinched, and Maggie dropped her hand. "As okay as I can be." She had too many conflicting feelings to ever be okay again.

"What's that?" Maggie gestured to the amethyst, which Audrey had put on the coffee table.

"I gave her something to ground herself before and after dream weaving." Morgan tried not to sound defensive.

"Good." Maggie nodded. "It's been so long since I taught novices, and so few of them were dream weavers, I'd forgotten that dream weaving falls into that category of needing grounding. Actually, now that I think about it, there was some debate."

Morgan frowned. How could her aunt have forgotten something so basic? "You didn't think to try it just in case?"

Maggie shrugged and rubbed her eyes under her purple lenses. "No, Morgan, I didn't. Please realize I'm no longer the assistant novice-master on Avalon. But from what I recall, I did feed her when I could, so the knowledge is still in there somewhere."

"How is Charlie?" Audrey asked.

"Resting peacefully. I don't want to move him."

"Then don't. He can stay as long as he needs." But she looked down at her mug. Morgan sensed the tug-of-war in her over what to do—allow Charlie to rest at her place or have them leave so she could have her private time with Damien?

"I'm fine," Charlie said as he walked out of the bedroom. "I had a good nap, and I had the strangest dream..."

25

Maggie stood and rushed to his side. She didn't think to slow her movements to human speed until she caught his bemused and admiring glance.

"What other things can you do quickly?"

She punched him on the arm. "Be good." Then she saw he leaned on the door frame, and his face remained pale under his perpetual Texas tan. "Are you okay?"

"Yes, but I think I'll take you up on that offer for a ride home."

The thought that she'd like to help put him to bed flickered through her mind, but she shoved it away. "No problem. Morgan, are you okay here?"

"Yep."

Maggie helped Charlie to her car. Once they were both settled in and she'd pulled away from Audrey's duplex, he said, "They seem to be getting along well."

The guilt that had been pulled to the surface of Maggie's awareness throbbed. "Yes, I'm glad. Morgan never had many friends growing up. There weren't any other kids her age at her parents' castle, which was really more of a fortress..."

"Fortress? You mean Tintagel?"

She nodded. She could still see it clearly, but for Charlie, it would be a place of legend, currently a pile of dark stones. She had so many more memories than he did, and she felt the chasm of years that separated them.

"Tell me about it," he said. He leaned his chair back, folded his hands over his stomach, and closed his eyes. "Was Igraine as beautiful as the legends say? Was she your older or younger sister?"

Maggie spun her words out like a bridge between present and past. "She was older. The second one. Morgause was first, a fiery redhead. Then Igraine, lovely as the poets said, with jet black hair and eyes the color of the autumn sky. I came along several years later, just a few years before Morgan was born." She didn't mention that her mother had died in childbirth with her or that Morgause had raised her. Maggie had done enough work un-teaching herself the harsh pragmatism that Morgause had instilled in her—necessary for women in a society that treated them as property—that she didn't want to have to explain. "As for Tintagel, it was dark and foreboding. It was mostly walls and a collection of long, low buildings that served different functions at the time. The actual castle part was built later."

"Like in Beowulf."

Maggie laughed. "Sort of, yes."

"So what's the deal between you and Morgan?" He opened his eyes. "Were you enemies?"

"I..." She swallowed the wave of regret and nausea. "It's too long a tale to tell here. Let's just say we both were caught up in the political machinations of some selfish people, and I inadvertently contributed to some very deeply hurtful events."

"And you still haven't forgiven yourself."

"I can't. Not until she's forgiven me."

He patted her leg. "You're being too hard on yourself. And giving her too much power."

"It's only fair considering the power I took from her. You know how the legends say she and Arthur had sex as part of the harvest festival, and she conceived Mordred?"

"Yes."

"What they don't say is that she was so horrified after, she lost her powers. Today we'd call it a psychic wound, but back then, it was seen as personal weakness. Until then, she had been our most promising trainee. But after, she could barely manage the basics." Maggie had to breathe around the tears. "I wasn't directly responsible, but I didn't think it was a good idea, and I didn't object hard enough."

"Wow. That's harsh."

Yep, that was it. He hated her now. He saw how awful she was, and he wouldn't love her anymore. Well, if it saved him, she could deal.

She pulled up to his apartment building, and he raised his seat. She braced herself for the inevitable, "It's not you, it's me" speech. Or in her case, "It's not me, it's you."

"Hey." He turned her face toward him. "You can't be so hard on yourself and keep beating yourself up for stuff that happened years—centuries—ago. You must've still been really young, just a kid yourself."

She nodded since she couldn't speak around the tears in her throat, and he brushed one from her cheek. What was it about him that made her let her guard down and cry?

He continued, "Whatever happened, I'm sure you've punished yourself enough for it."

"I don't know..." She took a shuddering breath. "I don't know how I can ever make it up to her."

"You will. You're smart. And you obviously care about her."

Maggie wasn't prepared for the wave of protectiveness that

washed through her. Dammit, she did care about her niece. She wanted Morgan to have the chance at happiness she'd been denied her entire life, if her current attitude and situation were accurate indicators.

She smiled and cupped Charlie's face. "And I do care about you. Which is a whole different problem. But thank you."

He closed the distance for a kiss, and she allowed herself to think that something might be possible between them. If she could figure out how to break the curse. For the first time in a long time, the solution felt almost within reach.

Then he broke their contact and leaned back, coughing.

"Let's get you inside," Maggie said. She didn't let him see her sigh. As per usual, her glimmer of hope faded, which left her with bigger problems, including how to save her niece, both from the Fae and from herself.

When Philippe woke, the apartment was quiet. The first thing he checked was his hunger level, which registered as mild to none. Thankfully. He didn't want to put Morgan, Maggie, or anyone else in danger.

Philippe shook his head before his imagination took him down the dark path of what could have happened. His thoughts had always run away with him upon awakening. At least now he wasn't stuck on an island and forced to feed off intoxicated birds. But he was stuck. He unrolled his blanket cocoon and blinked at the naked light bulb above him, which wasn't on even though the closet seemed to be lit by a diffuse dim light. Oh, right. He had excellent night vision now. Being with the humans at the end of the night had made him feel almost human again himself. But he couldn't forget what he'd become.

What did they refer to him as? Right, a nightmare creature.

He'd never truly known the meaning of the word *hangry* until becoming a vampire, when the need to feed turned into a physical sensation plus rage at anyone who dared get in his way. And he could see how his relationship to that person wouldn't matter until was too late for them. He'd never been able to understand why people did awful things to each other. Did others feel the need for power or wealth as terribly as he needed blood?

He curled around the despair that bloomed in the pit of his stomach. He'd had a sense of the finality of the situation, but his last shred of denial had been stripped away by the events of the past few days. He now had a label, an identity, and there was no going back to his former life, his real life, as a roadie for a Heart cover band in the Pacific Northwest. Sure, he could work nights, but he couldn't appear before sunset, and bands traveled during the day. So what could he do? He didn't want to be dependent on others, he didn't want to accidentally hurt anyone, and he had no desire to be anyone's pet vampire.

Especially the Fae queen's, as Morgan had told him. He didn't know much about the Fae or what they did, but he remembered enough tales from his childhood to know they typically didn't play fair. Now, his dislike of them felt visceral. Due to the threat? Or the fact that Fae and nightmare creatures didn't mix?

He pondered what to do as he pulled his socks on. He wished he could know what Morgan intended. She wouldn't turn him in, would she? He smiled when he remembered their kiss. She'd kissed him like a woman who had never known love before but who had a good idea of what she was missing. But had she been seeing that Elric guy romantically before she'd bailed on him with Philippe? He'd never gotten a clear picture of their relationship. But how could he compare with a handsome Fae charmer?

The thought of Morgan with another guy was enough to

propel Philippe to his feet. Whatever their understanding had been, it wasn't any of his business. And while he might want to stick around to find out, it wasn't the safest bet for him. He didn't like it that the return of Morgan's powers hung on her bringing him in, but he didn't owe her anything.

Or did he? She'd rescued him from Merlin's island, after all. But the purpose had been to capture him herself.

His thoughts bounced around his head like shoes in a dryer. She liked him, she liked him not... If her kiss had been any indication, she was definitely interested in him. But he'd thought the same about Maggie and had been horribly wrong.

Finally he concluded he didn't know what to think, so he turned to his gut instinct, which said, "Run!"

He slowly opened the closet door, ready to slam it shut at the slightest indication the sun was already up. The room was pitch dark, but he frowned at the clock. It was early to be so dark. But then he remembered—Daylight Savings Time had ended sometime during the night, so hunting time started earlier.

Perhaps that was why no one was home yet, although he didn't know what Maggie and Morgan could be up to. He didn't think they were church-goers. The thought made him almost laugh out loud. He was pretty sure lightning would strike him if he attempted to enter a holy place or step on consecrated ground. As for those two, they'd probably cause a tornado.

Philippe turned back to his makeshift bed. He could at least be a neat guest, but he didn't want to make it immediately obvious that he'd left. He needed time for a head start in case they decided to come after him.

After folding the blanket he'd wrapped himself in, he left it on the pillow in the closet. He considered covering a couple of the spare pillows in the closet with the blanket to make it look like he was still there, but he didn't think Morgan would fall for such a trick. Instead, he took off the pajamas Maggie had given him, put them in the hamper in the closet, and dressed in the spare set of clothes. He then used some of Morgan's cosmetics to make himself appear less pale on first glance. He couldn't do anything about the intensity in his dark eyes, but he'd just avoid eye contact whenever possible. He had his wallet from before, so he had a current I.D., but he was sure his credit cards had long been canceled. And could anyone track him that way? He didn't know what kind of tools the Truth Seekers used, but he guessed they combined modern technology and magic.

Philippe hated to do it, but he rummaged through drawers and cupboards, looking for cash. He found a stash of about a hundred dollars in Maggie's bedroom and took that. Then he crept through the living room and out of the front door, locking it behind him after one more mental check that he'd gotten everything he could and should. Finally satisfied, he went down the fire stairs to the exit and did his best to melt into the early night.

After Maggie left, Audrey looked at Morgan and said, "She's trying, you know."

Morgan looked up from her charm bracelet, which she'd been toying with since she'd found it at the bottom of her bag. She had usually not worn it on jobs since Elric was metal-sensitive, but she had taken it out that morning. The artisan who had made the charms was a dwarf, and therefore very long-lived, so she had one for each of her completed jobs. That last space taunted her. She already had the charm planned—a diamond set in a crescent moon to signify the return of her powers. But now the thought of turning Philippe over to Tatiana made her stomach flip. At least her previous bounties had had something about them that justified their capture, typically some crime they'd committed against Faerie. But Philippe was an innocent. Just as she had been an innocent who had been the victim of others' schemes.

She had to know what was going on. That's why they had to raise Elric's ghost.

Morgan didn't acknowledge Audrey's statement. Rather, she asked, "When do you think she'll be back?"

"Charlie doesn't live that far away. Maybe twenty minutes?"

"Hmm, okay." That wouldn't be enough time to get everything settled and aligned for the ritual and do it without Margaret. Besides, could a Truth Seeker truth-spell a high Fae? They shouldn't be powerful enough, but then, a were-bat shouldn't have been able to kill Elric. Or maybe Elric had been weakened by his bizarre attempt at metal inoculation. Or made vulnerable by the nightmare magic it contained.

Morgan shivered. What in the realms could have convinced the Fae to mutilate themselves so? Because Elric likely wasn't the only one.

"Can you show me how to ground?" Audrey asked. "So I can help?"

Morgan almost asked what she thought she could do, but she recalled her own novice days, how she'd been prickling with power and wanting to know how best to direct it before she drowned in it. Interesting—she hadn't remembered her abilities being uncomfortable, although they had been before she'd started learning to control them. Would she feel the same again once she got them back?

That was not a happy thought.

"Okay, sure. First, get in an aligned but relaxed position and close your eyes."

Audrey placed her feet on the floor and put pillows behind her so she would be sitting with everything in a straight line.

"Good, now imagine yourself being anchored to the earth through your first chakra point, your grounding point." Morgan smiled. "We didn't call it that back when I was learning this, but I learned it later, and it made sense."

"Okay, now what?"

"Just sit there with it. Feel the connection. Maybe imagine yourself as a plant or tree, rooted through that point to the ground."

Audrey squinted and opened one eye. "Is that it?"

Morgan laughed. "Close your eyes, we're getting there. Now picture a weight anchoring that root somewhere beneath you. It's tugging you into the cushion, through the chair, and into the ground. This is the place you will always be able to sense to return to no matter how far your spirit goes."

"I could've used this last month," Audrey grumbled.

"It may or may not have helped. If your spirit is trapped somewhere, there's no guarantee this method will allow you to break free, but at the very least, you won't get lost. And you'll have a place to draw strength from."

Audrey's breathing slowed, and Morgan wondered if she'd gone to sleep. Or into the C.U.

"Audrey?"

Nothing for the span of thirty heartbeats. Then Audrey asked, "Morgan? Was Elric tall with dark hair? Because there's a guy here looking at me, and he looks pissed."

"Hang on. I'll be there in a second." She hoped. Athena rubbed against her and looked up at her with yellow eyes as if to say, "I'll help."

Morgan closed her eyes and took a deep breath.

Here we go...

26

When Maggie arrived back at Audrey's, she found the door unlocked and Audrey and Morgan sitting cross-legged on the couch with their knees touching and hands clasped. For a second she thought they were meditating, but then the wave of magical energy hit her. They were in the C.U.

"Morgan? Audrey?" They were either too far gone to hear her, or they were ignoring her. Morgan frowned, and her mouth moved, but no words came out.

Maggie locked the door behind her, sealed it with a ward, and sat on the armchair near them. She tried to calm herself, but worry for both of them kept knocking her out of her trance. Finally the cat came and settled on her lap, purring soothingly but somehow anxiously. Still, the rhythm of the noise allowed her to settle, and she entered the C.U. She whispered a spell to allow her to bend time, which could be done in the dream world, and arrive nearer to the beginning of Maggie and Audrey's journey.

At first she was surrounded by mists, but they parted, and

she found herself again by the lake, but this time on the Avalon side. Morgan and Audrey stood nearby talking to Elric. As Maggie approached, she heard raised voices, and Morgan emphatically separated her hands—enough.

"I'm tired of the lies, Elric," Morgan was saying. "You set me up to fail, to lose my chance to get my powers." She crossed her arms.

"You used the Pathway to sneak off with the queen's bounty," Elric spat back. "Did you honestly think she would be all right with that? Besides," he said and reached for her, "I was saving you. The situation in Faerie has gotten...complicated. You don't want to go anywhere near that."

Morgan stepped back, and her chest heaved. "What is the situation?" she asked in a calmer tone. "What does she want with him?"

"Why? Have you gotten attached? What's the first rule of bounty hunting?"

"Don't fall for the quarry," Morgan said, and her words sounded rote. "But he's not an ordinary mark, is he? It's time to come clean, Elric."

Morgan acknowledged Maggie's approach, and Elric sneered when he saw her.

"Ah, Margaret. I should have known you'd be nearby."

"What's going on, Elric?" Maggie noted his spirit was at least whole, but she hadn't expected him to wear his injury once his damaged body had decomposed. "Why is Morgan in danger?" She put as much implied threat into her tone as she could. He had better not be messing with her niece.

Elric put up both his hands. "Stop acting like I'm the bad guy. I was trying to protect her and solve a major problem we've had since that one—" he pointed to Audrey "—defeated Zeus in the temple and bargained for the cracks in the barriers that separate the C.U. from the waking world to be fixed. Zeus had promised the nightmare creatures that they would have free reign to sneak into the waking world, feed, and cause chaos. They didn't like him making that agreement without their input."

Morgan looked at Maggie, and with a touch of their old understanding, Maggie knew that they were putting together the same set of pieces.

"So what bargain did they make with Tatiana to allow them to come into the waking world through Faerie?" Morgan asked.

Elric's lips curled into an almost-snarl. "That they would allow her to capture and keep one of their own—the fledgling vampire Philippe—and show her how to make her warriors immune to metal if she would allow them passage."

"Why Philippe?" Maggie asked.

"Because of his connection to you." Now Elric rubbed his forehead. "Tatiana wouldn't tell me why, only that you needed to be distracted."

Although the temperature of the C.U. was typically a comfortable neutral, Maggie went cold. What had she been distracted from? She'd been essentially in a holding pattern. "Wait—does this have something to do with Merlin? With him being missing and trapped somewhere?"

Elric shrugged. "As I said, she didn't give me details." Then he looked at Audrey, and his lips curled into a predatory smile. "But I would guess the answer is right in front of you."

"And what about Morgan?" Maggie pressed. If she needed to protect her niece and her friend, so be it.

Morgan rubbed her upper arms. "Tatiana wanted me to bring Philippe to Faerie, thus entering it of my own will. She wants to trap me there so she can use my influence over the nightmare creatures." She frowned. "But I'm still not seeing the big picture."

Elric shrugged, and now Maggie could see the shore of the

lake behind him. "Don't go to Faerie," he said and cupped Morgan's face. "Your powers aren't worth your freedom."

She nodded, and when Elric pulled his hands away, tears sparkled on them.

"Goodbye, Elric," Morgan said. "Thanks for your help and for what I did regain."

Elric shook his head. "There's no need to thank me. Remember—what isn't said is more important than what is." And he vanished.

The rumbling of the cat's purr vibrated in the air around them, and Maggie grabbed Audrey's and Morgan's hands. "It's time to return."

Morgan nodded. "I have some planning to do."

BY THE TIME Morgan returned to Maggie's apartment, she had decided not to take Philippe to Tatiana. She wasn't too worried about Tatiana trying to trap her and use her—she'd evaded enough snares in her life that she knew what to look for and how to manage. But she recognized Philippe was an innocent bystander in all this, and he deserved to be free to live his own life. Well, afterlife. And if he wanted her help... She smiled. She'd be willing to make a trade for a few more kisses like the one they'd had that morning.

Maggie unlocked the door and frowned. "Something's different."

Morgan followed her aunt into the apartment. "What?" Everything looked the same to her, but the condo somehow felt...empty.

"Philippe?" Morgan called. It was full dark, so he should be up. She walked into the bedroom she'd been using, but all looked the same. She approached the closet, her steps almost a creep. Was he sick? Dead? She'd heard of fledgling vampires spontaneously combusting, their systems unable to handle the changes. But he'd been fine, and she didn't smell any new smoke beyond the residual acrid hints from the mirror and then their failed ritual. She opened the door to find the pillow and the blanket folded neatly on top.

"He left?" Morgan thought she had been cried out, but her eyelids pricked. How could he have left?

Right, he'd thought she was going to bring him to Tatiana. But hadn't they shared something special that morning? Couldn't he at least have stayed to talk about it?

As much as the treachery she'd experienced in her life had hurt, the idea that he thought she would betray him and the fragile trust they'd built hurt deeper, a blow to the core of her soul. She wasn't like that.

Morgan walked into the living room to find Maggie holding her phone.

"He left," Morgan said.

"I know. And he took my emergency cash. I'm wondering whether I should call the police."

"I can't believe he didn't trust me," they said at the same time. Morgan sniffled.

"Oh, sweetie." Maggie opened her arms, and Morgan accepted the hug. She cried on her aunt's shoulder—literally—for a few minutes, then backed away. She reached for her phone, but hesitated.

"I guess I can't blame him." Maggie sat on the couch and put her phone on the coffee table. "It's my fault he's a vampire. I should have been more careful."

Morgan sat next to her. "I can't say I do, either. If I thought there was a chance someone was going to bring me to be enslaved in Faerie, especially if the Fae were my natural enemies, I would run, too. And," she added with a sigh, "I am known as le Fay. He has good reason to think I'm loyal to them."

They sat in silence for several heartbeats. Then Morgan

asked, "So you're sure there was nothing between the two of you?"

"Absolutely." Maggie sighed. "And the fact he thought there could be is hard to talk about. I don't like to discuss my failures, as you know." She glanced sideways at Morgan.

Morgan grinned. "You never did. Just like your sisters."

"Yeah. And this ended up being major payback for trading lockets with Niniane."

"Yeah." Morgan wrinkled her nose. "That was dumb. So you said Philippe was injured in the battle over the lockets, but you didn't say how."

"Right. I had rescued him from the coffee tunnels, and we had just escaped from a former Truth Seeker who had gone dark under Niniane's influence." She shook her head. "I still can't believe that."

The thought of a turned Truth Seeker using their knowledge and power for evil made Morgan shudder. "What happened to him? Is he still around?"

"I don't know. Beau vanished after the tunnels closed. But getting back to Philippe, he and I had made it to Boston, where one of the ghosts said she had information for me. She took me to her brother, who captured us."

"Bitch," Morgan muttered.

"No, I'd truth-spelled her, so I knew she had a good motive. But her brother had betrayed her. Philippe escaped, and in his efforts to keep Niniane's locket away from Beau and her, he swallowed it."

"Right. I'd forgotten that bit. Intentionally, I think." Morgan shuddered. "I mean, quick thinking on his part, but her energy —ick."

"Right? It poisoned him, and the Gray Monk swooped in and fooled Philippe into thinking, well..." She shrugged.

"That he had a chance with you." Morgan forced herself to

not ask again whether Maggie had reciprocated the feelings. She had denied it, but there was her curse, and Philippe had certainly ended up doomed.

"Not at all." Maggie fiddled with the moonstone ring on her right third finger. "I wasn't attracted to him, not like that. And I'd met Charlie." Her cheeks went pink.

"Uh, oh. Drama?"

"Something like that. And I told you the battle didn't go well for Philippe." Maggie took a deep breath. "But I didn't say yet that I had to leave him alone. And then the Gray turned him."

"Wow." Morgan could see why Philippe had some lingering anger over the situation."Why did you leave him alone?"

"An imp had run off with my locket, and I had to grab it before it disappeared into its realm with it. I left him with a friend, but... I chose myself and my responsibility to the Truth Seekers over a man's life. Worse, his soul."

Morgan couldn't find words amid the feelings crowding her head and chest. On one hand, she could see how Maggie wanted the locket—it could be used against her later—and if there was one thing Morgan understood, it was self-protection. And it sounded like Philippe had been seriously injured. "Who was the friend?"

"Madame Lucia, a powerful witch posing as a psychic. She lives in the other half of Audrey's duplex." Maggie frowned. "Now that I think about it, I wonder if that arrangement was as coincidental as it seems." She shook her head. "But Lucia had to go help fight, and she left Philippe alone."

"But you got Niniane's and your lockets?"

Maggie nodded. "I did. But lost Philippe. Merlin took him and promised he'd put him somewhere where he could manage his transition and not hurt anyone."

Morgan balled her fists. "Merlin left him to die. He put him on a tropical island where he had to dig a hole in the sand to sleep in until he found a cave, and he survived on drunken birds."

"Oh." Maggie's horrified expression told Morgan her aunt hadn't known the specifics of Merlin's plan. "I would never have allowed that to happen."

Morgan patted her aunt's hand. "I know you wouldn't have." And she believed it. "Things get hairy in battle, especially when supernatural creatures are involved. Wait, did you say Merlin is missing?"

"Yes, trapped somewhere. But we can't worry about him now. What are you going to do?"

Morgan looked at her phone. She needed to talk to Philippe, to tell him that she wouldn't turn him over to the Fae. And at this point, she knew she could trust her aunt with at least one of her secrets.

"I have an app," Morgan said.

"Oh? Dark Mirror?"

Morgan raised her eyebrows.

Maggie waved a hand. "We've been aware of it for a while. It makes sense that a bounty hunter would use it, although it does violate the Non-Interference and Freedom of Movement Act."

"So you're not going to turn me in?" Morgan asked.

Maggie smiled. "No, since you're using it to find a fledgling vampire who is still learning how to be what he is and is therefore a danger to himself and others."

"Okay, thanks." She opened it and focused on finding Philippe. "According to this, he's..." She frowned. "That can't be right. It says he's in the building."

A knock on the door made them both jump.

"Morgan? Maggie? I got dinner."

~

Philippe's mother had always said that bad news was best delivered with food, so he stood there like a fool holding a bag full of pho and fixings. He couldn't help but remember that was the last meal he'd had before being turned, and while the food smelled just as good—better with his heightened senses—the thought of eating it made his stomach flip.

Morgan yanked the door to Maggie's condo open. She opened her mouth to say something, but her stomach growled. She blushed and put a hand over her mouth.

"Hungry?" he asked.

"Are you?" She looked at him closely, her gaze like the light brushing of her fingertips over his face.

"No, I'm still good from last night."

She stood aside to let him pass. "Nice makeup job."

"Thanks. Didn't want to look too undead. I might get cast in something. There's a film crew on the Square." He walked into the condo, where Maggie stood looking at him quizzically. While he still thought her beautiful, she seemed faded next to Morgan's dynamic energy and presence. "I brought pho."

Maggie shook her head but didn't say anything. "I haven't eaten that in forever."

The two women fixed their bowls of soup, and they all sat at the table.

"You came back," Morgan said, and her voice cracked on the last word.

Philippe wanted to reach for her hand, but he didn't. His own shame flooded him. He'd been so preoccupied with the danger he was in that he hadn't considered her peril.

"I had to." He looked down at his hands, which rested on his lap. "After I left, I headed into a wooded area and overheard something."

"What?" Maggie asked and put her spoon down.

"There was one guy—the others kept calling him Captain— who was giving orders for capturing you, Morgan. They were making plans to grab both of us, but specifically to arrest you for Elric's murder. That's the guy you were running from, right? The one who followed us here?"

"Yes." Morgan had also stopped eating, and she looked ill. "Aunt Maggie, is there something you can do? You know I'm innocent."

"I do, sweetie, but you know Tatiana doesn't care."

Sweetie? Philippe looked back and forth between the two women. The tension he'd previously sensed between them seemed to have dissipated. So Elric had been murdered, and the two of them had reconciled. Dammit, why did he always have to sleep through the good stuff?

"So what do we do?" Philippe asked.

"We?" Maggie shook her head. "I'm going to figure out how to get the two of you as far away from here as possible. Then I'm going to figure out where the hell Merlin is. He's the only one I know who has enough influence in Faerie to stop the queen."

"But he's missing," Morgan said. "I can't think that's a coincidence. You're sure you banished Niniane far away?"

"I'm pretty sure I did, but she's a powerful being. And if she had help..." She picked up her spoon, but her thoughts had obviously strayed far from her soup.

Morgan and Philippe looked at each other, and he wished he could do something to fix the hurt in her gaze. She wasn't wrong that he'd tried to leave, but he'd come back to warn her. Didn't that count for something?

The two women finished their meal, both lost in their own thoughts. After they'd brought their dishes into the kitchenette, Maggie said, "I'm going to consult with Lucia. You two stay here."

"No worries on that count." Morgan flopped on the couch. "I'm not sure where I can go without the captain ambushing me. Damn Fae—why did the nightmare creatures have to give them a way to tolerate metal?"

"What?" Philippe asked. "Would you please fill me in?"

"I will." Morgan's lips curled into a small but sensual smile.

"You two be good," Maggie told them and left.

Philippe sat beside Morgan on the couch. "I feel like I've just been told to behave by a parent."

"Right. No boys in my room." Morgan giggled, but then her expression turned serious. "But I do need to catch you up on everything. And thank you for coming back to warn me."

"You're welcome." He caressed her cheek with his right index finger, and although he must feel corpse-cold to her, she didn't flinch away. He dropped his hand. "So does this mean you're not going to turn me over to the Fae queen?"

"I'm definitely not going to do that. I had already decided not to even before all this, I just didn't realize it." She held his hand and toyed with his fingers as she caught him up on the day's events.

"That's wild," he said when she had finished telling him about the ritual. "So Elric warned you, too."

"Yes, so I'm stuck here. At least I know I can trust Maggie now. But do you feel like you can? It sounds like she left you in a vulnerable position."

Philippe grimaced at the memory. "Yes, but I've forgiven her. If her locket was as powerful as Niniane's, I don't blame her for wanting to get it back. Not anymore. It sucks to be at the mercy of someone else."

"It's not so bad sometimes." She stood and held out a hand. "Let me plug my phone in, and I'll put on some music."

He allowed her to help him stand and followed her into the bedroom. The last time he'd been in a similar situation, he'd gotten lucky, but that had been another him in another life-time. He didn't even know if he could have sex like a human.

That was one thing vampire lore, what little he knew, disagreed on. Anne Rice said no. Stephanie Meyer said yes.

Morgan put her phone on its charger and pulled up the music app. The plaintive lyrics of Melissa Etheridge's "I Wanna Come Over" wafted out at them.

"Is that a hint?" he asked, his heart picking up tempo from its typical sluggish undead march.

She walked over to him, put her hands on his chest, and looked up at him through her eyelashes. "What do you think?"

27

Morgan couldn't believe she was being so forward. While she'd enjoyed the sexual revolution of the sixties, she'd always held back and had never had sex with a guy she'd only known for a couple of days. But now that her life had veered off course, and she no longer knew what her future held, she needed something to anchor to. And Philippe had given up his freedom, or risked doing so, to help her preserve hers.

Philippe lowered his lips to hers, and the passion of their kiss soon warmed his mouth so that she almost forgot he was a vampire. Almost. He smelled of fresh air and of something wild. She'd always been able to sniff out a predator. The fact that he held his strength in check to hold her gently and not hurt her while they kissed made her feel powerful. With Elric she'd always felt at a disadvantage, and she shoved the memories of him away.

The strength of the connection she felt to Philippe frightened her. And intrigued her. She wanted to discover more.

They tumbled on to the bed, and Philippe ran his hand over her curves until he found the edge of her shirt. He pulled it up to expose her skin, and he ran his hand up her back to unfasten her bra. Her breasts had never felt so full and heavy, and she pulled away to rip her shirt off, then recaptured his mouth in hers. He cupped her breasts and lightly thumbed her nipples, sending little bolts of pleasure through her to her core. She arched her back, wanting him to do more, but he pulled away. Morgan huffed.

"Why did you stop?"

He looked away, but she could see the glow around his irises. "This. What we're doing. I can feel your heartbeat and smell your blood, and you're driving me crazy. I don't want to lose control and hurt you."

"Oh." Morgan blinked to try and bring some blood back to her brain from her other parts. She knew she could bind him and command him to continue to ravish her, but she wanted him to freely choose his course of action. "Would it help if I were to give you some?"

"Some what?" But his fangs had already extended.

"Philippe." She put a hand to his cheek and turned his face toward her. "I trust you to only take what you need."

"Are you sure?" He closed his eyes. "You don't know how amazing you look. Smell. Feel." He jerked his head from her hand. "I'm not worthy of it."

He moved to slide off the bed, but she caught his arm.

"Yes, you are." And that little part of her that had always felt *less than* since losing her powers listened to her words. "Just because you've been turned into this doesn't mean you're any less of a person, a worthy human being." She blinked at the tears that wanted to come.

He brushed a droplet from her cheek. "What? Are you okay? Was it something I did?"

"No. And yes. You made me figure out something that I should have long ago."

He smiled. She kissed him once, quickly, and then pulled away.

"Take what you need."

"Wait, turn around." She did as he said, and he pulled his shirt off so they sat with her back to his chest. Although she couldn't see his physique, she could feel the planes of his muscles. He slid her bra all the way off and cupped her breasts so she arched against him again. She almost didn't feel it as he sank his fangs into her neck, and as he drank, he continued to drive her crazy so all the sensations melded together, and she gasped as the orgasm made her entire body shudder. He held her as she collapsed back into his arms. He kissed the wounds on her neck closed and then supported her as she drank from the bottle of water she'd placed on the bedside table.

"I don't think I took too much?" He leaned over her, his eyebrows drawn in concern.

She smiled at the languor that spread through her entire body. She felt drained, but in a sexually sated way. "No, you didn't. But do you feel better?"

"Amazingly. Let me show you." He ran his hands over her torso. "If you're up for it."

The exhaustion that had overtaken her fled at his touch, and she wanted him, this time inside of her. She took the opportunity to explore the dips and planes of his pecs and abs —even better than she'd imagined—and tugged at the waistband of his jeans. "Oh, I definitely am."

He stood and took off the rest of his clothes, and she did as well, and then they stood and looked at each other. The light of the waning moon illuminated the bedroom through the curtains, and it caught the paleness of his skin. And hers. But whereas she'd always felt insecure with her new lovers, she had no hesitation baring her body to him, not even the extra curve in her lower belly from her pregnancy so many centuries ago. Now the hunger in his eyes was only for her, not her blood.

And when they came together, they fit perfectly. She didn't remember tumbling to the bed, only the sharp thrill of his entering her and the wildness of his kisses as he claimed her with his mouth and body. Every time she ran her hands over him, whatever part, he moaned like her touch was magic. Maybe it was. They finished together in another perfect climax with each of his pulses igniting another wave of pleasure in her until every one of her cells flared with heat and ecstasy. And when she flamed out, she came back to herself with his weight on top of her.

It seemed like the time for the l-word, but she wasn't there yet. But she said what she could. "Philippe, I trust you."

"And I you." He rolled off of her and spooned her, then nuzzled her hair.

For the first time since she'd received her tenth and supposedly final job, she slept soundly and without dreams.

MAGGIE DIDN'T KNOW what would happen when she left Morgan alone with Philippe, but she sensed they needed some time together. Just like she and Charlie did.

When she got to her car and pulled out her phone, she almost called Charlie, but hesitated. He needed to sleep. She hoped he would call Rizzo in the morning if he wasn't completely better, and if he wouldn't, she would. And maybe once she got Morgan and Philippe away from the Fae, she would plan a weekend away for the two of them. They needed to talk. And she really needed time to work on breaking her curse. And figure out what had happened to Merlin.

And, and, and...

The weight of all her responsibilities, both personal and professional, would smother her if she thought too much about it. Instead she responded to Lucia's text, telling her that now was fine for a visit with, *B right there.*

She put her phone away and pulled out of her spot. When she arrived at Audrey's and Lucia's duplex, she saw that Audrey's lights were on, but she also noticed Damien's car wasn't there. Relief warred with concern, and while she had no explanation for why Damien's absence relieved her, she did hope everything was okay between the two of them. They'd been friendly to each other the night before while they helped Philippe hunt, but the tension was obvious. She wondered if Audrey had talked to Morgan about it.

Maggie sent a prayer of thanks to whatever deity was listening that she had Lucia to discuss things with and to help her with rituals she couldn't handle on her own. She wasn't prepared for the tangle of messy feelings that welled up in her when Lucia opened the door to her half of the little house, and she couldn't manage to choke out a greeting.

"Rough day, dear?"

Maggie nodded. Lucia guided her in and sat her on the red couch, then put a cup of tea in her hands.

"There now, drink this, and we'll talk. The spirits have been abuzz with the news of the Fae prince's murder."

Maggie sipped the tea, which was at the perfect temperature, and allowed the familiar and comfortable ginger-lemon bite to ease some of her tension. "Thank you."

"You're welcome." Lucia grabbed her own cup off the kitchen counter and came to join Maggie in the living room. "Tell me what's been happening."

Maggie sighed. She filled Lucia in on the events of the past few days, including Charlie's being the target of the fae-fire. "And so now we have something going on between us, and on top of everything, I have to worry about this curse."

"You've had something going on between you for a while." Lucia tapped her ring against her cup, a sign she was thinking.

"As for your curse... I have a sense your niece is somehow involved in the solution, but I cannot tell how. It's good that you've reconnected."

"Is she involved? Or is it just weird timing?" While she didn't necessarily believe in coincidence, Maggie didn't want to consider that some force had brought Morgan to her doorstep. Especially not with Philippe.

"You know as well as I that coincidence is the tool of fate. Do you really think that her appearing now in your long life so close to you almost being ready to open your heart to someone was by chance?"

Maggie looked down into her tea. "It's safer for me if I do because I don't see the solution."

"It will come in time."

Maggie smiled. "Is that a prediction?"

"Perhaps. You're the one who will decide. But that's not the most pressing problem. You need to get those two away before the queen's soldiers find them."

"You're right." Maggie stood. "Thank you, as always, for your advice." But she felt like she left with more questions than answers.

"Any time. Be careful. Oh, and your niece may appreciate this." She handed Maggie a paper bag. When Maggie looked inside, she saw a bag of chicory and a carton of half and half.

"Thank you. I'm sure she will."

They hugged. When Maggie left, she noticed Audrey's lights were off. It was still fairly early, but then, she'd had a long day. They all had.

Maggie recalled Elric saying that the reason for Tatiana wanting to distract her might be right in front of them and looking at Audrey. She shivered. Yet another person she cared about but didn't know how to protect.

~

AUDREY SAW Maggie's car pull up and waited for a knock on her door. But it didn't come. Instead, she heard Maggie go into Lucia's.

Fine, she didn't need to talk to anyone, anyway. Wait, that wasn't right. Since that afternoon, she'd had what could best be described as a case of the shivers. As in, every time she thought about it, tingles danced up and down her spine. She'd pulled her phone out about a thousand times, and she'd finally texted J.J. or Rizzo, or whoever he was.

She checked her phone again to see if J.J. had texted her back, but he seemed to have gone back underground or wherever it was he went. Or maybe it was time for his hospital shift as emergency room physician Arthur Rizzo, and he couldn't. She didn't know exactly what J.J. was, only that he was some sort of guardian spirit who lived a double life. After having grown up with him as a much-older stepbrother, she still struggled to get her mind around it all.

Yep, the holidays were going to be weird this year.

Finally she had to admit she wanted to talk to Damien. Things had felt strained between them the previous night when they'd helped Philippe hunt, and she wanted to make it right. She had told Morgan the truth—she wanted things to work out with Damien because she had fallen for him. Hard. Even if he put himself in danger every damn day. It's not like she led the most risk-averse life, and her role as a dream weaver would put her in peril at some point. That's why she was training with Maggie. And why her failures to make progress frustrated her. Hopefully the technique Morgan had shown her would help.

If she was going to be at the center of some strange fairy plot, she wanted Damien to be by her side.

With that decided, she requested to Facetime him. She also turned off her lights in case Maggie decided to stop by after seeing Lucia.

"Hey," he said, and she curled into the warmth of his voice. "What's up?" He looked like he was sitting in Charlie's office.

"I was wondering if you had a minute to talk." She chided herself for feeling so nervous.

"Uh, oh. Is this going to be the 'we need to talk' conversation?" he joked, but she could hear the anxiety in his tone as well.

"No, at least I don't think so." She sat, and Athena crawled on to her lap. "I went to the C.U. today. With Maggie and Morgan."

"And?"

Okay, that was something. She couldn't see all of him, but his expression only betrayed curiosity, not censure.

"We spoke with Elric, the dead Fae. He said his murder was part of a larger plot, and Tatiana is trying to distract Maggie."

He nodded. "That makes sense. Did he say from what?"

Here was the hard part. "No, but he looked at me and said something like, 'but the answer may be standing right in front of you.'" She braced for him to jump into overprotective mode, but he didn't.

Instead, he asked, "Do you know what he may have meant?"

She should have been relieved by his cool and professional tone, and her disappointment surprised her. "I don't, but I'm scared." She realized she was talking to detective Damien, not boyfriend Damien. The emotional distance between them stung. But then his lips softened the way they only did when he looked at her, and the gap closed.

"Why don't you come meet me at the station? I'm about to get off. We can grab dinner." He smiled, and the tension in the center of her chest loosened. "We can talk about things, figure them out." The resonance in his next words thrilled her. "I want to see you."

"I want to see you, too. When do you finish up?" She knew

he technically got off at seven, but he also ended up doing reports late sometimes.

"Does seven-thirty work for you?"

"Perfectly. I'll see you then." They disconnected, and she sat back and petted the cat. Then she packed an overnight bag in case the evening went really well.

28

———

Of course Morgan didn't sleep for long. The click of Maggie's keys in the lock of the front door of the condo jerked her awake. She never slept while on jobs, at least not much, and if she did, it was almost with one eye open. A certain amount of residual alertness kept her from going into deep sleep, no matter how much her body craved it.

I'll sleep when I'm dead had a different meaning for the almost-immortal.

In that half-second of forgetfulness between sleep and wake, she became aware of someone holding her, but she could also tell he wasn't sleeping. Then reality slammed into her.

It wasn't Elric, who had pretended to betray her but who had also kept vital information from her, and who now was dead. It was a vampire whom she'd allowed to drink from her. If it had been any other vampire, she would have shuddered. Combining passion and feeding bonded a vampire to a human. But he was no ordinary vampire, and she definitely didn't meet the criteria for typical human. So she'd have to see where this relationship—if it could even be called that at this point—went. But this wasn't the time to ponder romance. She'd get them away from the threat of imprisonment in Faerie and figure it out from there. Maybe they'd go north, where the nights would be longer.

Maggie turned on the coffee grinder, and Morgan jerked, as did Philippe. They needed to get going to take advantage of the darkness, but damn, a cup of coffee would taste really good right now.

"You okay?" she asked him.

"Mmmm. More than okay." He kissed her neck. She first stiffened from instinct at having a predator's fangs so close to her carotid artery, but relaxed almost immediately. Unfortunately he seemed to notice. "I thought you said you trusted me?"

She rolled over to face him. "I do. I know you won't drink from me unless I agree. But I'm dealing with centuries of caution."

He smoothed her hair away from her face. "And I trust you won't bind me and command me to do anything I don't want to, although if it will keep you safe, I give you permission."

"Don't say stuff like that." She put a finger on his lips. He captured it and gave it a little nip with his non-vamp teeth. "Seriously." She pulled it away. "Don't give power away to anyone unless you absolutely have to."

He rolled away. "What about emotions? Aren't they somewhat involuntary?"

Morgan wondered what he meant, but before she could ask, Maggie knocked on her door. "Morgan? Philippe? I think I have a plan."

They dressed and joined Maggie in the living room. She looked from one to the other, and although she raised her eyebrows, she didn't ask what they'd been doing. Morgan exhaled the breath she'd been holding. What had she expected, that Maggie would act like a pissed-off aunt who had trusted them to act with more decorum?

"What's the plan, Auntie?"

"I'll tell you, but first, coffee. Lucia had some chicory she let me have. Come let me know if I made it right. She also gave me some cream for you."

"I miss coffee." Philippe sighed. "Even if I have PTSD around it now."

Maggie looked down. "I'm sorry."

"Not your fault," he said. "I got myself into trouble. Besides, if it hadn't happened, I would never have met Morgan."

Morgan's blush heated her from her scalp to her toes, and she turned to the counter to fix her coffee so the others wouldn't see. What the hell? She hadn't acted like a besotted teenager even when she'd been a teenager. Sure, she'd become a mother at fifteen, but still, her emotions hadn't affected her like that, not even around Elric.

The first sip of coffee with the chicory and cream made all other thoughts fly from her mind. "This is amazing."

"Good, I'm glad." Maggie fixed herself a cup with the real cream and also closed her eyes after her first sip. "Oh, that is nice."

"Right? Philippe, do you mind if we drink it over there?"

"No, that's fine."

Morgan joined him on the couch, and Maggie sat in her armchair. Philippe sniffed Morgan's coffee.

"Huh, it doesn't even smell good anymore."

"What does it smell like?" Morgan asked.

"Kind of like dirt."

Maggie cleared her throat. "Tatiana likely has the complex surrounded, so when we leave, it will have to be through magical means." She placed her coffee on a coaster and pulled out her phone. "And she's likely got soldiers or minions stationed at the airport. That's the only means of transportation that Philippe has time to take."

Morgan studied her coffee. "So we're limited to magical

means of transport." Of course. Tatiana did have them trapped, and Morgan didn't know the area well enough to know where to zap them. Not that she could. She didn't need to be weakened that much if they were going to have to run.

"Exactly. That means I need to be able to zap the two of you someplace where you can pick up a Pathway that's not controlled by the Fae."

Morgan frowned. "I thought the Fae built the Pathways."

"Not all of them. Some of them were constructed by the Truth Seekers." Maggie grinned. "And there's one nearby that should take you across the country. Portland, specifically. That will buy you two several more hours."

"The Pacific Northwest." Philippe looked both hopeful and terrified. "That's close to home for me."

Morgan couldn't imagine how he must be feeling, so she held his hand. "Is it too close?"

"No." He squeezed her hand. "But it's somewhere I'm familiar with, so we should be able to navigate it fairly easily."

"And then the two of you can take off into the mountains. I'll be in touch once we figure out what the hell is going on here."

Morgan had never seen her aunt flustered, but also excited. For the first time, she understood why Maggie had become a Truth Seeker—she liked the challenge and control. And since Morgan had become a bounty hunter for similar reasons, she felt they might be related, after all.

Audrey waited in the lobby at the police station. She'd just sat down with her tablet to revise the article she'd written that afternoon on where to order organic, free-range Thanksgiving turkeys when she had the feeling again she was being watched. It didn't help that the Decatur police station had a two-story lobby and was completely glassed-in with tall windows. But she couldn't see anything looking at her. Even so, she scrunched herself down on one of the benches so she wouldn't be visible from outside.

But then she thought better of it. No, she wasn't going to hide from them. She'd faced down the king of the gods, Zeus himself. She moved to where she could see and be seen from all the windows and set up there. Nothing happened at first, but then all the hairs on her body stood to attention, and she smoothed the ones at the back of her neck as she looked outside. In spite of being in a busy area of town not too late at night, the street stood empty, but *something* watched. And waited. And wanted something from her, but she didn't know what.

A familiar set of footsteps told her Damien had come out of the door to the right of the volunteer booth. She turned around to look at him, and the elated feeling in her chest warned her she had better make this work in spite of both their doubts and fears. Yes, she had fallen for him. Hard. Sure, he looked exhausted, but as she'd thought before, he even made tired look good. The line between his dark brows eased when she stood and he saw her. Her motion also seemed to break the other spell, and she no longer felt on the receiving end of a predator's gaze. Being in the same room as him made her feel safe.

"Are you okay? Sorry that took so long." He gave her a kiss.

"Yes. I think my mind is playing tricks on me." She leaned into him and caught a whiff of crisp autumn air and leaves, which contrasted nicely with the smooth sweetness of his leather jacket. He'd shed his equipment except for his Glock, which he kept in a shoulder holster, and his black T-shirt hugged his chest. She couldn't help but run the fingers of one hand over his taut muscles, enjoying the feel of the soft cotton over the hard planes.

Desire slammed into her. She wanted more. She wanted to feel his skin.

Rather than pulling away, he tightened his grip on her and captured her mouth with his own. After a long kiss that she didn't want to end, he pulled back.

"I, ah, right." He ran a hand through his hair while holding on to her with the other arm. "This is probably not the place to have this discussion, but—"

She put a finger on his lips and tried to ignore the throbbing at her core. "Let's go back to your place."

His grin erased all traces of fatigue from his face. They practically ran to his car hand-in-hand, and he recaptured her hand in his after he started the car and pulled out on to the road. For once the traffic lights all cooperated with them, and they made it back to his apartment in less than fifteen minutes.

Once inside, he carefully put away his bag and removed his holster, leaving it with his gun on the dresser in the bedroom. She put her stuff on the right side of the bed and waited. She reminded herself not to cross her arms—she wanted him to know she was open—but breathless shyness overtook her. Sure, they'd done this in the Collective Unconscious, but what if it was different here? Different in a bad way?

He walked over to her and tilted her chin up so she could look into his gray eyes. His bedroom eyes, which almost shone against his olive skin. "Want to make sure I understand what *you* want." His deep voice thrummed through her body and calmed her.

"I want you." She play-stabbed his chest with her index finger. "All of you."

He smiled with a tenderness that she only saw when he looked at her, but concern shadowed his gaze. "Is your collarbone better?"

"Yes. Completely. I'm frustrated it kept us from doing this for so long." She tugged his shirt from his pants and ran her hands over the smooth skin and soft hair on his belly. Not belly —that word made it sound like he had extra fat down there. His abdomen, then.

Her feet left the ground, and she laughed as he picked her up and laid her on the bed. He pulled his shirt off before stretching out beside her, and she caught her breath.

"Uh, you're not doing yourself justice with your dream self," she said. "Damn, you've got some muscles."

He looked down and wrinkled his nose. "And I smell like I've been running the streets all day."

Audrey leaned up on her elbow. "Then how about we take this to the shower? I can help you clean up." The thought of rubbing soap over all his surfaces made her mouth water.

"That sounds like a fantastic idea."

MORGAN AND PHILIPPE PACKED QUICKLY. Morgan had already consolidated her important possessions into a backpack, and Philippe didn't have much, so it didn't take them long.

When they joined Maggie in the living room, they found she had changed her attire to all black, and she had a mini-crossbow in a holster on her hip. She also loaded silver bullets into a cartridge, which she placed in a holder on her belt with two others. She had a Glock in a holster on her other hip.

"Can you shoot with either hand?" Morgan asked. "And is the gun specially made to fire those?"

Maggie looked up with a grin. "In a pinch, yes. And yes to the custom job." She patted it. "I hate using firearms—I am English, after all—but Charlie has convinced me of their necessity. Are you ready?"

Morgan nodded, and they joined hands. She ignored the twinge of regret that she wouldn't be able to stay longer and get to know her aunt better. Survival first, mushy emotional stuff later.

Maggie closed her eyes, and the places where their skin touched tingled. Morgan recognized the feeling of an impending shift and held on tighter to Philippe. The walls of Maggie's condo faded, and they found themselves in a wooded area. Morgan shifted her weight to adjust for the softer ground under her feet and wrinkled her nose against the smell of stagnant water.

"Where are we?" she whispered, although she didn't know why.

"Near a pond the locals call Avondale Lake," Maggie replied, also in hushed tones. "We're near a sort of offshoot that doesn't circulate the water very well."

Morgan surprised herself by saying, "Our lake was better. It didn't smell nearly this funky."

Maggie squeezed her hand. "Yes, it was. The Pathway is this way." She led them away from the lake on a little trail.

Morgan could feel that they hadn't landed too far away from Maggie's condo and marveled at how much land in the city was still devoted to just trees. Of course, this would be a flood plain and therefore prohibitive to insure, but still. She hoped to return someday to explore the area more. When the trees had their leaves. She felt exposed under the naked branches.

Philippe hadn't said anything, and when Morgan looked at him, he shrugged. "Something feels off."

"I agree." Of course she had gone into hyper-alert mode when they'd arrived, but the only thing she could sense was that the air felt thick somehow. But that's how it felt around a Pathway, which connected dimensional folds.

Not thick, she corrected herself, crowded. Like when she walked through a gathering of people.

"Here we are," Maggie said. She pointed to a gazebo in

someone's backyard. "Hidden in plain sight. The humans can't activate it, so it's safe for them."

Philippe grunted and fell to his knees, a wooden stake through his shoulder. Anger flashed through Morgan—she couldn't lose him now, and she wheeled around, her knife in her hand, to defend him. But she found herself out of reach of the captain, who aimed a stone-tipped arrow at her.

"You're under arrest for the murder of Prince Elric," he said. "Round them all up."

Maggie hadn't had the chance to reach for her weapons, and one of the soldiers released her belt so that the gun and crossbow fell out of grasping range. Morgan heard her whisper an obfuscation spell so that if someone were to come across them, they'd look like an uninteresting pile of sticks.

Morgan cursed. How could they have found them? Then a man stepped out of the woods, and she got her answer. Not a man, a ghoul. Or something. He stood tall and spare to the point of being gaunt.

"Well done, Margaret," he said in a Southern accent. "I knew you'd bring them here."

"Did you set us up?" The words spilled from Morgan's tongue before her mind caught up with them. But Morgan had just decided to trust her aunt... Not that Morgan had had good judgment in the past. There was Elric.

No, Elric had tried to protect her.

Morgan blinked, the confusion whirling in her brain. So what did Maggie have to do with all this?

Morgan glared at her aunt. If the captain and another soldier hadn't been holding her arms, the possibility of this new betrayal would have knocked her to her knees.

"I didn't, I swear." But no one held on to her, like they knew she wouldn't run. "Beauregard? I wondered what happened to you."

"You know I wouldn't abandon you, my dear. But I've been

busy brokering the new alliance between the Fae and the nightmare creatures." He dragged Philippe to his feet. "You're looking well, Philippe. I have to say, this new look suits you."

"Fuck you." Philippe lunged at him, fangs extended, but Beau sidestepped him and tripped him. Philippe groaned, and Morgan tried to go to him, but her captors held her back.

"Let's go," the captain growled. They were ushered into separate waiting cars. Morgan wondered how it could have all gone so wrong, but she didn't have much time to analyze or plan on the short drive, which brought them to the area where Morgan and Philippe had first landed in Atlanta. Since the park closed at dusk, no one was there to help them. Or make the situation worse with the possibility of more innocent blood spilled.

The vehicle Morgan rode in was in the lead, so it stopped first. When they pulled her from it, she immediately looked for the others. Maggie emerged from the car with Beau. She looked unhappy, and two soldiers each had a hand clamped around her upper arm. Philippe staggered from the car he'd ridden in. Someone had bandaged his shoulder, but the glow around his eyes said he had lost blood and was getting hungry, and the proximity of fairy blood wasn't helping.

"Off we go." The soldiers holding her marched her up the trail. No matter how hard she struggled, she couldn't break away from them, and they repaid her by tightening their grips on her upper arms to bruising pressure that matched the sense of someone pressing on her inner ears. She stifled a groan and barely got a look around at the clearing before it blurred and faded. Maybe they were afraid she'd escape because they were bringing her through the Pathway first. She tried to resist the transfer, but the crisp autumn air softened to the neutral eternal springtime of Faerie. She felt like she dangled in midair before her feet settled on cobblestones, not leaf mulch. Then when the white granite walls of the queen's palace rose around Morgan, she knew she and the others were truly trapped. She bowed her head and didn't resist as she was marched to the dungeon, then shoved into a cell. She landed on her knees, which stung.

"That will teach you to defy Her Majesty," the captain growled. "And thanks for bringing the vampire. I'll be sure to let him know you were in on the plan.

"No!" She scrambled to her feet, but not fast enough. The door closed, and the boards expanded to fill the spaces between door and jamb, and an unearthly silence descended. Morgan knew that was one of the Fae's psychological tricks—most of their captives couldn't stand true silence. Although it was only made of wood, the door wouldn't be splintered except by magic. And Morgan didn't have that power back.

They'd taken her weapons from her backpack but left it in there with her. She used it as a pillow and curled up on her side, although she didn't sleep. Instead, she listened, not for noise, but for changes in the magic that flowed around her. And tried to figure out whether her aunt had betrayed her or not and whether Philippe would believe the guard and think she'd deceived him.

Gods, she hated irony.

29

After what could have been minutes or hours—time passed differently in the Faerie realm—the guards fetched Morgan from her cell and brought her into the antechamber to the throne room reserved for prisoners. Exhausted, she leaned against the wall since the room had no furniture. No comfort for the condemned. She hadn't slept at all, of course. Who could have with their entire fate hanging in the balance? Instead, she'd chased her thoughts and felt as though the pursuit had been physical.

She desperately wanted to talk to Philippe. What must he think? That she'd turned him over? Stupid Fae. And stupid Morgan. She should've figured out what Tatiana was up to when Elric had told her about Philippe.

Oh, Elric. The Fae died differently than humans, but it felt the same to her. Stuck in wherever their afterlife took place—a closely guarded Fae secret—he wouldn't be able to return to Faerie or her realm for centuries, not until he built his energy back up.

The guards brought her aunt in next. Maggie hugged Morgan when they met again and said, "I was so worried about you!" The gesture almost made Morgan cry, and Morgan knew then with certainty her aunt hadn't betrayed them. Maggie didn't say anything else, though, which Morgan appreciated. Perhaps Maggie had learned not to make false promises.

Philippe stumbled in a few minutes later and landed on his hands and knees. Although Faerie didn't technically have daylight, he was weak, possibly from his shoulder injury. Morgan wondered if he'd fed. She wanted to go to him and help him up, but she hesitated. Would he push her away? She fought her compulsion and knelt beside him.

"Need a hand?" Morgan held her breath waiting for his answer.

"Thanks." He reached out to her, and she grasped his hand, helping him first to his knees, then into a deep squat, then to standing. He leaned heavily on her. She looked into his dark eyes, afraid of what she'd see, but he only smiled.

"I'm sorry." She squeezed his hand. "I didn't know the guards were there, waiting for us. They lied."

He shook his head. "I didn't think you had betrayed me. But even if you had, I would have understood." He gestured to himself. "I'd give anything to go back to my old life."

Maggie looked away. This time Morgan felt compassion that her aunt would have to live with that mistake for the rest of her life. And others. But didn't they all have something to regret?

Before Morgan could say anything, the guards reappeared and marched them into the throne room. Tatiana sat on her throne, her golden hair up in ringlets pinned with diamonds that sparkled when she moved. Her dress, the color of a summer sky, made her look somewhat benevolent. Morgan knew better than to trust the illusion.

"I hope you've enjoyed my hospitality." Her lips spread into a smile. "It's the least I could do after what happened to Elric."

Morgan bit her tongue, almost literally. Elric had died

because he'd disagreed with the queen, but she'd never admit it. She only twisted what had happened to her advantage. Typical Fae.

"Do you know what today is, Morgan le Fay?" She sneered through Morgan's adopted title.

"It's a week after Samhain, Your Highness."

"And a very special anniversary." She leaned forward. "Whatever shall we do to celebrate? Oh, wait, I see here you've brought me the vampire I hired you to find. And just under the deadline, too." She crooked her finger, and the guards shoved Philippe forward. He fell on his knees on the steps of the throne dais. She put a finger under his chin, which was covered with perpetual day-old stubble as it had been when he'd changed, and turned his face this way and that. "Such a handsome fellow. I can see why you were attracted to him, Margaret."

Maggie only sighed but again kept her mouth shut.

"Whoops, did I get something wrong?" She looked up, her cobalt gaze narrowed. "Or did you? Let me offer you a choice, then, to redeem yourself. I'm well aware of the curse that will doom you and any lover. And I can tell you how to rid yourself of it."

Maggie took a sharp breath. Morgan squeezed her hand. That would be a tough choice. Maggie and Charlie were perfect for each other.

"And what is your price, Your Highness?" Maggie asked.

"The vampire stays here with me. As my plaything."

Philippe looked over his shoulder at the two women, his eyes wide. Morgan's heart broke for both of them. And strangely, in doing so, it healed for herself.

"No," Morgan said and stepped forward. "You will not do this to them." She spoke with as much authority as she could, but she quaked. Part of surviving had been avoiding situations where she'd risk herself for others. But Philippe had forgiven her even before he knew with certainty she hadn't betrayed him. And Maggie had changed, and Morgan realized she'd forgiven her aunt.

"Ah, Morgan. I was just about to give you your powers back." Tatiana leaned back and tapped her scepter against her palm. "But I've been concerned about doing so since it would make you the next most powerful being here aside from me. I saw this in you long ago, hence why I allowed Niniane to use you as she did. I knew it would break you."

Morgan and Maggie exchanged glances, and Morgan realized Maggie had been as much of a pawn as she had. Morgan clenched her fists, waiting for her own impossible choice. "What do you propose?"

"That you stay as you are, crippled in magic. In exchange, I will give your aunt the first clue to solving her curse and allow you to bring the vampire boy back to your realm. Or, you stay out of this and receive your powers in payment, as we agreed, for bringing him to me."

Morgan paused, thinking through the choice. Not because she considered the bargain, but because she needed to find the catch. She knew she could count on betrayal in there somewhere.

Then it dawned on her—Tatiana had admitted weakness, her concern for Morgan being at her full capacity. What had Elric said? When a Fae admitted weakness, they were distracting the listener from something way more important.

The truth struck Morgan like a lightning bolt, and she resisted the urge to smooth her arm hairs, which stood in excitement. Tatiana had screwed with her head, making her think she was getting her powers back with the queen's help, but she was regaining them as she stretched herself. And would continue to do so.

And even if not, Morgan was willing to take the chance for her aunt's happiness and Philippe's freedom in all senses of the word. If he decided not to stay with her, he deserved to live as he wished, not to be Tatiana's plaything.

Morgan lifted her chin and spoke with the authority she'd once had as a priestess of Avalon, albeit a very junior one. Her words rang through the vaulted space. "I accept your bargain. I will not ask you to return the rest of my powers to me, and in exchange, you will give my aunt what she needs and Philippe his freedom."

Tatiana's expression snapped into rage. Obviously she hadn't expected Morgan to take her up on her bargain. Margaret and Morgan exchanged a quick smile.

"Very well." Tatiana stood and pointed her scepter at Philippe. Morgan stiffened. But before she could react further, the scepter emitted a beam of golden light. It speared Philippe through his chest, and he crumpled to the ground.

"No!" Morgan felt like her own heart split in two, cleaved by a blade of regret. How could she have allowed Tatiana to trick her again? Morgan knelt beside the mortally wounded vampire.

"You are now free," Tatiana intoned in the words used for the rare Fae funeral. "May your soul fly swiftly and true."

"No, please." Morgan took Philippe's hand. "No, you can't do this. Don't leave me."

"Is. That. A. Command?" Philippe asked, and when he coughed, blood bubbled to his lips. Morgan's blood. It sang to her, a whispered treble note in the air between them, but she ignored it.

"Yes. No. I don't want you to live a half-life as a zombie." She searched for the solution—what could she do to save him? His skin warmed under hers, and she knew he would combust soon if she didn't do something.

Tatiana's mocking laughter continued, and the Fae in the throne room joined in, the sound melodious and jarring. "Oh, this is too rich. Did you fall for him, Morgan?" She wiped tears from her cheeks. "You, the commander of the nightmare creatures falling for one. I should have known."

Another slip. That's right, Morgan could command the nightmares. She looked around the throne room. They stood in the background, obviously having been shoved aside so the queen could look upon her beautiful subjects. That infuriated Morgan more—who was Tatiana to decide who was worthy of being seen?

The link Morgan had with Philippe after he'd drunk from her and after they'd made love told her he was fading quickly. What could she do? She focused on the block that had been in her soul since that night she'd unknowingly committed incest and finally saw the disappearance of her powers for what it was —an unnecessary atonement for what she'd unwittingly done. It shrank to insignificance, and her powers—all of them— flooded through her. She looked for the one she knew she needed the most at this moment, the power to call the life force of fire and to command it to heal or destroy.

She bent down to kiss Philippe, prompting more peals of derisive laughter. When she did, she poured the power of fire/life into him and harnessed the combustion process that threatened to turn him into ash. The hole in his chest healed, and when she peeked, red sparks whirled in her peripheral vision. The laughter turned into horrified gasps.

"What is this?" Tatiana asked.

Morgan pulled away from Philippe and helped him to stand. She lifted her hand. "Nightmare creatures, stand ready!"

They moved forward from the shadows. There were more than she realized. They all looked at her—lagoon creatures dripping fetid salt water, vampires with their fangs extended and eyes aglow, werewolves with their mouths open and tongues lolling in their half-human forms. And ghosts and ghouls and all manner of things that go bump in the night.

"What are you doing?" Tatiana's question ended on a breathless squeak.

Morgan didn't know how long she could hold the creatures in thrall, but Maggie took her hand, lending her strength. "You will stop allowing them passage through Faerie to the waking world, give my aunt the key to breaking her curse, and you will then allow all of us to go free. Healthy, alive, and free," Morgan clarified.

"Or what?"

"Or I will have the nightmare creatures commit a slaughter so massive it will go down in the annals of Fae history."

The gathered courtiers looked around nervously, but all the exits were blocked by something mean and hungry-looking.

"Very well." Tatiana sighed and sat back on her throne. "You may go, vampire. Good luck. Fledglings don't last long without direction. As for you..." Now she pointed the jeweled scepter at Margaret. "The first key to the answer you seek is in your hand. The second is just within reach, and the third can be found in the Library of the Heart, which, as you know, you approach at your peril." She smiled, but it wasn't a nice one. "Make sure what you want is really worth it, Margaret. You know there will be a price."

"Library?" Philippe whispered to her. "What kind of library isn't free?"

"She must mean the Library at the Heart of the World," Morgan whispered back. "And it holds the answer to every question ever asked, and more. Consequently, it's heavily guarded to keep out those who seek their own gain over true knowledge. This is a tricky question."

"Thank you." Margaret bowed, no sign of what she felt evident in her expression. Morgan couldn't help but grin with pride for her. And she made a silent promise to help.

"You're welcome." Tatiana smiled. "Is that all, Morgan?"

"Yes." Morgan dropped her hand, and the nightmare creatures stood down, many of them shaking their heads. Were they not there of their own volition?

Tatiana looked at the slender timepiece she wore on her wrist. "That should do. And you all are dismissed." She stood, and like a demented fairy godmother, smiled and waved her scepter. The walls of the palace faded around them, and Maggie, Philippe, and Morgan found themselves standing in the middle of the woods where they'd been taken. The cold air slammed into them, and Morgan shivered, but she didn't care.

Had she really just survived an encounter with the Fae queen and come out with more than she'd hoped? Would someone else pay a price?

Morgan looked around and hoped the nightmare creatures hadn't been hurt in Faerie. Then she saw a lagoon creature, who bowed to her and disappeared in a puff of sulfur smoke. Morgan sensed it had returned to its own realm.

The air had more of a chill than the last time they were there, and the trees didn't give them any time clues since they'd already lost their leaves.

"Do you know what the date and time are?" Maggie asked.

Morgan pulled out her phone. "It's 10:00 p.m. The same night we left."

"Good." Maggie sagged against a tree. "I was afraid we'd been gone for years." She shook her head. "The last key would be in the Library."

"I'll help," Morgan said. She looked up. "You deserve your happily ever after, at least for this lifetime."

"Do I?" Maggie stood and walked over to Morgan. She put both hands on her niece's shoulders. "After all the harm I've caused, especially to you, do I, Morgan?" She blinked and rubbed her eyes with the backs of her hands. "Can you ever forgive me?"

Morgan said the three words she never thought she'd speak. "I forgive you."

Just as the air had been thick with the hard feelings between them, now it almost shimmered with their release. Maggie smiled as her shoulders slumped, losing some of the tension Morgan had always observed in them. "Thank you. That means more to me than I can ever tell you." She took Morgan into her arms, and Philippe joined them in the group hug. "Then let's go tell Charlie. We have a journey to prepare for." Then she stopped. "Oh, crap, I just realized why today felt so familiar. Tatiana mentioning Niniane shook the memory loose."

Morgan smoothed the hairs on her arms. "What is it?"

Maggie looked at her. "You don't know?"

But Morgan did, and dread rooted her to the spot. She'd only been a small child, but she remembered that particular night clearly. The feeling had been too strong and consistent to be simple déjà vu. "It feels the same as the night you and Morgause brought Uther to my mother. And Arthur was conceived." She closed her eyes so she could better feel the current of magic, which was subtle but still there in the modern world. "It hasn't happened yet."

Maggie nodded. "We have to find Audrey and Damien. They can't consummate their relationship tonight." She grabbed the others' hands. "Hold on. We're going to Audrey's. And if she's not home, Charlie's. He'll know where Damien lives."

MAGGIE ZAPPED them to Audrey's place, and when they found it empty, to Charlie's place. Charlie answered the door looking— thankfully—healthy and whole.

"We have a problem," Maggie said. "We need to stop a disaster from happening. Where does Damien live?"

"Virginia Highlands area. In a basement apartment. Why? What do we need to stop?"

"The thing the Fae have been aiming for all along. At least now they've revealed what they're after, so we have the advantage. To a point."

"Wait, what?" Charlie followed Maggie to his car and tried to call Damien. It went straight to voicemail.

"I finally remembered what's familiar about this evening, the feel of it." She hopped in the driver's seat. "Give me the keys."

He didn't argue—smart man. Morgan and Philippe crawled into the back seat. Charlie handed the keys to Maggie, entered on the passenger side, and had just barely buckled himself in when she took off. Maggie wheeled around and headed out. A gust of wind rocked the car, and Maggie dodged as a tree came down from the side. A shower of sparks and a loud bang said a transformer blew behind them. Of course they'd be pursued. She didn't slow the car, and Charlie held on to both the oh-shit handle and door as she careened into traffic and whipped left to turn on to the next street.

"And did someone try to kill you the last time, too?" Charlie asked. He'd texted Damien, but Maggie suspected his attempts to communicate weren't getting through for whatever reason.

"No, but that's because I was doing what they wanted me to do." She wove in and out of traffic like something chased her, and she muttered a curse and a spell when they approached the light at the six-way intersection at Scott, North Decatur, and Medlock. The light turned from green to yellow and held at yellow for one second. Two seconds. Maggie wiped her right hand on her pants, leaving a sweaty streak. Three seconds. She put more force behind the spell, switching from English to Celtic. Four seconds. She gunned it, turned left again. She glanced in the rearview mirror to see if it had changed, and the traffic light itself popped, let out a plume of smoke, and went dark.

"I'm going to have to do some explaining about that to the guys in Dekalb," Charlie said.

Maggie shrugged. "You won't be able to tell them the truth. That's the problem with this job."

"I'll come up with something. Got any advice?"

She smiled and shook her head. "You'll figure it out when the time comes."

"So are you going to explain why we're going to interfere with my friend's sex life? I'm assuming that's what he and Audrey are going to do."

"The Fae can only spend as much magic as they did this week very occasionally. Like every thousand years or so. It weakens the queen, and it takes her a while to recover. The last time they did this—" She hit the gas so they'd make another yellow light, which they did just barely, the third one in a row.

"There probably weren't cars to be driven like a madwoman," Charlie grumbled, but he sounded like he was having fun.

She smirked. "No, just carts and horses. Which we did, Merlin and I. To sneak a certain king in to see a certain duchess who was married to someone else."

"You're talking about the night Arthur was conceived."

"Bingo."

"So wait—what are they doing with Audrey and Damien?"

"No human comes away from an encounter with Zeus unscathed, and he's known for impregnating human females in nontraditional ways. Maybe all it will take is a sexual encounter here to make it happen. The Fae are aiming for the birth of a new King Arthur, who will bring the power of magic back into the world. They want to steal and control the child."

Maggie had to slow the car as they got closer to Virginia Highlands because the area became more congested. She drummed her fingers on the steering wheel. Charlie tried to text and call again, but his efforts were futile. Finally, when they got off the main road, she sped up, and they pulled up behind Damien's beat up Civic.

Charlie got out of the car as Maggie set the parking brake and ran to the door of the basement apartment, which was around the side of the house. It was locked, of course, and he pounded on it. She thought she could hear running water.

"I think they're in the shower," he told Maggie when she joined him. The look he gave her made her wonder what it would be like to have him in the shower, and—*focus, Margaret.* Morgan and Philippe joined them.

"Can you break the door down?" Morgan asked. Her face had gone pale, and although she'd forgiven Maggie for everything she'd done to her, Maggie hated to think how many bad memories this situation must be bringing up for her. Or maybe she was carsick.

Before Charlie could reply, the window above them opened, and an older woman looked down. Gravity and time had pulled the lines of her face long, and her frown deepened them.

"What's all the racket down there? I told Officer Lewis not to bring his work home with him. Go away!"

"Ma'am, this is an urgent matter," Charlie said and showed her his badge. "We believe Officer Lewis might be in danger."

"Of what? Having a good time? I saw him go in there with that young lady. She's fine. They've been seeing each other for weeks."

Maggie took off her glasses and put a hand on Charlie's arm. "Ma'am, I'm really sorry to bother you, but he may be gravely ill and not realize it. Can you help us get in?"

"No, lost the spare key a week ago. But I can get him out of the shower so he'll hear you." She disappeared from the window, and Maggie counted the seconds, her heart beating in triple time against the small ticks from Charlie's watch. The landlady's wizened face reappeared. "Give it a minute. He's used too much damn water tonight anyway."

A shout of dismay came from inside Damien's apartment, and the water shut off. Charlie knocked as Maggie asked, "What did you do?"

"Shut off the hot water." She grinned, showing not too many teeth. "That'll deflate his pecker and get him moving. Now do what you need and get off my property."

She slammed the window as Damien opened the door wearing only jeans. His hair was wet, and suds still clung to his shoulder.

"What is it?" he asked. "I just looked at the phone and saw your texts."

Maggie looked him up and down, her heart sinking. He looked happy and satisfied and—

"Did you and Audrey have sex?"

Damien folded his arms over his chest. "That's none of your business."

"I'm afraid it is," she said.

"Yes," he finally said. "We were enjoying ourselves with some afterplay in the shower when the water went cold. Then when I came out, I heard the knocking and saw the texts."

Audrey pushed past him, and if Damien was irritated, she looked downright pissed off. "What the hell is going on?"

"I'm sorry," Maggie said. "Something is going on with the Fae."

Audrey shoved her wet hair from her face. Her clothes had wet spots and looked like they'd been thrown on in a hurry. "Something is always happening with them. That's what they do." She enunciated the words. "What does that have to do with us?"

"They wanted you to have sex and conceive the next King Arthur," Charlie said. "Or something like that." He gave Maggie a sideways glance. She recognized how odd it sounded to talk about such things under electric streetlights with them all carrying little computers in their pockets.

Now Audrey and Damien turned to Maggie, their expressions incredulous. "That's the most ridiculous thing I've ever heard," Audrey said. "I'm on birth control."

"They're powerful," Maggie interjected. She sent a pleading glance Charlie's way. "They could potentially do something to make it not work. Remember, at their hearts, they're nature spirits, and they excel at manipulating natural processes."

"Well, what's done is done," Damien said and put his arm around Audrey. "Goodnight, all." And he shut the door in their faces.

"I guess we deserved that," Charlie said. He put his arm around Maggie, and she wanted to find it comforting, but her thoughts whirled. What should she do now? What if Audrey did turn up pregnant?

And what, if anything, should or could she do about it? She couldn't help it—her shoulders slumped in defeat.

"Hey," Charlie said and tilted her face up to his. "You're not alone in this."

"Not at all," Morgan added. She and Philippe held hands. "We'll help in whatever way we can. Assuming you'll let us continue to stay with you until we can figure out what we need to do."

Maggie turned to look at all of them. "You don't have to. This is my fault. I allowed myself to get distracted." She looked at Philippe. "Again."

"You can't save the world by yourself," Charlie told her. "And you don't have to."

She allowed him to fold her into his arms and closed her eyes. Maybe she didn't have to face everything alone. But how was she going to handle this new wrinkle and solve her curse?

She'd figure it out. She always did. At least now she had help.

30

Audrey and Morgan looked into the pool in the field that Maggie had been using as Audrey's training ground.

"Show me the were-bat," Audrey said, and then held her breath. The breeze rippled the surface of the water, and as before, gray clouds gathered overhead. Also as before, something filmed the surface of the water. As they'd all expected. Audrey exhaled—expected was good—and nodded to Morgan.

Morgan inhaled and then blew on the water before saying, "Obfuscation, begone." The were-bat appeared in what looked like a section of woods. A circle of glowing mushrooms and an old smelting chimney came into view as well.

"It's hanging out near the Pathway," Morgan said. "The one I took here. It's probably trying to get home."

Audrey nodded. "That makes sense. We need to tell Maggie and the others."

"Wait here and watch it. I'll be right back." Morgan vanished in a puff of smoke, which she said she could only do from the C.U. Audrey shook her head. She suspected her friend liked stretching her magical abilities now that she had them back.

Audrey turned her attention back to the pool. Although it would take the team time to drive and then hike to the site, Audrey didn't have to wait long, thanks to the way time bent in the Collective Unconscious. Maggie, Charlie, and Damien entered the clearing. Now Audrey put a hand to her heart and said a prayer for all their safety, especially Damien's. Morgan popped back in beside her.

"Is it still there?" she asked.

"Yep."

Audrey couldn't look away. The were-bat looked disoriented, and she wondered if the Fae blood it had ingested had made it ill. And even more unpredictable. The others seemed to think so as well.

They held hands, Maggie in the middle. Audrey could see the telepathic words floating between them. They all seemed reluctant to harm a sick creature, but they also knew it would become more violent as it worsened. She watched them plan their strategy.

"That will work, right?"

Morgan nodded and squeezed Audrey's hand. "Sometimes simple is best."

Finally, they spread out to surround the were-bat. Maggie said some sort of spell in a language Audrey didn't recognize. As she spoke, a golden glow surrounded the nightmare creature, which howled, its distress increasing with the intensity of the glare trapping it. Then Damien and Charlie shot it. It combusted into flames, but green ones rather than the usual fire colors of orange, yellow, and red.

"She did something to allow it to go straight back to the realm of nightmares," Morgan said. "It shouldn't have to pass through Faerie to get back there, and it won't be able to get back here."

"Good." Audrey relaxed and rolled her shoulders. They were tight even here in the C.U.

"Great job locating it, by the way," Morgan told her. "You're getting better and better at this."

"Thanks." Audrey stood. "I'm glad I can finally help." And she was. Even better, now that she had gained her magical security clearance, she and Damien didn't have to keep secrets from each other anymore. She smiled—she couldn't wait for him to come join her so they could celebrate the banishment of the were-bat. And since Morgan had forced the Fae queen into their bargain, no more had come through.

A FEW WEEKS LATER...

"OH, good, the stuffing is almost ready."

Morgan looked up from the copy of Rolling Stone she'd been flipping through. "How can you tell?"

Audrey took an exaggerated sniff. "Can't you smell it?"

"Well, yes, but I've been smelling it for the last twenty minutes." Morgan patted her growling stomach. "Doesn't it have ten more to go?"

"No, it smells just about done." Audrey stood and stretched. "I've always cooked with my nose, but it's been really sensitive lately. Maybe all that time we've spent in the C.U.?" She didn't wait for an answer, just went into the kitchen to check the stuffing, which would really be dressing for the turkey at Maggie's later. They were waiting until sunset to celebrate Thanksgiving so Philippe could be a part of it, even if he couldn't eat anything.

Maggie had shooed Morgan out so she could have some time to herself to decorate and relax before everyone came over. Morgan didn't blame her—they'd been spending a lot of time together. Morgan, having shown dream weaver potential in the past, had joined in on the training sessions in the Collective Unconscious, and Audrey had gotten much better with the competition. Outside of that, she and Maggie had been trying to solve the riddle of the keys to Maggie's curse and to do rituals—safe ones—to find Merlin. So far they hadn't had any luck, but Morgan was willing to keep trying. She'd gotten good at figuring out puzzles and finding people.

Meanwhile, she'd been back to New Orleans to check on the shop and had found Lacey to be perfectly capable of managing it. Somehow she'd even managed to turn a bigger profit. Morgan had given the girl a raise and hinted the shop may be hers someday.

And perhaps Maggie wanted to share a glass of wine with Charlie. Morgan thought she'd seen him coming up the street carrying a wine bag when she'd left. Good. Maggie smiled a lot more when Charlie was around, and he seemed to not suffer any lasting ill effects from the fae-fire.

Morgan sipped her own wine and noticed Audrey had hardly touched hers. Morgan had been relieved when she saw Audrey drinking—surely that meant she wasn't pregnant. Like the others, Morgan hoped they'd managed to foil the Fae's involvement in Audrey's and Damien's relationship, but she wasn't sure. One never could be with *them*. Even if their plan had backfired, and now Maggie and the others watched over Audrey to the point that Audrey had confided in Morgan she felt like a goldfish in a bowl.

"Yep, done!" Audrey called. "What temperature does the oven need to be on for the cookies?"

"Three seventy-five." Morgan stood and drained the last sip of wine from her glass. "I'm going to grab more Chardonnay. Do you want any?"

"No thanks, I'm not feeling it today. My stomach's been off."

A chill made the little hairs at the nape of Morgan's neck stand. "Are you okay?"

Audrey poked her head out of the kitchen and rolled her eyes. "Not you, too. And I'm fine. Peed on a stick this morning. It was negative. I've been buying so many pregnancy tests I think the clerks at CVS think I'm trying to get pregnant."

"At least you're being careful." A slight pressure on Morgan's hip made her look down to see Athena the cat sitting on her haunches, her paw on Morgan's pocket. Her eyes pleaded, but for what, Morgan didn't know. She scratched the cat behind the ears, and Athena purred and slow-blinked.

"No cookies for you," Morgan told her. "Or oyster dressing."

Although it had been a few weeks since her powers returned, Morgan still hadn't become accustomed to her new abilities or senses. She knew the cat tried to communicate with her, but she couldn't figure out what or why. Nor had Athena spoken in Morgan's head again like she had that one afternoon.

"Maybe a cat is just a cat," she murmured to herself. Athena dug her claws into Morgan's jeans. "Hey!"

"What?" Audrey walked out of the kitchen. "Are you okay?"

"Yes, I think so." She looked at Athena and said telepathically, *"Message received. I'll keep one eye on her and the other alert for danger."*

Athena rubbed against Morgan's leg before jumping off the sofa and on to her window perch. Morgan rubbed her leg through her jeans. Would Philippe be jealous someone else had drawn blood?

"I pulled the sable cookie dough out of the freezer," Audrey told her. "It's all ready for you."

"Thanks."

Later that evening, as they all waited for the turkey to rest and the last bits of Thanksgiving dinner to heat, Morgan looked around. Charlie teased Maggie in the kitchen. Maggie threatened to do something to him with the meat thermometer in response. Audrey and Damien snuggled on the couch and talked about the old movie that was on the television. And

Morgan and Philippe sat on the loveseat. She held a glass of wine, and he had his arm around her. Since she'd given him her fire, he had ceased being vampire-cold.

For the first time in over a millennium, Morgan felt truly thankful for her life and circumstances. Audrey winked at her, and Morgan grinned. Whatever happened from this point on, she knew none of them would have to handle it by themselves. And for the first time in her life, Morgan wasn't afraid to depend on someone else...or have another person rely on her.

Maybe family wasn't so bad after all.

AUTHOR'S NOTE

Thank you for reading Web of Truth! I hope you enjoyed it. As more and more books come into the market, it gets increasingly difficult for my books to be found by other readers who may like them. Reviews are one way an author can stand out from the crowd, so I would be so grateful if you would leave a review on Goodreads and/or the web site where you ordered the book. Even a single sentence is great and so very helpful. Thank you so much!

ABOUT THE AUTHOR

Cecilia Dominic wrote her first story when she was two years old and has always had a much more interesting life inside her head than outside of it. She became a clinical psychologist because she's fascinated by people and their stories, but she couldn't stop writing fiction. The first draft of her dissertation, while not fiction, was still criticized by her major professor for being written in too entertaining a style. She made it through graduate school and got her PhD, started her own practice, and by day, she helps people cure their insomnia without using medication. By night, she blogs about wine and writes fiction she hopes will keep her readers turning the pages all night. Yes, she recognizes the conflict of interest between her two careers, so she writes and blogs under a pen name. She lives in Atlanta, Georgia with one husband and two cats, which, she's been told, is a good number of each. She also enjoys putting her psychological expertise to good use helping other authors through her Characters on the Couch blog post series.

Find Cecilia Online

Mailing List (you'll receive a free short story set in the same universe as this series – excerpt below): https://www.subscribepage.com/CDbackofbookWebsite

Facebook - CeciliaDominicAuthor

Twitter - @ceciliadominic

Instagram - @randomoenophile

You can also look for Cecilia on Goodreads and Pinterest.

Cecilia's books available everywhere e-books are sold. Look for paperbacks in select brick-and-mortar stores. They can also be ordered online via most major retailers or (coming soon) from her website.

If you'd like to see what exactly happened between Maggie and Philippe in the first book in the Dream Weavers and Truth Seekers series *Truth Seeker*, please continue reading for an excerpt or grab a copy.

ABOUT TRUTH SEEKER - OR, WHAT DID HAPPEN TO PHILIPPE?

Dream Weavers & Truth Seekers Prequel Novella

Any second now...

Phillippe's watch had stopped fifteen coffee shops ago. One of those "atomic clock" things that re-set itself according to time zone, it had given up. He hoped it wouldn't detonate in a mini mushroom cloud on his wrist.

He slouched in his chair, his back against the display case of blue and silver coffee and travel mugs. Snow swirled outside the window and obscured what he assumed was the business district of a medium to large city. He would have preferred to sit in a warm corner away from the window, but at this point information equaled survival.

In spite of his annoyance, he willed the muscles in his face to be pleasantly neutral. He didn't want to draw any more attention than he already did with his lack of overcoat and snow boots. Maybe people would think he came from some northern clime where people were more accustomed to the cold. He wore his black tennis shoes, blue jeans, green T-shirt, and open flannel under a blue denim jacket. Philippe, just as glad he wouldn't have to go outside, wondered what *she* would wear this time. The only constants in her wardrobe were colored lenses and all black clothing. He had never seen her eyes without the glasses.

No matter what jump he made, she always arrived twenty minutes after him. They never spoke or acknowledged each other's existence, but she always gave him a clue as to where he was. He guessed that he was in Ohio or north-central Kentucky from the assortment of Cincinnati, Cleveland, and Kentucky papers left at the front or on the tables. That would fit with the weather and the neutral Midwest accents.

He thought about the chart he'd made on the back of a napkin of all the places he'd been since he'd stumbled into this unique mode of travel. What had begun as an accident was now a game of cat and mouse, and Philippe imagined the jaws of the trap as they closed a little more each time he used the tunnels. He wasn't sure that *they* knew who he was, and he had no clue about *their* identity. His one certainty was that he hadn't been back to his origin point. Now he wanted to solve the puzzle so he could bail out somewhere close to home in the Northwest.

He glanced at his watch, remembered it didn't work, and looked at the clock. Any second now...

The door opened with a whoosh of cold air, and *she* walked in. Philippe's resolve cracked, and he smiled at her windblown beauty. Her long, thick strawberry blond hair hung straight and breeze-tousled below her black beret, and blue-tinted lenses partially hid her eyes. He sat straighter as she studied the pastries. He knew every one of them intimately by now, but he didn't dare make a recommendation. She waited for the portly lady in front of her to pay for a hot tea and scone and ordered a tall nonfat latte. The barista told her the total.

"$2.55, please. Are you having a good day?"

"I am, thank you." She smiled. "Everyone seems so friendly here in Cincinnati."

Philippe snuck his napkin out and made a notation—he'd been right.

The barista returned the girl's smile. "We have our meanies, but in general, yes, we're pretty nice."

Philippe studied his makeshift map, unable to discern a pattern. The locations ranged from small towns to large metropolises. He rarely landed in the same state twice a day, and he never left the shops for fear that he would be stranded.

The air changed—a low hum that he felt in his bones from his jaw to his tailbone to his feet. Time to go. The sensation propelled him out of his chair. He threw away his white cardboard cup and folded the newspaper he'd left at his table. On a whim, he took out his pen and scrawled a note on a paper napkin, which he dropped by the spiked wooden heel of the redheaded woman's left boot as he walked past.

The storeroom of the coffee shop was located off a small hallway. Philippe wondered if he would ever be able to tolerate the smell of coffee beans again after he got out of this mess. Burlap sacks lined the walls of the small closet, regular to the right, decaf to the left, and espresso in the back. One of them glowed a warm mocha, the aroma of coffee translated to a visual sensation. He looked over his shoulder one more time and touched the rough burlap sack.

The glow moved up his arm—a warm, electric tingle and all his hairs stood on end. The room receded into a dark brown fog, the bag melting away under his pinching fingers. He peered into the tunnels, a series of hallways diffused with coffee-colored light. His footsteps made no sound as he ran down the hall, the sense of someone after him even stronger this time. There was one door, which he yanked open. He could almost feel the breath of his pursuer on his neck as he tumbled out on to the burlap sacks, and he finally felt he could exhale without someone hearing him.

He pictured himself as a rodent who crept through the shadows of that strange world, glimpsed in the peripheral vision, but gone before seen.

This new closet opened on to a long, red-tiled hallway. He made sure no one was around, then slipped out and turned to the left. What luck—restrooms! The ones in the last place had been outside the store, which he'd been afraid to leave. He went into the men's room and stood at a urinal. A young man in a suit came in with a wheeled carry-on and laptop case. Philippe looked away. Two more men came in, both with luggage, and a middle-aged guy with a little boy. The kid pulled a miniature red and yellow wheeled carry-on behind him.

Philippe exited the bathroom and the hallway to find ticket counters. This was his first airport stop, and he noted that on his napkin. Security guards patrolled the checkpoint and kept watch at strategic intervals. For the first time in days, Philippe felt safe, and he didn't even need the redhead to tell him where he was this time. A sign over the exit blinked, "Welcome to San Antonio!"

He pondered his options. He didn't make enough money at his waiter day job or cover band night job to pay for an airline ticket home. With a thrill, he wondered if the redhead had read his note or if she'd even noticed it. He strolled into the coffee-shop to wait. Sleep deprivation made him incautious, and he forgot to order something before he sat down.

"The seating area is for patrons only, sir," one of the baristas snapped.

"I'm waiting for a friend."

Philippe studied his list. Downtown Cincinnati to the San Antonio Airport. Even though he hadn't had a choice, he felt pleased. At least it was warm here. He imagined what it would be like to just walk outside, catch a shuttle to the Riverwalk, and have some real food and a margarita. He guessed this place would be open all night, or at least most of it, and he could sneak back into the closet whenever it called to him. He hoped.

"You're getting careless, Philippe."

He jumped up and found himself face-to-face with the redhead. She wore the same all-back outfit as in Cincinnati, except she carried the sweater and wore a black spaghetti-strap top under the leather jacket. This time her sunglasses had light purple lenses. She tossed his note on the table, and his scrawl mocked him with what must have seemed desperate words —*Talk to me, please – Philippe.*

"Now that we've met, I can buy you a cup of coffee," he offered.

"You've been traversing the tunnels for four days now." She looked at him, and he realized how disheveled he must appear. "Allow me to buy you dinner."

Four burritos, a margarita, and a chalupa later, Philippe was ready to talk. The woman, who had introduced herself as "Margaret, but everyone calls me Maggie. Don't even think of calling me Mags," sat across from him and picked at her taco salad. He'd panicked for a moment when they left the airport and the coffee shop—was he shutting himself off from his only route home?—but he sensed he could trust her.

"You've hardly touched your sangria," Philippe said. Or thought he did. The earth tilted, and his tongue felt loose in his head. He'd been stupid to order the margarita, but he needed to unwind.

"I'm not supposed to drink on the job." She smiled. "But you can. First question: how did you end up in the tunnels?"

Philippe wished he could make full eye contact, but even though they sat in shadow, she wore her purple lenses.

"A couple of my buddies and me went for coffee after work

on Monday," he explained. "One of them, Arnie, dared me to slip past the baristas into the back and snitch some beans."

Maggie raised an eyebrow.

"Childish, I know." His cheeks heated. "I went, but someone came in behind me, so I looked for a place to hide. I ducked into the closet and decided, while I was in there, to just grab some beans from one of the sacks." He paused and tried to figure out how to explain what had happened next.

"Go on." She leaned forward.

"I found one with a little hole in it, and then this warm tingly feeling washed up my arm, and then, whoosh, I was in this place full of tunnels and doors." He watched her. Was she buying it?

She looked over her glasses at him.

What the hell? Her eyes were yellow. No, gold.

"What happened then?"

He had to keep going. The words spilled from him before he could help it. "I freaked out and opened the first door I came to. Let me tell you, I was surprised as hell to find myself in someplace with palm trees."

Maggie pushed her glasses up her nose. "Sorry, they slip. Go on."

Maybe he'd been so sleep-deprived he'd dreamed up her weird eyes. They looked normal now. "So then I took a few minutes to get my bearings and figure out where I was by looking at the papers. Tampa, Florida. Across the freakin' country." Now he looked at her to make sure she didn't think he was nuts.

"That's not surprising. Go on."

"Well, then a bus full of old people pulled up, and they stampeded inside, so I took the chance to go back to the storeroom and try to find my way back. This time I saw the bag glow, so I touched it, and zap! Back in the tunnels."

"Did you have any idea what you needed to do to get back?"

Philippe shook his head. "I just kept trying, figuring that I would get to the right one eventually."

"Your friends are really worried about you." She leaned back and studied him with crossed arms. "When you didn't reappear from the back, they told the baristas, who looked for you. A day later, you were listed as a missing person. A buddy of mine at the police station saw how you'd disappeared and gave me a call."

"Are you the coffee police?"

Maggie chuckled, a sound like wind-chimes. "Hardly. I've been trying to get into those tunnels for almost a year now. I even took a job as a barista, but I got fired for some spurious reason."

He knew how that went. "So what do you have to do with all this if you're not the one who built the tunnels?"

"I'm afraid I can't divulge that right now. Let's just say that my organization is not the only one that's very interested in you."

Philippe's heart thudded, although her statement confirmed what he'd sensed. "Me? Why?"

"You're the first unauthorized breach of the tunnels, and the builders, and whoever's behind them, are panicking. They would like to interrogate you, I'm sure."

"I have some questions for them." Philippe's face flushed. "They had no right to keep me from getting home."

"And if they caught you, they'd kill you, so being trapped away from home is the least of your worries." She fiddled with her napkin and spoke in a low, intense tone. "It's how they think, Philippe. They consider you to be equivalent to an animal, like a research rat who's escaped. They figured that if they kept you running scared and away from home, they could catch up to you. Luckily I did first."

He checked to find the nearest exit. "What do *you* want with me?"

"I want to know everything in the smallest detail, what the tunnels are like, how you get in them, how you get out, and how they work. I want to know who built them, what their purpose is, and how to destroy them."

"You're a lady with a lot of questions." Philippe yawned. "Can we talk about this later? I've been running on caffeine and sugar for the past four days."

Maggie nodded, pulled a black leather wallet out of her jacket, and laid down enough cash to cover the meals and leave a tip. She stood and gestured for him to do likewise.

"I have a good friend here. We can stay with him. If anyone asks, we'll tell them you're my boyfriend."

She turned, and Philippe studied her slender back and nice ass. "No problem."

Rat or no, he liked this maze.

Truth Seeker is now available in paperback. You can find it through your favorite book retailer or have your local bookstore order it from Ingram using ISBN 978-1-945074-45-5

BONUS STORY

Please enjoy this preview of *Perchance to Dream,* a Dream Weavers and Truth-Seekers story...

Emma stood in the doorway and squinted into the peach-colored light that had appeared without warning to disrupt her sleep. She put a hand out to steady herself and snatched it back when she touched the rough-hewn wooden door frame. The walls of the room seemed to have just been put up, the beige dry wall barely set. Sawdust and wooden curls littered the plywood floor. The sounds of others murmuring and moving about reached her ears. She backed up until her back touched the wall and...

Emma woke, her hands still clenched. She lay in bed, awakened by her husband bumping into her. He rolled away when she gently shoved him back. She snuggled into the flannel sheets, twitched her shoulder blades until they were comfortable, and closed her eyes. With a sigh, she slept...

...and found herself back in the room, standing in the door. What kind of hella-vivid dream was this? The sweet-sharp smell of the wood filled her nose, but at least the sawdust on the rough plywood floor didn't make her sneeze. Normally in her dreams she had difficulty moving, but this was no different than her waking life. She walked through the room and found a door on the other side, also unfinished, and a hallway. More rooms lined the hall, some with only wooden framing, others further along but not complete.

Voices carried down the hall, lively conversations and laughter. This comforted and frightened her simultaneously. Where were these people? She heard footsteps behind her and turned around...

...and woke again to the sound of a car alarm going off outside the window.

"Just effing steal it already," Greg mumbled into a snore. Emma nudged him.

"Turn over," she said. He did. She didn't want to go back to sleep, but drowsiness overtook her...

She found herself in the same doorframe in the same room off the same hall. *What the hell?* She knew that in the past, she had continued a dream upon awakening once, but twice was unheard of.

"Oh, there you are."

She spun around and found herself face to face with a person, mid-twenties, who seemed to be simultaneously gender-less and dual gendered. Slender and with dark hair, they wore a simple tunic and pants outfit of navy blue. The person's large brown eyes captivated her, as they seemed to belong to someone far older than the chronological age of the rest of the being.

"Who are you?"

"Adrian." The person's voice gave no clue as to gender, as it could be a low-pitched female's or tenor male's.

"I'm Emma."

"I know. Lucy told me about you."

"Lucy?"

"The Madam Lucia? The psychic you spoke with today? Yesterday, actually."

Emma shook her head. She knew that had been a bad idea, but, really, what could she have done?

She'd gone to Target for packing supplies and was headed back on Highway 29 when her cell phone rang. Lightning overhead had made the reception poor, but she could hear the voice of Grace, her mother-in-law.

"Hello, Emma," Grace snapped. "Is this a bad time?"

The corners of Emma's mouth tightened. "Yes, actually."

"Well, I won't keep you but a second. Is my son there?"

"I'm driving right now. In the rain." *And Greg's at work, as you well know.*

"I just wanted to ask him if this would be a good weekend for us to come see the house. We're so excited for you."

Of course she'd called to ask him, not them. "We're excited, too, but we need to see how the move goes before we can make any plans. As it stands now, we're planning on having a house-warming party at the end of the month."

Emma swerved to miss a puddle and earned a honk from a driver whose lane she'd invaded.

"Sure, but don't you want us to come up before that? To help out?"

Not really. "I really appreciate the offer, but I'm sure we'll be fine."

"Well, I'll just talk to Greg and see what he says. Go on with your errands, and we'll see you soon."

Emma sighed and tossed the telephone into the passenger

seat. She knew how it would all play out. Grace would call Greg and guilt trip him for not inviting them up before the house-warming—*"But honey, don't you want to spend time with us?"*—and then they would come and pick and nag—*"I don't mean to tell you how to set up your kitchen, but I've had my glasses in the cabinet by the sink, and it's just worked out so well for me for twenty years"*—and do it so sweetly that protesting would make her, Emma, look like the bitchy, ungrateful daughter-in-law.

She hadn't seen the glass bottle until she rolled over it and heard the pop under the right rear tire. The car groaned and pulled to the right. She drove into the first parking lot, put her forehead on the steering wheel, and cried in frustration.

A tap on her window startled her, and she looked up to see a tall, dark-skinned woman dressed in blue jeans and a black linen top embroidered with flowers in red metallic thread. The woman wore her hair long and in braids, and it faded from copper-colored at her crown to blonde at the bottom. She looked at Emma with friendly black eyes.

"You are having a rough day, yes?" she asked in a lilting accent.

Emma looked up and saw that her car was one of two parked in front of a small whitewashed frame house with purple curtains in the windows. The sign over the door said, "Madame Lucia, Palm Reading $5."

"Yes," she sniffled.

"Come inside, and you can call a tow truck from there."

Emma straightened. Did everyone think she was completely helpless? "Thanks, but I can change a tire."

"Then let me help you." Madame Lucia, Emma presumed, held a large red and white golf umbrella. She helped Emma change the tire—an unwieldy process since it involved unloading and reloading the trunk. By the end of it, Emma felt doubly grateful she'd had someone to hold an umbrella over her.

"Um, thanks," Emma said once they'd completed the task. The woman inclined her head. "Do you have anywhere I could wash my hands?" Emma held up her grease- and dirt-stained fingers.

"Of course. I have a bathroom inside. You may clean up there."

When Emma emerged from the bathroom, Madame Lucia had an old-fashioned tea set on the small coffee table in the living room. Emma thought of excuses she could make to leave, but her growling stomach gave her away.

"This is all really very nice," she said, "but..."

"But nothing. It is a slow afternoon, and I had the kettle on for tea anyway."

Emma sat on the couch. "Thank you."

She sipped her tea in awkward silence and nibbled at a scone. "These are very good," she finally said.

"Thank you. I made them myself."

"Do you usually serve them to, ah, clients?"

Lucia shook her head. "Oh, no. Only to, how shall I say it? Equals? Colleagues?"

Emma put the scone back on the delicate china plate. "What do you mean?"

"Your palm, when you showed me, said that you have some sort of perception beyond that of normal people."

"No, nothing out of the ordinary here." At least nothing helpful.

"Then please forgive me. I can make mistakes sometimes."

Tea ended amiably enough when an actual customer drove into the parking lot. Emma hoped it wasn't anyone she knew as she ducked out, got in her car, and drove home.

"I didn't really consult her," Emma said to Adrian. "It just happened that I ended up in her parking lot. I had a blowout."

Adrian shrugged. "Regardless of what brought you to her, it was meant to be that you saw her."

Emma wasn't going to argue. "What is this place?"

"A new extension of the dream world, the CU."

"CU?"

"Collective Unconscious."

"Oh." She'd heard something about that in her intro to psychology course. "So the repository of dreams?"

"Yes, the archetypes that visit people's dreams." Adrian walked down the hall, so Emma followed. "This is a new phase to allow those with talent to have easy access to the place." They lowered their voice. "They're trying to improve customer service."

Emma peeked in rooms. Some were completely finished and decorated in widely ranging styles from a seventeenth-century boudoir to a twentieth-century New York penthouse. Some lacked even drywall.

"I don't have any talent."

Another shrug. "You must have some if you were able to get here."

Emma decided this was a very interesting dream and that she might as well play along. "Like what?"

"Clairvoyance, psychic, ESP, whatever you want to call it. Strong intuition beyond that of 'normal' human beings."

"I tried to tell Lucia—there's nothing special about me. I must have gotten let in by accident."

Adrian gave her a patient *you must be a dolt* smile. "You were invited, and you accepted. You may not realize that you accepted, but you did. And now you have a room."

Obviously arguing wouldn't make a difference. "Why are they all the same size and shape?"

"It's how they're doing all the new developments these days. There are also some lovely amenities, like free access to most of the Manor parties."

"Manor parties?"

"The dwelling places of those who live here."

Emma shook her head. "This is all very confusing. Where are we going?"

Adrian didn't reply but continued to walk, so Emma followed. They passed down one long, straight hallway that seemed to have no end in sight.

"Where are the windows?" Emma finally asked to break the silence.

"Oh, they'll be put in last," Adrian replied with a wave of one hand. "That way they won't interfere with ideal object placement."

"The windows will be cut out after the rooms are done? That will be a mess."

"No." Adrian gave Emma a quizzical look. "They'll be hung."

"I don't get it. How can you look out a hung window?"

Adrian turned to her with the same infuriatingly patient expression. "The same way you look out any other kind."

"But won't there be a wall behind them? What will they overlook?"

"Whatever the resident wishes."

"Oh, so they're more like screens?"

"They'll have screens if you like. Especially if you decide to look over scenery where things may fly in."

A faint beeping floated through the air and grew louder. Adrian halted, cocked their head, and looked at Emma with gray eyes. Before Emma could ask why they had changed color, Adrian said, "That will be your alarm, I think. Bother, I had wanted to take you to the manor. Ah, well, another night, then."

"Right."

Adrian and the scene melted away, and Emma rolled over to turn off the alarm and turn on the bedside lamp. She sat up and swung her feet over the side of the bed. For a moment, the light caught something that fell from her foot to the floor. She picked it up—a curl of wood.

"What's that, hon?" Greg asked.

"I'm not entirely sure." Emma crushed it in her palm, then threw it in the small wastebasket by her side of the bed. "I had a very interesting dream this morning..."

Wait, what's happening to Emma? Is the Collective Unconscious a real place? Can dreams really come true, and if so, would you want them to?

*If you'd like to read **Perchance to Dream** for free and get updates on when new Cecilia Dominic novels will be released, please go to https://www.subscribepage.com/CDbackofbook to sign up for my newsletter. I hate spam and promise to keep your information safe!*